CHALKBOARD PREACHER
A Clean Slate

Book 3

Vinegar Bend Series

"Behold, I will do a new thing; now it shall spring forth, shall ye not know it? I will even make a way in the wilderness and rivers in the desert."

Isaiah 43:19

KAY CHANDLER
A MULTI-AWARD-WINNING AUTHOR

To Donna

God Bless!

Kay Chandler

This novel is a work of fiction. Names, characters, places and incidents are products of the author's imagination or used fictitiously.

Scripture taken from the King James Version of the Holy Bible

Cover Design by Chase Chandler

DEDICATION

CELESTE COXWELL, PAT WARD, JAN COOPER

Writing the Vinegar Bend Series provided a sense of restoration for me during the Covid-19 lockdown. I had minimal contact with friends and family, so the Reverend Marlowe family became beloved companions. The number of characters in the series grew with each new book and each new character brought with them their own personal insecurities and levels of desperation.

I generally know exactly to whom I wish to dedicate a book shortly after I begin to write. With *A Clean Slate*, three names came to mind. In the 1980's, I taught a Ladies Sunday School Class. It was an amazing group of Godly young women. One Sunday morning a homeless mother showed up in our classroom. Her clothes were tattered, and she needed food for her family. I'd never noticed how well-dressed "my girls" were until Syndy walked in. My heart went out to her, for fear she'd feel uncomfortable among a roomful of immaculately dressed women who seemed to have it "all together."

But I had nothing to fear. Those precious ladies welcomed her with open hearts and immediately set out to meet her needs and that of her family—physically, emotionally, and spiritually. I watched as *Celeste Coxwell, Jan Cooper*, and *Patricia Ward* became God's hands and feet as they lovingly befriended this destitute family. Syndy, her husband and three young children responded to the genuine outpouring of love and became an active part of our church.

As I considered the insecurities and dire circumstances of the characters in *A Clean Slate*, and their desperate need for restoration—it brought back sweet memories of *"my girls"* and how a destitute, insecure family of five was restored, through redeeming love

Recalling the Characters from Books I & II

Reverend Castle (Cass) Marlowe, *(the Chalkboard Preacher)*

Amelia (*His first wife, and mother of the following children:*)

Gazelle *(15-year-old daughter, Christian name is Esther)*

Goat (*14-year-old son, Christian name is Eli*)

Gander (*7-year-old twin to Goose, his Christian name is Elkanah)*

Goose (*twin to Gander, her Christian name is Elizabeth)*

Gopher *(3 ½ year-old baby boy, Christian name is Enoch)*

MyEwe *(infant daughter)*

Rebekah (*The Chalkboard Preacher's 19-year-old wife*

Lonnie (*Rebekah's Papa*)

Nellie (*Rebekah's aunt, Lonnie's sister*)

Elsie *(Family friend, Cass's high school sweetheart)*

Liberty – *Elsie's husband*

Ryker – *Gazelle's boyfriend*

Kay Chandler

CHAPTER 1

Bryce Psychiatric Hospital
Tuscaloosa, Alabama
December 29, 1919

The Reverend Castle Marlowe covered his nose as he trudged down the putrid-smelling hospital hallway, looking neither to his left nor to his right. Walking silently beside him was his friend, Liberty McAlister, whose singular purpose for the trip was to have his wife, Elsie, released from the horrifying institution.

A short, bulldog-looking nurse by the name of Althie Whitaker waddled slightly ahead of them, rattling a large ring of keys with each step she took. Cass suspected she could handle any patient in the hospital with ease, regardless of physical size or degree of madness.

As they walked the long corridor with rooms on one side and a rail overlooking a dungeon below, blood-curdling screams rang in their ears. Cass stopped, leaned against the railing, and looked

1

down at the frightening sight of deranged females of all ages. Some looked as young as ten, while others appeared to be in their eighties. An elderly woman sat clawing at her skin, drawing blood. Another crawled around on all-fours, howling like an animal, while others sat on the cold concrete floor, rocking back and forth in a steady rhythm, unaware of their surroundings.

Liberty laid his hand on Cass's shoulder. "Pitiful, isn't it? Do you now see why it's imperative that I remove Elsie from this horror-pit? The patients aren't even called by their names but are simply identified by a number. It's inhumane."

"I'm so sorry, Liberty. I hope it works out for you."

"Hey, thanks to you, my friend, it's a done deal. I can't thank you enough for convincing Governor Kilby that I'm capable of taking care of my wife at home."

Cass ran his hand across the back of his neck. "Liberty, I've tried to make you understand. I *never* said I convinced him. I made your case as best I could and he listened, but he made no commitment. His exact words were, 'I'll do what I can.'"

"Well, that's good enough for me. As the Governor of Alabama, he has the authority."

Cass pressed his lips together while contemplating how to handle the situation if—and the possibility was real—they couldn't convince the doctor to release her. How could he make him understand that even the Governor is subject to certain regulations and though it was simple to get her committed, it was going to be much harder getting her released.

"Liberty, I'll do all I can to back you up, but you need to be prepared to leave without her, because from what I hear—"

"No, Cass. I know what you've heard. Don't think I haven't heard it, also, but I can't leave her. I won't. If I'd known when I brought her here what I know now, I would never have left her in this place. I honestly thought she'd get the medical help she needs, but I was wrong."

When someone came up behind him and grabbed the tail of his coat, Cass jerked around to see a frail woman in her forties, holding on tightly, while whispering, "Please take me home. I've got to get home." Her hair looked as if it hadn't been combed in years. Her prison garb was tattered, and the stench stole his breath. An orderly ran over and popped her on the arm with a strap, causing her to release her grip. The pleading in her eyes as she was led away would haunt him forever.

Liberty cried unashamedly. "Do you see what I mean? This is no place for Elsie. She'll only get worse in this horrible environment. But if I can take her home, I'll devote every minute to getting her well."

Nurse Whitaker stopped several feet ahead and waited at a cell door for them to catch up. As she unlocked the door, she smirked, "We'd better be quite so we don't wake the baby. You ain't never seen a woman get riled the way Four-forty can when I go in making a racket. It's hilarious. Watch this!" She threw open the door and yelled, "Yoo-hoo, time to wake up, baby."

Cass glanced at Liberty, then shook his head slightly, hoping he'd get the message to hold his tongue. Cass's throat tightened, seeing Elsie sitting in a rocking chair, cuddling a doll. Without looking up, she whined, "You're a mean old woman. You know Rebekah Lou is sick. Why won't you let her sleep?"

Cass breathed easier when Liberty remained calm, though he could tell from his clenched jaw that it was an effort. As difficult as it was, he understood he couldn't afford to get on the bad side of an employee who might have influence over Elsie's discharge.

Liberty eased across the room and knelt at Elsie's feet. Blinking back the tears, he whispered, "Good morning, darling."

Her hollow eyes searched his face. "I know you."

He smiled. "Of course, you do. I'm your husband."

She leaned down and kissed the doll's head. "No, you aren't my husband. My husband is Rebekah Lou's father."

Cass licked his dry lips. He'd suspected all along that Elsie had convinced herself that he was the father of her imaginary baby. What if she blurted it out? Would Liberty understand that it, too, was a figment of her unstable imagination? As bogus as the baby in her arms?

"Elsie, I've brought an old friend to see you." He turned and motioned for Cass to come closer. "You remember Cass."

"How do you do?"

Cass pulled at his shirt collar. "I'm good, Elsie."

She looked down at the doll, then said, "You gentlemen should go now. I need to feed Rebekah Lou. Please, do come again, sometime." Cass heard the nurse snicker.

When Elsie began to unbutton her dress, Cass turned quickly facing the door, but Liberty didn't move.

Cass heard her say, "Who did you say you are?"

"I'm Liberty, sweetheart. Your husband."

"You can't be my husband. My husband is dead."

"Then I want to be your husband. I want to take you and little Rebekah Lou home with me to take care of you. Will you marry me, Elsie?"

"Marry you? Do you love me?"

"Oh, honey, I love you very much. And I love little Rebekah Lou. May I hold her?"

"You're a good man. I think she's full, but you might try to burp her."

Cass eased the door open and he and the nurse stepped out together. She said, "If you ask me, Four-forty's husband oughta be locked up in here with her. I think he's beginning to believe that stupid doll is real. He's almost as batty as she is."

Minutes later, Liberty stepped out and the two men walked down the hall ahead of the nurse, who stayed behind to lock Elsie's door.

Cass was afraid to ask. "Forgive me for asking, Liberty, but after seeing her, do you still feel it's time to take her home?"

"I'm more convinced than ever. Let's go convince the doctor."

After almost two hours pleading with the doctor, Liberty felt he'd convinced him that it would be in Elsie's best interest to go home. He told him what a great visit he had and that she'd agreed she was ready to leave with him.

The tall, lanky doctor stroked his goatee, picked up his cigar and drew a long puff. "Well, Mr. McAlister, it does sound as if you're capable of looking after her, and regardless of what rumors you may have heard, it's the policy of this hospital to release patients as soon as we deem it practical to do so. Frankly, I've been quite busy transitioning patients for the past few days and I had no idea Four-forty had made such amazing progress. However, we've discovered the mind can sometimes snap back at a mere recollection. I suppose with your wife, this has been the case. And you say, she recognized you and realizes she has no baby?"

He glanced at Cass and wrung his hands. "That's pretty much it, sir."

"Well, I wouldn't normally let a patient go without my thorough examination, but after speaking with the Governor, he seems to think you're an honest, upright fellow, so I see no reason to keep Four-forty any longer."

Liberty grabbed his hand and shook it with such force, Cass whispered, "Let it go. You aren't priming a pump."

Embarrassed, he turned loose. "Thank you, doctor. Thank you, very much. You've made me a very happy man."

The doctor turned to the young, attractive secretary and glanced at his watch. "It's after five, Miss Coggins. Sorry to have kept you late. I'll see you Monday morning."

"Don't worry about a thing while you're away, Dr. Manley.

Enjoy your trip. I'm sure your wife is eager to see that new grandbaby."

"Yes, she is. I'm just sorry I won't be here to welcome Dr. Truett, the new doctor."

"I suppose he'll be working your shift while you're away?"

"No, I don't foresee any problems that my staff can't handle until I return. I'm leaving Althie Whitaker in charge. I have no doubt she'll keep a tight ship while I'm gone."

Miss Coggins's lip curled, in apparent agreement. "She'll do that for sure, sir."

"Dr. Truett will work the midnight shift, beginning Thursday night. Please inform the night staff to welcome him and to help answer any questions he might have."

He held the door open and wished her a goodnight, as Liberty waited impatiently for the gabbing to cease. He shifted from one foot to the other in his eagerness to get Elsie and get out of that wretched place. "Doctor, pardon my impatience, but we have a long trip ahead of us. May I go get my wife, now?"

Smiling, he said, "I understand you must be very eager to get her home. Wait here, until I find Nurse Whitaker, who'll help your wife get her things together."

"Oh, but sir, I'll be happy to help her."

"It's policy, Mr. McAlister. It shan't take long. Have a seat, and I'll return shortly."

After the doctor closed the door behind him, Cass said, "You made it sound as if Elsie was ready to throw away the doll and open her shop, Liberty. You know he'll find out differently as soon as he sees her."

He ran his hands through his thick white hair. "I know. I only wanted to convince him I need to get her home. I kept trying to read his expressions and I suppose I got carried away, waiting for him to look as if he approved."

"Well, with the beautiful picture you painted, how could he say no? But it was a lie, Liberty, and you may have made things worse."

"How could they be worse? Nothing could be worse than leaving her in this place."

"I just meant it may make it harder to remove her when she does get better. He doesn't seem like a very forgiving man to me, and he has the authority to hold her here for as long as he declares her insane."

"I hate that word. She's not insane. Mixed up, but not insane."

The door flew open and the doctor stood beside the nurse. His voice was sharp. "I think our business here is concluded."

Liberty's brow furrowed. "Where's my wife?"

"Four-forty is in no condition to leave these premises. Good day, gentlemen."

Liberty's teeth ground together. "You can't do this. She's my wife, and I'm taking her home."

"Your wife is being prepared for shock treatments. It seems your little visit disturbed her so much, she's in worse shape than she was the day you brought her in. My recommendation, Mr. McAlister, is for you to stay away from this hospital for a period of six months, until the therapists have an opportunity to undo the damage done here today. I shall give the Governor a call and let him know exactly what transpired. I don't know what your reasoning was for coming here and making up such a ridiculous story, but I don't take to being lied to." He walked over to his desk and shoved something in the drawer. "Now, if you'll excuse me, I'm ready to go home." He cupped his hand over his mouth and shouted. "Guards!"

Cass gently took Liberty by the arm when three hefty men in white suddenly surrounded them. "We have no option, Liberty. We have to leave."

CHAPTER 2

Liberty didn't stop talking all the way home Monday night, which was out of character for the reserved man Cass considered to be his dearest friend. He contributed Liberty's constant chatter to a combination of extreme disappointment at having his hopes shattered and the fear that he'd lost his beloved Elsie forever.

"I can't believe I left her there, after I promised I'd bring her home. I've got to get her away from that dreadful place." He gnawed on his fist. "And somehow—someway, I will. I made her a promise."

Cass kept his eyes on the road as he drove. He didn't have the heart to remind Liberty that Elsie was so out of touch with reality that she wasn't even aware of who they were, and she sure as shootin' wouldn't remember a conversation that took place. He tightened his grip on the steering wheel. "Liberty, I know you want her home with you, but you saw the same thing I saw. She's not the same woman you married . . . and possibly never will be. You have to face that fact."

"Why do you keep telling me what I have to do?" He leaned his head back and moaned. "I'm sorry, pal. I know you mean well. But I need someone to believe with me."

"I understand and I wish I could be that someone, but to agree with you would be to knowingly solicit false hope, setting you up for a downfall. I honestly thought from what you told me, that she was much better. I even relayed that to the Governor, though I discovered today that she was in even worse shape than when she left Vinegar Bend."

"Well, maybe she is, and maybe she isn't. But if she is, that should be even more reason why we need to get her away from that place."

"Liberty, as much as I wish it weren't so, the truth is, Elsie is insane and the sooner you admit it to yourself, the sooner you can get on with your life."

"You don't understand. Apart from Elsie, I have no life."

It was well past eight o'clock Monday night by the time they reached Vinegar Bend. "Liberty, should I take you to the house or do you prefer I let you off at the farm?"

"The farm."

"I'm sorry, you're disappointed. I know you were hoping—"

"Yeah, well, what's that verse in the Bible about a man without a vision?"

"Without a vision the people perish?"

"Yeah. That one. Well, I don't intend to perish. I have something to live for, so that means I need a vision. Right?"

There was so much Cass wanted to say, but he imagined Rebekah whispering in his ear that it was best to say nothing. And since his little wife seemed to possess a Godly talent for discernment, he fought to keep his thoughts to himself. He stopped in front of the gate and Liberty grabbed his coat from off the back of the seat. "Thanks for driving me there, friend."

"I'm just sorry, things didn't work out."

"Maybe it wasn't meant to be today, but don't worry, I don't intend to perish."

Cass had never been so glad to get home to his wife. He couldn't even imagine the desperation Liberty felt, having to leave Elsie behind. He supposed it was a blessing she didn't give birth. He knew firsthand how difficult it was for a man to take care of an infant, alone. But on the other hand, perhaps Elsie wouldn't be in the shape she was in, if it hadn't been for the traumatic experience. He parked and laid his head on the steering wheel, reliving the horrible events of the day. When he raised his head, he saw Rebekah waiting for him on the porch.

Trudging slowly up the steps, he forced a smile. "Sorry, I'm so late. It took longer than we anticipated."

"From the look on your face, I'm guessing you weren't successful in getting her released."

"No, it was terrible. If it's alright with you, hon, I'd rather talk about it later. I'm exhausted."

She held her head back for a quick kiss. "I understand. Have you had supper?"

"No. We didn't stop."

"Then go to the kitchen and I'll whip you up some eggs and bacon."

"Don't bother. I'm not hungry. I just want to go to bed. Are the kids asleep?"

"They are. Get ready for bed and I'll be in as soon as I finish up in the kitchen."

Rebekah put away the last dish and tiptoed into the bedroom. She found Cass leaning over little MyEwe's crib.

"She's beautiful like her momma."

She pulled the quilt around the baby. "She's a little joy, but why aren't you in bed, already? I expected you to be asleep."

"I'm worn to a frazzle, but I guess I'm too wound up to sleep. It's been quite a day."

"I can only imagine Elsie's disappointment in not being able to leave with Liberty."

"You only *think* you can imagine. I'm glad you weren't there to see it, Rebekah. The Elsie you knew is gone. That crazed woman inhabiting Elsie's body doesn't have a clue where she is."

"Oh, Cass, how sad. Does she still have the doll?"

"Have it? Why, she put in to nurse it while we were in the room with her."

"You don't mean it."

"I wish I didn't. I almost choked when she began to unbutton her dress. Liberty sat right there with her acting as if it were perfectly normal for a woman to nurse a doll. I turned my back and the nurse who let us in the room, laughed as if she were enjoying the show. The weird thing is that even after that little episode, Liberty still insisted on bringing her home."

"What's so weird about that, Cass? He loves her."

"I understand, but honey, you didn't see what I saw. She'd require someone watching her twenty-four hours if he had her at home. Yet, the way he talked after we left, it sounded as if he really believes he can get her out of there and that everything will be hunky-dory when he does. I'd be afraid to close my eyes at night if she were in the same room with me. I'm telling you, she's a basket case. But enough about my day. How did yours go?"

"It was good. Papa and Badger stayed in Papa's room all afternoon. Those two are up to something. I could hear them both laughing and at one point it sounded as if they were tearing up creation in there, I've never heard such a racket."

"What were they doing?"

"Who knows? But whatever it is, they've included Goat in their plans. Papa insisted they were working on a surprise. It's hard to imagine that sweet, funny man is the same mean ol' codger who made my childhood so miserable."

"I'd say he's not the same man. The Lord can take the old man and create a new being."

"Well, I sure love the new Papa. He's made such a difference in Badger. It's amazing how quickly the other kids have caught on to the signing. It's sometimes easy to forget he's deaf, the way he picks up on what's going on around him." She glanced over and realized her husband had fallen asleep. What a sweet man. It was plain to see the day had taken its toll on him. He and Elsie had been friends forever. It must've been incredibly stressful seeing the first girl he ever loved going through such a dreadful illness. Rebekah had never loved anyone until Cass came into her life, so she had nothing to compare it with. Even though she liked to pretend her husband had never loved anyone but her, the fact remained that another woman gave him five beautiful children. And even though Amelia was evil, wasn't it possible that he might have certain feelings for her, simply because they'd experienced a husband-wife relationship?

And though Elsie was her best friend, Elsie hadn't been shy in reminding Rebekah that Cass was her first and only love until Liberty came along. There must've been something very special between them for Elsie to find it so hard to let him go. Her throat tightened. Where were these jealous feelings coming from? Just because she wasn't Cass's first or even his second love, was no sign that he didn't love her more than he'd ever loved Amelia or Elsie. Cass reminded her often that he loved her and her only. And she had no right to doubt him.

She rolled over and went to sleep.

Tuesday morning, Cass kissed his wife goodbye and pleaded with her to make his apologies to the children for having to leave before they awoke. She promised to do so, as he knew she would, but in his heart he questioned if he deserved their forgiveness. For the past twelve months it seemed all he ever did was apologize for his constant absence. The pull between ministry and family was taking its toll.

With three lectures and a speaking conference lined up back-to-back in neighboring counties, it would necessitate his being away for three full days. He loved doing the Lord's work, but he understood the sacrifices his family made so that he could continue accepting the many invitations.

Though it wasn't yet public knowledge—Cass hadn't even told Rebekah—the church in Vinegar Bend was looking for a new Pastor. Brother Mack was planning to retire, due to ill health, and Cass had been approached by the deacons as a possible replacement.

He loved doing the Chalkboard Lectures but knowing how much it would mean to his family to have him home, didn't he have an obligation to consider the offer?

CHAPTER 3

Wednesday night, dressed in a starched, white shirt and new black suit, Liberty gazed at his reflection in the Tuscaloosa Hotel mirror and straightened his bow tie. He picked up a new leather briefcase that he bought at Sears and Roebuck and shoved it under his arm. It was the perfect prop.

Smiling, he muttered, "By crackity, I don't think I've ever seen a more prosperous looking doctor." He tipped his hat and chuckled at the image as he rehearsed his lines. "Good evening, Madam. Dr. Bo Truett at your service." Since Dr. Manley only mentioned Dr. Truett's last name to the secretary, Liberty decided to use the common nickname, Bo, when making his introductions to avoid any slip-ups.

Perhaps he should've felt guilty for planning such a deceptive act. But he didn't. He'd considered the possibility of getting caught and should it happen, he'd go straight to jail. But if he couldn't get his Elsie home, did it matter where he spent his days? As slim as his chances were that he could pull it off, it was worth a try, since he had nothing to lose.

He sat watching the clock, waiting for the shift change. The night employees wouldn't recognize him since he and Cass were there during the day when Dr. Manley informed the secretary the new doctor would arrive Thursday night. He'd make an excuse for his unscheduled Wednesday night arrival, then he and Elsie would be long gone before the truth would be discovered. It would work. It had to.

****

Miss JoElle Jernigan, the bookkeeper who worked night shifts at Bryce's Hospital sat at her desk Wednesday night and turned the page of the romantic novel. She reached for her handkerchief to catch a falling tear. How special it would've been to have known such love. For the past thirty years, she'd given the best part of her life, holding out for something that never happened. With the passing of time, her hair grayed, she lost her girlish figure and the lines on her drawn face made her look even older than her fifty-four years. She'd given everything and gained nothing. If only she could turn back the clock, she'd do things much differently. Her first mistake was to accept the job at Bryce Hospital for the Insane. As much as she wished she could walk away, it was too late. She couldn't afford to leave now.

At the age of twenty-four, she was engaged to a nice young man who worked at a sawmill. She thought it her lucky day when she spotted an ad in the newspaper for a bookkeeper at the local hospital. With plans to build a home on a prime piece of property, which her fiancé had his eye on, JoElle landed the job, hoping to save enough money to make their dream a reality.

Her thoughts wandered, carrying her back to the day of the interview. A handsome young doctor, Dr. Theodore McDuffie hired her immediately to work the midnight shift and he wasn't at all shy about complimenting her beauty. Though embarrassed the way he carried on, she couldn't help being flattered that he found her so attractive. With very little activity taking place in the hospital at night and being the only two in the office, there was ample time to—well, become better acquainted. Naturally, falling in love with the smooth-talking doctor was the furthest thing from her mind, since she was practically a married woman. Exactly when it happened, she couldn't say. All she remembered about that first year was the painful look on her fiance's face when she broke their engagement.

Theo, as she called the doctor in private, led her to believe there was a future for them. For years, she waited—hoping, dreaming, and trusting that one day she'd be Mrs. Theodore McDuffie, living in a big house on Main Street in Tuscaloosa. After eight years of waiting, Theo boldly walked into the hospital with his arms around Maggie Doss, the Senator's daughter and announced their engagement.

Tears welled in her eyes, as she recalled the excruciating pain in her heart the day she attended the wedding along with the hospital staff. Pretending to be happy for him was the hardest thing she'd ever had to endure. Looking back, she realized she should've walked out of his life and out of the hospital that day and never looked back. Why she didn't, she couldn't fathom. But she didn't. In less than a year after his marriage, Theo cried on her shoulder one evening at work and told her he'd made a terrible mistake, but his wife wouldn't agree to a divorce. He convinced her—and maybe she wanted to be convinced—that he loved her and her only.

She continued to be the doctor's secret mistress for many years, when he made it plain that he'd lost all interest in her. Last week he retired, and he and his wife left for a South Sea Island cruise.

Reaching in her desk, she pulled out a lace handkerchief to dry the tears flowing from her eyes. How could she have been so stupid?

She laid her open book aside and pulled a Stanback powder from her pocketbook, hoping to thwart a developing headache. An ignorant, immoral decision made long ago had led her to no good end. Life had passed her by and now old and tired, she worked out of necessity—spending long nights at the hospital and long, lonely days, alone. In a tiny apartment. Above the dry cleaners. On Tippytoe Street. With nothing left to live for and too cowardly to die.

****

At five past eleven o'clock, Wednesday night, Liberty shoved his shoulders back and walked into Bryce Hospital for the Insane, wearing spectacles and holding a Stetson hat. Would Elsie recognize him? Perhaps he should stick the spectacles in his pocket before going into her room. What if she refused to leave? He threw his head back and stiffened. This was no time to allow negative thoughts to enter his mind.

An elderly woman sat at the desk, and without giving her time to question him, he said, "Good evening ma'am. Dr. Bo Truett. I suppose Dr. Manley informed you I'd be coming?"

Her brow creased, making his heart skip a beat. Then, with a big smile, she quickly arose and held out her hand. "Welcome, doctor. My name is JoElle. JoElle Jernigan. We weren't expecting you until tomorrow night."

"Actually, I'm not scheduled to begin until tomorrow, but I arrived in town early and decided to drop by and take a look around."

"Sure. I'll be happy to give you a tour and introduce you to the staff, although as I'm sure Dr. Manley told you, we only have a skeletal crew working nights."

"You're very kind, JoElle. That's a beautiful name. May I call you JoElle?"

She blushed. "I'd like that. Thank you. It makes me feel so old when everyone around here calls me Miss Jernigan, even if I am a few years older."

"You don't strike me as old, JoElle. I thank you for your hospitality, but I prefer to check things out on my own, if you please. I could be here fifteen minutes or several hours. Keys, please?"

"Of course." She pulled a large ring of keys from off a nail on the wall behind her and handed them to him. "There are numbers taped to each key, designating the hall numbers. Are you sure you wouldn't like for me to guide you?"

"Thank you, but this is not my first trip to this hospital. I'm familiar with the hall numbers, but if I should have questions, I'll be sure to let you know. I shall return the keys upon leaving."

Liberty took the elevator to the fourth floor and went directly to Room 440. He glanced from left to right. Relieved that the hall was empty, he quickly unlocked Elsie's door. She was sitting in a chair, holding the doll. Her eyes lit up. "Liberty? Is that you?"

His heart beat like a jack hammer, hearing her call his name. "Yes, sweetheart. It's me. I've come to get you and Rebekah Lou, but everyone here is asleep, so we have to be very, very quiet."

She placed her finger over her lips. "Shh! I won't make a sound. I'm glad Rebekah Lou finally went to sleep. I've rocked her for hours. I think she has colic."

"Honey, let's don't talk until we get in the car. We don't want her to wake up."

She nodded, and once again placed her finger on her lips, signifying she understood.

Liberty led her down the stairs to the basement, unlocked the back door of the hospital, then walked her to his automobile. "You and the baby wait in the car. I need to take the keys back to the nice lady. I'll be right back."

He entered through the back door, locked it, then took the elevator from the basement to the first floor.

Walking into the office, he laid the keys on the desk. "Thank you, JoElle."

"You're leaving so soon?"

"Yes, you've been more helpful than you can imagine."

"I'm glad I could be of service. I'm looking forward to working with you, Dr. Truett."

He hurried outside, and gave a whoopee, as he drove away.

Elsie put her finger over her lips. "Shh!"

He laughed. "It's okay, now, sugar. You can talk all you want to. I have a feeling Rebekah Lou is not gonna be sick any longer. I think you're both on your way to getting better."

****

JoElle was impressed with the new doctor. He had a gentle way about him. It was thoughtful of him to come by a night early, just to familiarize himself with a few of the patients. But perhaps he wasn't as caring as he appeared to be. Was it possible he was up to something? She hated that she'd become so pessimistic, but it was difficult to trust anyone after having been fooled so completely.

****

Liberty drove for a couple of hours after the escape, Wednesday night, talking non-stop to Elsie, who barely said a word, but the sweet smile plastered on her face was enough for him to know he'd done the right thing. He'd planned to drive all the way back to Vinegar Bend, but she looked exhausted. Driving through Grove Hill, Alabama, he saw a light on at a Boarding House in town. Walking Elsie to the door, he knocked.

A kindly looking old soul opened the door with a broad smile on her face. "Well, who do we have here? You folks must've been driving all night to stop at a Boarding House at four o'clock in the morning."

Liberty attempted to apologize, but she wouldn't hear of it.

"Land sakes, don't you say another word about being sorry, sugar. I always get up about this time of the morning, and to tell the truth, I'm glad you chose to stop here. This time of year, I don't get many boarders. I'm Nan. Folks all around just call me Aunt Nan. I'd like it if you would, too."

Liberty said, "Nice to meet you, Aunt Nan. My name's Liberty and this is my wife, Rebekah."

The woman smiled tenderly and placed her hand on Elsie's shoulder. "What a precious baby. Is it a boy or a girl?"

Liberty swallowed hard, but before he could respond, Elsie said, "A girl. Her name is Rebekah Lou."

"What a lovely name. Do you mind if I hold her?"

Liberty blinked away the moisture filling his eyes when Elsie handed Rebekah Lou to the little old lady, who cradled it gently and cooed soothing words to the lifeless object.

"You folks follow me upstairs. I have the perfect room for you. It even has a crib for Rebekah Lou. How long ya'll plan on staying?"

Liberty bit his lip. He'd only planned to stay long enough for Elsie to rest before continuing on to Vinegar Bend, but perhaps this stop was not a coincidence. Could it be an answer to a prayer he hadn't yet prayed? It was comforting to know that God knew his need even before he asked.

"I'm not sure, ma'am. Could I give you an answer after I've had time to think on it?"

"You take all the time you need."

Observing Elsie getting antsy, Liberty reached for the doll, and mouthed a "thank you."

Aunt Nan's gaze locked with his, and without speaking a word, he knew without a doubt she understood his pain. She said, "Breakfast is at seven o'clock, but if y'all choose to sleep in, I understand. I'll keep it warm for you."

Liberty took the doll and Elsie stood beside him as he laid it in the crib. It took all he could do to keep from bawling. He was thrilled his attempt to rescue Elsie was a success, but his heart couldn't have felt heavier if loaded with a sack of bricks. He gazed teary-eyed at the doll in the crib and longed for it to be as real as Elsie believed it to be.

He led her to a rocking chair in front of the fireplace, then stoked the flickering embers. "You're shivering. Why don't you sit here and warm while I unpack our night clothes?"

"Thank you, Liberty. You take such good care of me and the baby. I should've given Rebekah Lou a dose of Paregoric before putting her to bed. Do you think she'll be all right? It breaks my heart to see her in pain"

"Hon, I think she's outgrowing the colic. See how peacefully she's sleeping?"

She smiled. "You're right. She does look peaceful, doesn't she? She was never peaceful at that other place. Poor baby cried constantly. Can I tell you something, Liberty? I cried too. I wanted to go home."

His voice cracked. "I wanted you to come home, too, dear."

Then looking around the room, her brow furrowed. "Where are we? This isn't my house."

He knelt in front of her and laid his hand on her arm. "We're at Aunt Nan's house, sweetheart."

Her eyes squinted as if she were trying really hard to get the facts straight. "Oh, I remember now. I like your Aunt Nan. She's very kind."

"Yes, sweetheart. She is kind, indeed." Liberty pulled a gown from his suitcase and handed to Elsie. She held it to her nose and sighed.

"This smells so good—like sunshine. Is it mine?"

"Yes, darling. It's yours. You made it."

"I did?" She looked confused. "Why can't I remember, Liberty? The nurse was right, wasn't she? It's true that I'm crazy."

"No, hon. You aren't crazy. She was." He held the covers back for her to get under. "We've had a long night. Try to get some sleep."

Her eyes focused on the doll. "I like it here, Liberty. I don't want to go back to that hospital. There was an evil woman there who'd make loud noises and wouldn't let Rebekah Lou sleep. Sometimes our sweet little baby would be so tired, she'd cry all night, which made me very sad."

"Well, you don't have to worry about that woman anymore. You'll be with me from now on." He held her in his arms as she closed her eyes and drifted off, but he couldn't sleep for wanting to look at her. *Please help me, Lord. I need my wife made whole again.*

CHAPTER 4

Thursday morning, nurse Althie Whitaker made the usual rounds with the hospital breakfast trays. Shoving open the door to #440, her eyes frantically searched the room. "Four-Forty?" Why she called, she couldn't fathom, for it was apparent the patient was gone, since there was no place to hide. Had she forgotten to lock the door after taking her supper last night? Frightened that she'd be fired, Althie sat on the edge of the cot to collect her senses. *Don't panic. She's here . . . somewhere.*

The meek patient couldn't have gone far, but Althie had to find her before someone else did There were a couple of staff members who would be delighted to see her fired for incompetence. But after searching the huge building all morning, Four-forty was nowhere to be found.

Althie went back to the room sat down, ate the breakfast meant for Elsie, then picked up the tray and took it back to the kitchen. She laid it on the counter and in a voice loud enough to be heard above the racket of pots and pans, remarked, "Four-forty had a real appetite this morning. Ate near 'bout everything on her plate." None of the kitchen crew paid her any attention, though she was sure they all heard if she needed witnesses to confirm the patient was in her room at breakfast.

Just as she was about to walk out, she heard one of the dish washers remark, "I'm surprised Dr. Manley left, knowing the new night-shift doctor will be starting tonight. Knowing how protective he is of this hospital, I would've expected him to stay around to show him the ropes."

The other dish washer said, "I'm sure it wasn't his idea to leave. He'd hang out here twenty-four hours a day if it were up to him. But no way was Mrs. Manley gonna miss seeing that new grandbaby."

Althie's hopes elevated to a new height. That was it. She'd make sure everyone understood that Four-forty was still in her room all day Thursday. Then she'd wait until first thing Friday morning to report the missing patient, which would point fingers to the new doctor, who would be responsible for making night rounds.

She went downstairs and ran into Miss Coggins, the secretary.

"What are you doing down here, Whitaker? Lose somebody?" Then, laughing as if she'd cracked a joke, she said, "We couldn't be so lucky. Right?"

Althie licked her dry lips and forced a chuckle. "You're right." Then quickly added, "If all the patients on my ward were as gentle as Four-forty, it would make my job a lot easier. As long as she has that stupid doll, she won't give nobody no trouble. I think she's beginning to adjust. She ate every mouthful of her breakfast this morning."

It wasn't as if the secretary had any idea who Four-forty was, but she'd be one more witness to confirm Althie's story. With so many witnesses, it would be easy to convince the board that the patient disappeared Thursday night on the new doctor's watch.

****

Liberty lay in bed beside his wife until nine o'clock Thursday morning. He'd never slept to such an hour in his entire life. Growing up, there was too much to do on the farm to sleep late. His Papa had him up plowing a field before sun-up. After he was grown, he continued the routine, but now, for the first time in his life, work was not the driving force in his life. His mind was geared toward getting his wife well and the way she tossed, turned and groaned in her sleep, he feared it would take a very long time to erase the images in her mind of the time spent in such an awful environment.

She awoke with a start. Flinging her arms, she popped straight up in bed and screamed, "Where's my baby?"

Liberty wrapped her in his arms, then pointed to the crib. "Did you forget? We put her to sleep in the crib and she slept through the night. Didn't I tell you she's getting well?"

Bursting into tears, she said, "Liberty?" Then rubbing the back of her hand across his cheek, she said, "You're here."

"Yes, dear. I'm here."

She walked over and picked up Rebekah Lou, then gazed about the room. "I remember."

"What is it you remember, sweetheart?"

"I remember coming here."

With raised hopes, he declared, "I'm so glad you're remembering. Not only is Rebekah Lou getting well, Elsie, but you're getting well, too. I knew you would. I'm getting hungry. Why don't we get dressed and go eat breakfast?"

"Yes, I'm hungry, too." Then, looking confused, she said, "Where's your grandmother?"

His hopes plummeted as quickly as they had arisen. "Uh . . . my grandmother's dead."

"Dead? Oh, Liberty. That makes me so sad."

He quickly added, "It's okay, hon. Please don't cry." Wrapping his arms around her, he said, "She died before I was born. I never knew her."

With her head buried against his chest, she sobbed. "Help me, Liberty. Please help me."

"I will, sweetheart. Tell me what I can do to help you."

"I don't know. I'm so mixed up. I thought this was your grandmother's house. I suppose I dreamed it. I wish it had been true."

He smiled. "Oh, you aren't talking about my grandmother. You meant Aunt Nan. This is her house."

She nodded. "Yes. Yes, Aunt Nan. Did she die?"

"No, sweetheart. She's cooking our breakfast. But she isn't really my aunt. This is a boarding house and everyone calls her Aunt Nan."

"I remember, Liberty. Isn't that wonderful? I remember Aunt Nan. She loves Rebekah Lou."

He nodded. "Yes, she does, and she loves you, too. I think we should stay here for a while. What do you think?"

"I'd like that."

They walked downstairs and Aunt Nan met them at the bottom of the stairs. "Good morning Liberty and Elsie. I've kept your breakfast on the stove, so why don't you let me hold Rebekah Lou while you two sit down and eat?"

Liberty paused, waiting for his wife's reaction. She smiled and without hesitation, handed the doll to Aunt Nan.

He let out a heavy breath. Elsie was full of surprises this morning. Maybe it wasn't much, but it was enough to give him hope.

Liberty and Elsie spent the day Thursday exploring downtown Grove Hill. Though Elsie was a long way from being well, things were going much better than Liberty had even dared to hope.

Seeing a church on the corner, she ran toward it and sprinted up the steps. "Isn't it beautiful? Can we go inside, Liberty? Can we?"

"Why not?" He opened the heavy wooden door and Elsie appeared to be in awe as she walked slowly down the aisle gazing at the beautiful painted backdrop behind the Baptismal pool. She stopped at the altar, while holding Rebekah close to her breast.

"Liberty, I think when we get home, we should dedicate Rebekah Lou to the Lord. But she'll need a new dress. A long white one with lots of lace and a little bonnet to match."

He reached for the doll and held it, just as he would have if it were real. "I have a better idea, honey. You're a wonderful seamstress. For years, women from all around the country have gone to your shop in Vinegar Bend to buy their clothes. Besides, Rebekah Lou is still very young. Let's wait until you can make the dress. It'll be much prettier than a store-bought one."

"My shop?" She rubbed her temples. Then repeating herself, she mumbled, "My shop."

His thoughts ranged from what if she remembers to what if she can't? He watched with mixed feelings as she closed her eyes while rubbing her temples.

"What's wrong with me, Liberty? I feel as if I have memories locked inside my head, but when I try to retrieve them, I get a terrible headache."

"Nothing at all is wrong with you, my sweet. You're perfect. The memories will come back in time." Leading her out of the church, he said, "Where to now, Princess?"

"I've had a lovely time, dear, but I'm a bit exhausted. Perhaps we should head back to your Grandmother's house"

"Aunt Nan's," he muttered.

Her brow furrowed. "What?"

Did it really matter? "You're right. We should get back."

****

Cass had just finished speaking at the Men's Conference, Thursday at noon, when a preacher slipped him the following note: *My husband, Castle Marlowe, is speaking at the Conference. Please have him call home, immediately. Rebekah Marlowe.* He quietly eased outside and asked a gentleman where he could find the closest pay phone. After being directed to the corner drug store, he ran the three blocks.

Holding the phone to his ear, he said, "Rebekah? Can you hear me? What's the trouble?"

"I'm not sure, Cass, but I heard this morning that Liberty sold his farm."

Letting out a loud sigh, he said, "No, that has to be gossip. He'd never sell."

"But it isn't gossip. It's true. I heard Josh Abrams at the grocery store say Liberty sold the whole shebang, Tuesday— equipment, acreage and the house to Mr. Abrams son."

"That doesn't make sense. He told me Monday on the way to the hospital that because of the boll weevils destroying his cotton crop, he planned to plant peanuts this next year. Why would he be planning his next crop on Monday if he intended to sell the next day?"

"Don't you get it, Cass? Monday morning, he thought he'd be getting Elsie and taking her home with him. When the doctor refused to release her, he lost all hope. He must've felt he had nothing else to live for."

"You aren't suggesting suicide?"

"What else can you make of it? He left here, Monday morning, thinking he'd bring Elsie home. I'm afraid he couldn't take the disappointment when he had to leave her there."

Cass rubbed the back of his neck. "I wouldn't think he'd do anything that desperate, but now that you mention it, he didn't seem to be thinking straight when we left the hospital that evening. I have one more lecture after lunch, but I'll be home in time for supper, and I'll give him a call."

"But if he's sold his house, how can you call him?"

"Before Elsie was committed, they stayed every night at her old homeplace, and he'd leave for the farm in the wee hours of the morning. I'm sure he's at her house in town."

"Well, I probably panicked for no reason. I shouldn't have bothered you."

"You did the right thing, dear. For sure, he's not thinking straight, or he would never have sold the farm." *But suicide?* He rubbed his hand across the back of his neck. Could she be right?

He hung up the phone with his mind made up. It wasn't fair to Rebekah to shoulder so much responsibility and be burdened with guilt when she needed to consult him. He'd accept the Pastoral position at the church. Perhaps he'd have time to work on that book of Sermon Sketches that people had been encouraging him to write.

CHAPTER 5

Cass was later getting home Thursday night than he'd anticipated, and everyone was asleep except Rebekah. She'd kept his supper warm, though he was too exhausted to eat. "It looks good, hon, but I'm ready to crash in bed. It's been a very trying day. After I had a flat tire in the middle of nowhere, I had to walk for miles to the nearest town to buy a pump, thanks to Goat."

Clearly exasperated, his jaw jutted forward. "I don't know how many times I've told him to put it back when he takes it out of the car. If I could've gotten my hands on that kid at the time, I'm afraid his growth would've been stunted for the rest of his life. The way I'm feeling now, he may be grounded that long."

"I'm sorry you had such a bad trip, darling, but don't be too hard on Goat. He's had a lot on his mind lately."

"Rebekah, he's almost fifteen years old and his mind shouldn't be so crowded that he can't remember to put things back where he finds them."

"Well, at least you were able to buy a new pump."

"Wrong. The store was closed."

"Oh, m'goodness. Then how did you get it fixed?"

"As I was walking back, a fellow picked me up who had a pump. If he hadn't come along when he did, I suppose I'd still be stranded out there."

"Honey, aren't you going to call and check on Liberty before going to bed? I know it's late, but I'm dreadfully worried about him. I'd feel much better if you'd call."

Whether he made the call for his wife's sake or for his own peace of mind, Cass reluctantly picked up the phone and addressed the operator. "'Evening, Josephine, would you please ring Elsie McAlister's number."

"Reverend, Elsie ain't home. Ain't been there for a spell. I hear tell she's—"

"Thank you, Josephine, I'm quite aware of all the rumors. Now, would you please ring that number?"

"Suit yourself, but I'm telling you, she ain't home."

After countless rings, Josephine said, "Told you she wasn't home."

He hung up and crawled in bed beside his wife.

Rebekah raised up. "Well? Did you talk to him?"

"He's not home."

"Oh, Cass. Now do you believe me? Where would he be this time of night? In bed. That's exactly where he'd be if . . . if—" She burst into sobs.

"Rebekah, I don't know where he is, but I assure you, you're wrong. Liberty's long-range thoughts are centered on Elsie. He has no intention of killing himself. After I've had ample time to think about it, I now understand that selling the farm was a well-thought-out decision."

"How do you figure that? Frankly, I don't think Liberty would know what to do with himself. All he's ever known was farming."

"That's true, but it looks as if Elsie will be in the hospital for a very long time—perhaps forever."

"Oh, Cass, you aren't serious?"

"I wish it weren't so, but you didn't see her, hon. I'm confident Liberty recognized it, just as I did. I'm sure it would be difficult for him to run the farm in Citronelle and continue making that long trip to the hospital week after week. I suspect he's planning to buy a farm in or around Tuscaloosa to be near her."

His explanation seemed to satisfy Rebekah, though he wished he were as convinced that Liberty didn't commit suicide as he pretended to be.

****

Thursday night at precisely eleven o'clock, a skinny little fellow with a pointed goatee and an attitude equally sharp sashayed into Bryce Hospital, glanced around, then stalked over to JoElle Jernigan's desk. Leaning in to read her name tag, he gruffed, "Mrs. Jernigan, is it?"

"Miss. That would be Miss Jernigan. But who are you and

what are you doing here this hour of the night?" Her initial thought was that a former patient must've made his way back.

His high-pitched voice, squeaked. "You're asking who I am? This is no less than what I expected. Complete incompetence on the part of the staff. Well, mark my word, there'll be some changes made around here, sooner than later." Seeing the opened book on her desk, he grabbed it and tossed it in the trash. "If you think you're being paid to sit here and read trashy novels all night, I have news for you. I can get rid of you so fast, missy, you won't know what happened."

JoElle tried to hide her fear. He didn't look dangerous, but she'd seen some very frail patients who were capable of out wrestling the strongest guard. But one thing for sure, the man was at the right place and the sooner he was committed, the safer she'd be.

"Please, have a seat, sir, and I'll have someone come help you." She pressed a button under her desk and a big, burly guard walked in. "Need help, Miss Jernigan?"

"Yes, thank you, Robert. Please take this gentleman and show him the men's quarters."

"Sure, thing."

The scrawny fellow yelled, "Take your hands off me, you big brute. I'm Dr. Woodfin B. Truett and I am employed at this hospital."

The guard held tightly but glanced questionably at the bookkeeper.

The man's little pointed chin jutted forward. "Look in my briefcase and you'll find my credentials, along with a letter from Dr. Manley with instructions for me to begin tonight at eleven o'clock."

Miss Jernigan tried to catch her breath, then exclaimed, "I'm so sorry, Doctor. But I thought—"

"I don't care what you thought, you incompetent nincompoop. You're fired."

She lowered her head. "Yessir. I'm so sorry, sir."

"Sorry, is right. Now, get out of here and don't show your face at this institution ever again."

JoElle took her pocketbook from the desk drawer and cried all the way back to her room in the boarding house. How would she afford to make the rent at the end of the month?

****

Nurse Althie Whitaker arrived at the hospital forty minutes before time for her shift to begin Friday morning. She stopped by the kitchen and placed breakfast trays on a cart. The cook stirred a pot of oatmeal and croaked, "Whatcha doing here so early, Whitaker? We ain't hardly got enough food cooked to fill up a cart."

"Dr. Manley put me in charge until the new doctor arrives, and I want to get everything done in a timely manner, to prove his confidence in me was not ill-placed." She rolled the cart down the Four-Hundred hall, stopping at the first three cells, dropping off trays. Her heart pounded as she turned the key to room #440. Then rolling the cart inside, she stopped and let out a blood-curdling scream, making sure she was heard all the way down to the kitchen. Then taking the elevator to the main floor, she rushed over to the new doctor's office, screaming. "Doctor, a patient is missing."

Dr. Truett stood. "What do you mean, missing?"

"Four-forty is gone."

"Gone? Are you saying you left the cell door unlocked?"

"Of course not. I stayed late last night because I was worried about her."

"How so?"

"Well, I ain't got no chil'un, and my patients are like family. Poor, sweet Four-Forty has been upset for the past few days, ever since her husband showed up for a visit. She was in bed asleep when I left after my shift. But I went to drop off her breakfast just now, and although her door was locked, she's not in her room. I suppose you made the rounds last night. Was she in her room?"

"Uh . . . Four-forty, you say?" He scratched his head. I walked the halls, but I didn't actually go into the rooms. I assumed all the patients were asleep."

"Oh, dear. So, you have no idea what time of the night she went missing." Althie managed to shed a few tears before choking out the words, "The staff should be notified to check every floor and scour the grounds. We must locate the poor dear."

"Nurse, I'll thank you not to tell me how to run this hospital." He picked up the telephone and made a call to the Sheriff's office.

Minutes later the sheriff and two officers arrived at the hospital and asked to speak to the staff member who last saw the patient in her cell. Dr. Truett pointed to Nurse Whitaker.

The older officer said, "Ma'am, are you positive the patient was in her room when you left yesterday."

"Of course, I'm sure. I stayed late, taking care of loose ends, hoping to impress Dr. Manley when he returns. The last thing I did before leaving last night was to check on her. I tucked her and her baby in bed, turned out the light, locked the door and left."

The officers exchanged glances. "Baby? No one mentioned a baby. Did she take it with her?"

"Oh, it isn't a live baby."

The younger officer said, "You're saying she kept a dead baby in the hospital?"

"No. She has a doll that she *thinks* is her baby, God bless her. Four-for . . . the patient, Eloise . . . uh, Elvira, is really quite attractive." She gave a little tsk-tsk. "It's a crying shame such a beautiful, sweet soul has done gone bat crazy. Who knows why it happens? The only reason I work here is to try to bring a little sunshine into their sad, pitiful lives, but I can tell you right now, it's draining on the nerves."

"Ma'am, just the details that could help in the investigation, if you please."

"I was getting to that. Well, as I said, I stopped to check on her before going home and she was sound asleep, but her baby doll was in the rocking chair, so I picked it up and laid it in the bed with her, so she'd have it when she woke up. Then, like I said, I tucked 'em in and that's the last I saw of her."

The young guy said, "You sound like a very caring individual, ma'am."

"Most folks tell me that. But these poor wretched souls are like family to me. Can't help but love 'em, don't ya' know."

The officer in charge said, "We've checked all the windows and doors, and nothing appears to have been amiss. The only thing I can figure is that she managed to cajole someone to let her out."

Althie nodded. "It appears that way to me too, sir."

"Then you have no idea who that someone might be?"

She placed her forefinger on the side of her cheek. "Now, that you mention it, I do have my suspicions, but I hate to accuse anyone."

"Just tell us what you know."

"Well, her husband and a preacher came to see her Monday and her husband was all set to carry her home. Dr. Manley would've approved it, if it hadn't been for my recommendation that sweet Elma needed further treatment. Oh, m'goodness, when the doc refused to discharge her, the man was fit to be tied. He ranted and raved and I heard him swear he'd get her outta here, one way or t'other. Yessir, that's exactly what he said. He'd get her out one way or t'other."

Her eyes squinted as if she were concentrating on trying to pull up the memory. "You know, looking back on it, I suspect the husband brought the preacher to help him get her out, but they must've realized I was too sharp for 'em and they'd have to attempt it when I wasn't on duty. I got a feeling they slipped in here last night and got her." She nodded, as if to confirm her own story. "That's exactly what happened."

"But how would they have gotten in?"

"Beats me, but you might ask the doctor who was on call that question, since the disappearance happened on his watch. That would be Dr. Truett."

"We've already talked to the doctor, but we'll be investigating further."

"I'm just shocked, to be honest. Nothing like this has ever happened here before, but then, of course, it was the doctor's first night. Maybe he let 'em in and they overpowered him. I reckon if that was the case, he'd be slow to admit it." She shrugged. "Or maybe he forgot to lock the front door and they slipped in when he wasn't looking. I sure wish I could be more help, fellows. I just hope she's safe. I won't sleep a wink until that sweet little thing is found and brought back where she belongs. I can't imagine her fright."

"Well, I suppose if you're right and her husband is the one who kidnapped her, she's likely to be safe. He must love her very much to go to such lengths to get her out."

"You'd think. But have you considered that he may be the reason the poor thing is in the shape she's in? Who knows what goes on behind closed doors?"

"You've been extremely helpful ma'am. Where can we find

the name of the men who came to see her Monday?"

"Come with me. They would've had to register with their names and addresses in the office. I'll find it for you."

After writing down Liberty and Cass's information, they thanked her, then called the Police Station in Vinegar Bend and Citronelle with instructions to take the men into custody and have the patient returned to the institution.

****

Friday morning JoElle Jernigan waited until after she was sure the obnoxious new doctor had left the hospital, before going back to retrieve her raincoat and galoshes she kept in the office cloak room. She was grateful to see that the guard whom she instructed to carry Dr. Truett to a cell had not been fired.

"Oh, Robert, I hope I didn't get you in trouble, but I honestly thought—"

He chuckled. "I know what you thought, and for good reason. He sure acted like a candidate for a padded cell. He whooped and hollered after you left, but to tell the truth, I think he decided he might need me around. Of course, he may not be around long, after the kidnapping that occurred on his shift."

"Kidnapping? What are you saying?"

"You haven't heard? A woman on the fourth floor was kidnapped sometime after midnight by her husband and a preacher."

"You don't say. Would you happen to know who she is?"

"They said her last name is McAlister, but she went by Four-forty. I only remembered her name because my Grandmother's last name was McAlister. According to Nell, who works in the kitchen, the woman has a doll that she thinks is a real baby. Sad, ain't it, how many women don't give a pigs eye for the young'uns they bring into this world, and yet other women like her go crazy, longing for a little one to love."

He had no idea how much truth was in his musings. For years, JoElle had longed to hold a child close to her breast while humming Rock-a-bye-baby and to hear a sweet little voice calling her Mama. She cleared her throat. "Oh, m'goodness, I remember her well. Nurse Whitaker would often take her out to the Courtyard for no other reason than to make a spectacle of her. It broke my heart the way that old hag taunted the poor soul. Can I tell you something, Robert? I'm glad her husband kidnapped her, and I hope Whitaker is fired because of it. She does nothing but cause anguish to the patients incarcerated here."

"That won't likely happen, since it wasn't on her shift, but I'm quite sure the new doctor will have a lot of explaining to do when Dr. Manley returns. Lucky for you, the new doc sent you home at the beginning of your shift, so it can't be blamed on you."

"Maybe not, but I'll never find another job after Dr. Manley hears what happened the night before Dr. Truett arrived."

"You've lost me. Wednesday night? What happened?"

"You don't know?"

"I know nothing."

If Robert hadn't encountered the phony doctor posing as

Truett, it meant she was the only employee who had seen him. And now, she knew exactly what he'd come for. The thought that he'd gotten away with his plan made her smile. "Robert, didn't you wonder why I didn't realize Dr. Truett was the new doctor, since Dr. Manley informed us he'd be arriving Thursday night?"

Grinning, he said, "Not at all. He seemed crazy enough to me. I was ready to lock him up. Well, I gotta get back to work. I sure hope things work out for you, Miss Jernigan."

"Thanks, Robert." After he left, JoElle opened a file drawer, and thumbed through every file until she found the name, McAlister. She quickly jotted down the address, then retrieved her raincoat and galoshes, and hurried out the door.

CHAPTER 6

Shortly after seven o'clock Friday morning, Cass got dressed to go speak with the church deacons concerning the pastoral position. He kept mum, not wanting to raise Rebekah's hopes until it was a done deal.

Rebekah frowned. "I thought you were staying home, today. Where are you going?"

He straightened his tie, then pecked her on the cheek. "Don't look so gloomy. I'm not leaving town. I have a little errand to run, but I'll be back shortly." He was putting on his shoes when someone pounded on the front door.

Rebekah said, "I wonder who that could be this early?"

"Probably one of Dempsey's boys hung out at the still all night. Those boys are drinking up the moonshine faster than Dempsey can get it in jugs. I'll go point him toward home."

She pulled the curtain back and her jaw dropped, seeing the

Sheriff's car. Thrusting her hand over her heart, she clutched Cass's upper arm. "Oh, Cass. It's Sheriff Lloyd. They've apparently found Liberty." She burst into full blown sobs.

Liberty? Suicide? No wonder there was no answer when he called last night. His throat ached. Why couldn't he have seen the signs? Rebekah's spiritual gift was discernment, yet he blew her off when she tried to warn him. But what could he have done? "I suppose since Liberty's only kin is Elsie—and she's in no condition to do it—they've come for me to identify the body."

The knocking continued as he tied the last shoestring. Making his way down the hall, he opened the door, then motioning them inside with a slight toss of his head, his voice quaked. "You fellows come on in. But please keep your voices down if you will. My father-in-law is still asleep across the hall and he hasn't been well lately."

The men followed him into the parlor, and Rebekah joined them, while fastening her robe around her waist.

Cass said, "I'll make it easier for you, Lloyd. I know why you're here, and as soon as I can grab my hat, I'll be ready to go with you."

The Sheriff appeared stunned. "Oh, Preacher, I kept hoping it wasn't true. This is so hard to believe. But why?"

Cass lowered his head in his hands. "I know it doesn't make sense, Lloyd, but Liberty didn't want to go on living without Elsie. Being one of my dearest friends, I can't tell you how it affected me Monday, seeing him in such pain."

Rebekah let out a gasp. "Poor Elsie. What will become of her now?"

The younger officer blurted, "Missy, I 'spect you ought to be worrying more about what's gonna become of you and your youngun's. Your husband is in hot water for making it possible for Mr. McAlister to pull it off."

Cass's brow shot up. "Hold on, just a cotton-pickin' minute. Did you just accuse me of aiding him? Why would I do that? Liberty is my friend."

The officer chuckled. "Do you always answer your own questions?"

Rebekah shrieked. "My husband has been out of town since last Tuesday. He only got home late last night."

Sheriff Lloyd lowered his head. "I appreciate your honesty, Rebekah. Preacher, would you please come with us."

Cass gave her a hug and whispered, "It's okay, hon. Pay no attention to the egotistical pipsqueak. He's trying to exert his authority, but he has no idea what he's talking about. I'm sure Lloyd needs me to make a positive identity. Try not to worry. I'll be home shortly."

When Lloyd bypassed town and headed northwest, Cass leaned forward from the back seat. "Say, where are you going?"

"We've had instruction to take you to the jail in Chatom."

"Why Chatom?"

Lloyd said, "Sit back, please. You're breathing down my

neck."

Cass hoped he was wrong, but it seemed he detected a sharp reversal in Lloyd's attitude. He sounded almost belligerent. What caused the change?

Butch looked over his left shoulder and with a smirk on his face, said, "Just because you're a preacher, I reckon you thought you could get away with it. But I bet you didn't think your wife would be the one to rat on you."

"Rat on me? Lloyd, what's he talking about?"

The sheriff made no comment, but Butch rattled on like a bunch of tin cans tied to the back of an automobile. "You heard her. She admitted you were in on it. Said so, plain as day."

"In on it? That's crazy. Weren't you listening? She told you I was out of town."

"Yes, she did, and we know exactly where you were."

"Then you know I was in Montgomery and didn't get home until late last night."

"Likely story. I suppose someone can collaborate your whereabouts?"

"Well, no. I left Montgomery late, then I had a flat tire on the way—" Concluding no one was interested in hearing the truth, he clamped his mouth shut and leaned back.

Cass was booked in the County jail in Chatom at nine-forty-five, Friday morning and asked permission to call his wife. He told Rebekah where they had taken him and urged her to remain strong.

After hanging up, he asked to call his lawyer but was informed he could only have one phone call and he'd used it already.

He heard Lloyd and the jailer talking in low tones, then minutes later the front door to the jail slammed shut and all hopes of going back to Vinegar Bend with Lloyd were squashed. Sitting on the hard cot in the jail cell, his thoughts were concentrated on what would happen to his family while he waited for a trial, which left little time to grieve for his friend, He buried his face in his hands and muttered, *"Thanks, Liberty. Not only did you take your own life, but you may have robbed me of mine. What were you thinking?"*

Young Butch strutted over to the cell and with his legs spraddled out and his hands on his hips, he quipped, "Being an officer of the law, I'm qualified to instruct you that the sooner you cooperate, the sooner you'll get out of here. It could mean the difference in spending a considerable time in the slammer and a slap on the wrist. Are you ready to talk?"

Sheriff Lloyd rolled his eyes. "That's enough, Butch. Go wait in the patrol car. I'll be out shortly."

Cass couldn't hear the conversation taking place between the sheriff and the jailer, but he had a feeling he was in serious trouble. Did they honestly think he could've participated in Liberty's suicide? How utterly bizarre. Yet, they must've had reason to suspect him, lest he wouldn't be here.

The jailer picked up an apple from his desk, and bit down on the crisp fruit, then walked over to Cass's cell. "You ain't gotta stay here, you know."

Cass jumped to his feet. "Really?"

"'Course not. Just tell the truth." Chomping on the apple, he said, "Ever'body knows you helped your friend pull off his little shenanigan, and the sooner you confess, the easier it'll go on you."

Cass rolled his eyes. "Shenanigan?" What a strange way to describe a hopeless man's last act on this earth. Unaware of what the punishment for aiding in a suicide would be, should he be falsely convicted by a jury, he supposed it would be . . . *murder*? The thought made him shudder.

"It's like this, preacher. We know Mr. McAlister didn't do it alone. Who else would be interested in kidnapping a crazy woman, other than her husband and the cohort who went with him to the asylum to stalk out the joint three days earlier?"

Cass's jaw dropped. "Wait! You aren't saying . . . Elsie? Liberty kidnapped her? This gets more bizarre by the minute. I thought I was being accused of aiding in a suicide. I haven't kidnapped anyone."

"Well, that ain't what I'm hearing. But maybe you should tell us about the suicide."

"Apparently, there's been no suicide. I did go with Liberty McAlister to the hospital Monday with hopes of bringing his wife home, but the doctor refused to release her."

"Well, your story checks out up to that point. But we have a hunch you two went back last night and kidnapped her. What we can't figure out is how you did it."

****

Rebekah went downstairs and knocked on her Papa's door, before slightly pushing it open. He hadn't been well lately, and she'd expected to find him still in bed. "Papa?" She was surprised to see him sitting in his chair in front of the fireplace.

"Come on in, sugar. I've been sitting here praying, ever since those fellows came for Cass."

"Then you heard?"

"Yeah. Ain't no way Cass took part in Liberty's death. Why, he's dedicated his life to saving souls, not killin' 'em."

"You're right, Papa. They've booked him, but I know they'll set him free just as soon as they realize they've made a terrible mistake."

"So, you've heard from him since they took him away?"

"Yes, Cass called a few minutes ago. They've booked him in the County jail in Chatom. I'm going there to help clear up this mess. Gazelle will get the twins dressed and ready for school and I'll have her watch the two little ones until I get back. Breakfast is on the table."

"Sure, hon. But Gazelle will have her hands full with the baby. I'll keep Badger. Me and my little man will be just fine. But I didn't know you could drive. I learn new things every day."

"I can't, but Goat can. He's been driving on the back roads since he was eleven or twelve. Cass doesn't allow him to drive on the pavement, but this is an emergency."

"Well, you go on and do what you have to do, and don't you

worry about us, you hear?"

Rebekah ran upstairs to Goat's bedroom and squealed. "You aren't even up? Get dressed and hurry."

He rolled over and mumbled. "Good granny, Rebekah, you don't have to holler."

"Goat, I said get up. Now!"

"Aww, shucks, Rebekah. Five more minutes? Please? I'll have plenty of time to dress for school. I promise."

"You won't be going to school today. I need you to drive me somewhere."

His eyes popped open and his voice rose an octave. "Drive you? For real? Sure! Why didn't you say so to start with? Where are we going?"

"Stop asking so many questions and get dressed. I'll fill you in on the way."

Five minutes later, he was dressed and downstairs. He chirped in a sing-song voice, "Chauffeur Eli Nathan Marlowe is at your disposal, Madame. Where shall I take you?"

Rebekah feigned a smile. She couldn't discern whether this outburst of excitement was spurred by permission to drive the car or over the news he wouldn't be going to school, or the combination. However, in a few short minutes that enthusiasm would drain when she'd be forced to reveal the heartbreaking news that his father was in jail for aiding in a man's death.

She related the whole horrible scenario as he drove and was

pleasantly surprised at his mature response. Rebekah assumed she'd be consoling Goat and instead, she found he was consoling her.

Goat drove to the parking lot on the west side of the jail. She stepped out of the car and took a few steps before turning back around and looking at her stepson. "I don't know how long this will take but stay here until I come back. And Pray!"

He gave a salute and winked. "I've been praying all the way. God's gonna take care of it, Rebekah. You'll see."

If only she could have that same assurance. She ran into the building and after catching her breath, announced to the fellow sitting at the desk. "I'm here to see my husband, the Reverend Castle Marlowe."

Without looking up from the book he was reading, he simply pointed to the hall. "Fourth cell on the right."

The hall was dark and dingy, but she heard her husband's voice.

"You shouldn't have come here, hon."

She ran up and grabbed the cell bars with both hands, and felt comforted when he clasped his big, strong fingers around hers.

He said, "Are the kids okay? I hope they aren't worried."

"No one knows but Goat. He drove me here."

"That's good. What about your Papa? Does he know?"

"Yes. I spoke with him before leaving this morning to let him know I'd be gone. He said he was awake when the officers came, so he heard everything. He loves you, Cass. He said after they took you away, he'd spent every minute praying."

His voice broke. "Thank him for me. For sure, I need all the prayers I can get." Cass wanted to appear confident and relieve her fears, yet it would be wrong to give her false hopes.

CHAPTER 7

Rebekah stared the jailer square in the face, and in a voice, which she barely recognized as her own, shrieked, "A *hunch*? Seriously? Are you saying my husband was dragged out of our home and thrown in a jail cell because you have a *hunch*? I demand you turn him loose. You can't jail a man on a hunch."

He puffed on his cigar and leaned back in his desk chair. With a sarcastic chortle, he drawled, "Apparently, I can ma'am." Then pointing to Cass, he said, "Here's proof and we plan to keep him here until he tells us where Mr. McAlister and his wife can be located." Laying his cigar in the ash tray, he said, "It would be to his advantage to do so."

Cass groaned. "How can I tell what I don't know? I haven't seen Liberty McAllister since I let him off at his house, Monday night, after returning from the hospital."

Rebekah plunked her hands on her hips. "My husband has kidnapped no one and I demand he be released." She stomped a foot. "Now!"

Though he fully realized the charges levied against him, Cass smiled in spite of it. Never had he seen his little wife so fired up. "Honey, don't you see what this means?"

"Yes, it means they've convicted you falsely."

"But besides that. It means Liberty is alive and well, and he has his Elsie back. That's something to rejoice over."

Butch said, "There, Lloyd. Did you hear what he just said? He said he's glad he done it."

Rebekah rolled her eyes.

****

Friday morning, Liberty lay in bed awake, staring at his beautiful wife, but not wanting to disturb her since she'd had a very restless night.

Shortly after eight o'clock, her eyes popped open and she jumped out of bed and ran to the corner of the room, screaming.

Yesterday had been so good, he had high hopes of a quick recovery. What caused her to slip back into these deliriums? She glared as if she had no idea who he was.

"Elsie? Baby, it's me. Liberty."

She screamed, "No. You stole my baby. Don't come near me. I hate you." Braced against the wall, she slowly slid down and sat on the floor.

The door eased open and Aunt Nan tiptoed inside, walked over to the crib and picked up the doll. In a soft, soothing voice that would make the angels sing, she said, "Little Rebekah Lou needs changing." Then slowly walking toward Elsie, she said, "Would you like for Aunt Nan to change her dear?"

It was as if someone had taken an eraser and erased the fear from her drawn face. Her eyes lit up. "Yes, please. If it wouldn't trouble you too much."

"No trouble at all, but maybe Rebekah Lou's father would like to do the honors."

Elsie lifted her shoulders. "Her father? Where is he? Is he here? I want to see him."

Liberty's throat couldn't have ached more if someone had slit it with a butcher knife.

Aunt Nan said, "Yes dear, Liberty is here, and he loves his little Rebekah Lou very much, don't you, Liberty?"

His chin quivered. Were they simply prolonging the illness by going along with Elsie's heartbreaking hallucinations? His gaze locked with his wife's. "Yes ma'am, I love our little Rebekah Lou." He slowly walked toward her, wanting to hold her in his arms, yet fearful that it might set off another panic attack. He eased down on the floor and sat next to her and waited.

Elsie laid her head on his shoulder. His heart was too full to speak but he reached for her hand and held it.

Aunt Nan said, "Elsie, I've changed the baby. Would you care to hold her, or shall I put her in her crib and let her sleep?"

Elsie lifted her head. "What do you think, Liberty?"

"I think she might like to sleep. Why don't you and I go downstairs and eat breakfast, while she naps?" He stood and reached down to help lift her from the floor. When he did, she threw her arms around his neck and kissed him, passionately.

He smiled. "What was that for?"

"For loving me. I know I'm not well, Liberty. I get so confused at times, but you've never given up on me. Please, don't ever leave me and the baby."

He held her tightly. "Never. I could never leave you."

Before they reached the bottom of the stairs, the comforting smell of chicory in the Luzianne coffee wafted in the cool air. Sitting down at the dining table, Liberty picked up the platter of ham and forked a slab on Elsie's plate.

She smiled. "This looks good and I'm very hungry. Thank you, Grandmother."

Aunt Nan glanced at Liberty and winked. "I'm glad you have an appetite this morning, dear. I hope you enjoy."

Liberty said, "Won't you sit down and eat with us?"

"Oh, I ate hours ago, but I will have another cup of coffee and visit with you before I have to get a room ready for a guest."

Liberty assumed she saw the fear on his face, because she added quickly, "You'll like her and she'll love all three of you."

He bit his lip. "I don't know. Perhaps we should think about heading back to Vinegar Bend."

Aunt Nan shook her finger back and forth. "You'll do no such thing. You aren't ready, yet."

He knew she was right. She was a big help. Not only did she

cook their meals, but it seemed whenever he didn't know what to do, Aunt Nan always came to the rescue. But the thought of sitting across the table with another boarder made him cringe. It wasn't that he was ashamed of Elsie, but the thought of someone making crude remarks about her cuddling a doll could make him say something he might regret.

As if reading his thoughts, Aunt Nan said, "I can hardly wait for you to meet my cousin, Bunny."

Liberty's fears eased. If Bunny was anything like her cousin Nan, he'd have nothing to worry about. "I'm sure you're looking forward to her visit."

"Indeed, I am. Poor dear just lost her job and though she was trying to be brave, I'm sure it was traumatic for her. She's worked there for years."

"That's too bad. I suppose she'll be staying with you while looking for work in Grove Hill."

"I wish that were true. I tried to convince her it would be perfect, but she's always been very independent. I could be wrong, but I got the distinct feeling she's embarking on a mission."

"Religious, is she?"

"Well, she's a fine Christian woman, if that's what you're asking, but that's not the kind of mission I meant. She's looking for someone, although she didn't go into detail on the telephone. Said she'd fill me in when she gets here." With a twinkle in her eye, she snickered. "Just between the two of us, I have a feeling she may be looking for an old beau."

Liberty smiled. "Sounds intriguing."

"I'm merely speculating, mind you. But she was in love with a man for many years. Why two grown people who were obviously meant for each other wouldn't go ahead and get married was a mystery to me, but I'm sure they had their reasons. He came here with her several years ago. I lose track of time, don't ya' know. Coulda been five years. Maybe even ten. Oh m'goodness, he was such a distinguished-looking fellow and she seemed crazy about him. I have a feeling something dreadful happened between them, because when I asked about him, she didn't want to talk about it."

Liberty glanced at Elsie, who'd been curiously quiet during the conversation and smiled. "You weren't kidding. You really were hungry, weren't you sweetheart?"

She nodded. "Liberty?"

"What's on your mind, sweetheart?"

"Rebekah Lou . . . she's sleeping upstairs. Isn't she?"

"Yes, hon. Remember, Aunt Nan put her in the crib?"

Her brow creased. "Yes, Aunt Nan. I sometimes forget and think she's a grandmother."

Aunt Nan said, "Well, I'm flattered, dear. I'd like to think of myself as Rebekah Lou's grandmother. Every child should have a grandmother, don't you agree?"

The lines on Elsie's brow relaxed. "Yes, I do agree. I had a grandmother and she lived in a big house on Main Street in Vinegar Bend. I called her Big Mama and every year for my birthday, she'd bake me a twelve-layer chocolate layer cake, and let me lick the pan, after she iced it."

Liberty's pulse raced as she spouted off vivid details of her childhood, though he tried not to get his hopes up. He'd allowed his hopes to rise on numerous occasions whenever she'd show signs of recalling past events, only to have them crushed time and again.

****

The phone rang at the Marlowe home, and Gazelle grabbed it to keep it from waking little MyEwe. "Marlowe Residence."

"Rebekah?"

"I'm sorry, this is Gazelle."

"Gazelle, this is Liberty McAlister. May I speak with your father?"

"He isn't here."

"Oh? Then, please call Rebekah to the phone."

"She isn't here, either."

"When do you expect them?"

"I don't know. I suppose Father is on the lecture circuit and Rebekah asked me to get the twins ready for school and to stay with little MyEwe. She didn't mention where she was going or when she'd be back." She giggled. "Rebekah acted so mysterious, I have a feeling she and Father are planning a surprise. May I take a message?"

"No, thank you. Just tell them not to worry about us. Everything is gonna work out just fine."

"Yessir. I'll pass it on."

****

Cass's attorney arrived at the jail with proof that Cass had been in Montgomery at a Conference from early Tuesday morning until Thursday afternoon. He'd also tracked down the only man in the county with an automobile fitting the description of the Good Samaritan who gave Cass a ride back to his car. The fellow confirmed that he let Cass borrow a pump to pump up his tire and that he couldn't possibly have driven from Montgomery to Tuscaloosa Thursday night, taken part in a kidnapping, and made it back home in Vinegar Bend by the time the officers arrived Friday morning.

Walking to the parking lot, Rebekah said, "You look troubled. I'd think you'd be thrilled to be out of there. What's on your mind? Liberty?"

"I'm no longer worried about Liberty. I don't claim to know the law, but he'll probably be charged with breaking and entering but I don't see how they can charge him with kidnapping his own wife if she went with him of her own accord."

"If it isn't Liberty that's troubling you, what is it?"

"Rebekah, I've been inside that same jail many times to minister to men awaiting trial and I've heard some of them tell stories, claiming their innocence. But I never took a single one of them seriously. I assumed they were guilty, or they wouldn't be behind bars. Do you think the Lord allowed me to experience what it feels like to be falsely accused in order that I might be more compassionate?"

They reached the parking lot and Rebekah stopped short. Looking around, her jaw dropped.

"Where's the car, hon?"

Rebekah threw up her hands. "I told him not to leave until I got back. Where could he have gone?"

Cass stepped out in the street and pointed. "That's my car in front of the drug store." They walked the two blocks, went inside and found Goat sitting at the counter, flirting with the cute soda jerk who was at least four years older than him and from appearances, Cass surmised she'd been around the block a time or two.

Goat saw them coming in the door, and quickly slurped the last sip of his malted milk before sliding off the stool. "Nice meeting you, Jessie. Got to go drive my parents back home."

If Cass hadn't had more important things weighing heavily on his mind, he would've had plenty to say to his son, but at the time it didn't seem worth pursuing.

CHAPTER 8

The minute the car drove up in the yard, Gazelle grabbed MyEwe in her arms and ran out screaming, "Where in the world have y'all been? Rebekah, I assumed when you and Goat left, you'd be back shortly, and I could go to school. I had a report due today."

Her father said, "Don't blame Rebekah, hon. It was my fault."

Rebekah took the baby from her arms. "Gazelle, I'm sorry. It's a long story but I'll explain everything after I get supper on the stove. I'll write your teacher a note to let her know it was a family emergency and I'm sure she'll allow you to give your report tomorrow. How's Grandpa?"

"I took him a slice of pound cake and a cup of coffee about an hour ago and he said he was fine, but to tell the truth, he didn't look so good to me. Badger was playing with blocks on the floor and I tried to get him to come with me, but Grandpa said he was fine and to leave him be."

Rebekah smiled. "Those two have a very special bond."

"MyEwe was a little angel all morning. She's no trouble at all, unlike Badger at her age. Oh, I almost forgot! Liberty called and asked to speak to Father and when I told him he wasn't home, he asked to speak with you."

Cass's eyes widened. "What else did he say?"

"Nothing."

"Nothing? Surely, he said something. Think, Gazelle. Think! It could be very important."

Rebekah said, "Calm down, Cass. I'm sure he'll call back."

Gazelle's brow furrowed. "What's going on?" Not waiting for an answer, she added, "When I told him you weren't home, I asked if I could take a message and all he said was 'tell your Father not to worry about us, we're gonna be okay.' Then we hung up."

Cass leaned down and kissed the top of her head. "Thank you, honey. You did real good."

****

JoElle Jernigan arrived at her cousin's boarding house at a quarter past eight, Friday night.

Nan met her with hugs at the front door. "Oh my lands, Bunny, I've walked this floor for two solid hours, waiting for you. I was afraid you might've had an accident."

Her cousin giggled. "You're still the worry-wart. I came as soon as I could pack the car. Gee, Nan, it's good to see you. I miss those long talks we used to have, lying on Grandmother Jernigan's big feather bed." Walking down the long hall, she glanced about. "You said you had boarders. I suppose they left?"

"Oh, no. They retired to their room shortly after supper. The wife is precious, but rather fragile, so her sweet husband sees to it that she doesn't overexert."

"I look forward to meeting them at breakfast."

Nan bit her lip. "Bunny, there's something I should warn you about before you meet them. Of course, since you've worked in a mental hospital for decades, I'm sure nothing shocks you. They're a lovely couple, but the woman may come to breakfast holding a doll."

"A to baby doll?"

"Yes. Poor dear thinks it's real and her sweet husband goes along with it. Sad, isn't it?"

"Very sad. How long will they be staying?"

"I'm not sure." Nan clasped her hands together. "But enough about my boarders. I'm interested in knowing about this mysterious hunt you're on, although I have a feeling that I already know who you're searching for."

"You do?"

"It wasn't hard to figure out. You and your gentleman friend, Theo, were perfect together. I heard the pain in your voice the last time I asked about him. But when you called and said you were going to look for someone, you didn't fool me for a minute."

"Got me all figured out, do you?"

"Shucks, Bunny, you know we've never been able to fool one another."

"Nan, it's been a very trying day. Would you mind terribly if I went to bed?"

"Of course not. I wish we could spend more time together, but I believe you said you'd be leaving shortly after breakfast. I normally have breakfast at seven, but if you need to leave earlier, we could have our meal at six."

"I did say I'd be leaving after breakfast, didn't I? However, you're right. We need more time together. Seven o'clock will be fine. If it won't inconvenience you, I think I'll stick around for a while."

"Oh, honey, that's wonderful. I've put you in the Rhett room. If I'd known you were coming, I would've saved the Scarlett room for you. I know it's your favorite, but Bonnie Belle's crib is in there."

Bunny smiled. "I suppose that's where the baby doll sleeps?"

"Yes. In a way, it'll break your heart, yet, seeing how the woman cares for that doll makes you wish every child could be so blessed as to have such a caring mother." Then, throwing up her hands she said, "My goodness, how I do go on. You need to get some rest. Goodnight, my dear. I'll ring the breakfast bell at seven."

****

Liberty awoke at six-thirty and ran his hand over Elsie's empty side of the bed. Hearing a creaking sound, he sat up and stared at the beautiful scene of his wife sitting in a chair, rocking back and forth while humming to their baby. *Our baby?* His throat tightened. If only—

He walked over and kissed his wife, then placed a kiss on the side of the doll's face. "Good morning, beautiful."

He swallowed hard, reminding himself that if he didn't help her overcome this fantasy of hers, he'd be sucked into it with her. He was already beginning to act as if Rebekah Lou was real. It began as a way to reach Elsie. Now, as hard as it was to admit, he found he sometimes enjoyed pretending along with her. How happy they would've been if only the pregnancy had been real.

Elsie's smile melted his heart. It would take time and patience, but things were going to be better, he could feel it. She even picked out the dress she'd wear this morning and brushed her own hair.

"Liberty, I've enjoyed our visit, but I'm ready to go home. Besides, I'm sure you need to get back to the farm."

"About that—I sold the farm, Elsie."

"Sold it? But why?" Then, answering her own question, she said, "To take care of me. Oh, Liberty, I am so sorry. I know how much the farm meant to you."

"Honey, the farm meant a lot to me, but you mean more than all the farms in the whole world. I don't regret my decision."

"But how will we live?"

"Money is something you'll never have to worry about. I didn't work the farm for income, I worked it because farming is in my blood. One day, you'll be well, and we'll consider buying another farm," At the sound of the bell, he said, "I believe breakfast is ready."

"I'm glad. I'm starving. Your grandmother said last night that we'd have pancakes for breakfast. Sounds good, doesn't it?"

Grandmother? He smiled. Though she was still confused, she'd begun to communicate. It wasn't his imagination. The Elsie standing beside him was not the same Elsie he observed in the asylum. She'd come a long way in such a short time. Had they been feeding her drugs in the hospital that contributed to the heart-wrenching stupor? There were still hills to climb but together they'd make it to the other side. Her memory was definitely improving. The next step would be to help her realize there was no baby and never had been. His gut twisted in knots when she picked up the doll. Was it time to tell her? Did he dare take the chance of losing her again? He placed a hand on her shoulder. His hands shook. "Elsie, sweetheart, may I hold it?"

"It?" She giggled.

"Yes, darling." He swallowed hard.

Holding it with both arms extended, he said, "Sweetheart, do you understand that Rebekah Lou is a doll?"

"Yes, she is. She has your beautiful blue eyes. Let's go downstairs. I'm hungry."

Disappointed, that it hadn't gone as he'd hoped, he handed the doll back to her.

When Liberty and Elsie entered the dining room, Aunt Nan invited them to have a seat.

"My cousin will be down shortly." Then reaching out her arms, she said, "Elsie, hon, why don't you let me hold sweet little

Rebekah Lou while you eat your breakfast."

Liberty mouthed a "thank you," then pulled the seat out for his wife. Before he could be seated, a petite lady with salt and pepper hair walked into the room and extended her hand. "Good morning, my name is—"

Elsie jumped up. "Let's go, Liberty. I want to go home. I want to go now."

Liberty grabbed her hand and held tightly. "We haven't eaten, sweetheart. Let's eat our breakfast and if you still want to leave, I promise, we will." His words seemed to settle her, and she eased back down in her chair.

Nan's cousin took a seat across the table from them. Liberty tried not to stare, but the woman looked suspiciously like the receptionist who worked at the hospital the night he rescued Elsie. Yet, he couldn't be sure since his thoughts at the time were not on the woman at the desk, but on how to sneak his wife out without getting caught. He could feel Elsie's hand trembling. In an effort to calm her, he said, "Aunt Nan, I think Rebekah Lou may need her mama to hold her. Would you mind?"

Aunt Nan nodded and handed the doll to Elsie, who clutched her beloved Rebekah Lou, then pushed away from the table and rushed up the stairs sobbing.

Cass mumbled an apology, then hurried up to comfort his wife. He found her scrunched down, hiding in the small closet.

When he couldn't get Elsie to speak, he crouched down beside her. With no way to tell how much time had passed, he surmised it must've been half-an-hour, maybe longer, before she spoke. "Liberty, why? Why did you do it?"

His heart raced. It wasn't his imagination. The woman downstairs was indeed from the asylum and Elsie had recognized her, also.

"You called the hospital and they've sent that woman to come get me. I thought she was my friend but she's not. She's come to take me back, hasn't she?" She squealed, "You tricked me. Well, I won't go. I won't. You can't make me."

Liberty placed his palms on either side of her face, forcing her to look at him. "No, no, no, sweetheart. You have it all wrong. I went to a lot of trouble to sneak you out of the hospital. Why would I do that if I intended to send you back? I'll never let anyone take you away again. Do you understand? Never! Now, let's put Rebekah Lou in the crib and go back downstairs. Maybe Aunt Nan saved us some pancakes."

"But that woman—she's still down there."

"I told you I'll never let you go back. Trust me?"

She nodded, then holding his hand tightly, walked with him to the dining room.

Nan and her cousin were still sitting at the table, visiting.

Elsie kept her head lowered with her gaze focused on the floor.

The woman said, "Elsie, you remember me, don't you? Nan calls me by the nickname I went by as a child, but my name is JoElle. You and I were in a very bad place but we're free now. It feels good to be free, doesn't it?"

Liberty clasped his wife's hand. "I'm sorry, Elsie. I don't know how she found us, but you have nothing to worry about." His face flushed. "Aunt Nan? You?"

Aunt Nan glanced from Bunny to Liberty. "What's going on?"

JoElle said, "Sir, you have it all wrong. I don't want Elsie to go back. I don't work there anymore. I'd like to help you both."

"I'm listening."

"I was fired from the hospital after the real Dr. Truett showed up Thursday night. I mistook him for a mental patient, since I was under the impression that I'd already met Dr. Truett . . . who, coincidentally looked amazingly like you."

Liberty's lip curled. "I apologize, ma'am, for getting you fired, but I'd like to have seen that doctor's face when you attempted to have him committed."

She chuckled. "The way he fought the guard, I was about to recommend solitary confinement—but then he pulled his credentials and fired me on the spot. The next day, I went to gather my things and heard that Elsie was missing, and that you were the suspect. I wanted to find you, so I pulled your records to locate your address."

"I think I'm beginning to understand. Fine! I suppose I do owe you since I was the cause of you losing your job. How much are you asking?"

"Is that what you think? I don't want your money. I left Tuscaloosa intending to spend the night at Cousin Nan's on my way to Vinegar Bend. When she told me about her new boarders, I knew it had to be you and Elsie. The Lord works in mysterious ways, his wonders to perform. I don't believe in coincidences, Mr. McAlister. God led me to you."

"If not money, then what is it you want from us?"

"I want a job."

"I don't know how I can help with that, but if a recommendation is what you need—"

"I want to work for you and Elsie. I figure as the breadwinner, you need to go to work every day, and Elsie could use a companion to stay with her while you're gone. I'd like to be that companion."

Elsie sat quietly listening, then laid her hand on her husband's wrist. "Yes."

He scratched his head. "I don't know, hon. You were frightened when you saw her."

"I'm no longer afraid. She's kind."

"Are you sure?"

Elsie stared intently at JoElle for several seconds, then nodded.

He ran his hands through his hair. "Frankly, ma'am, I have mixed feelings about this arrangement, but it seems my wife trusts you—" He sucked in a lungful of air and blew out slowly. "You'll be expected to treat her with the utmost dignity at all times, as if she were your own daughter."

JoElle's face lit up. "Thank you, sir. I'd like nothing more than to see your sweet wife completely well. I'm encouraged by the great strides she's made in the short time she's been released into your custody."

Elsie glared at Liberty. In a monotone voice she said, "But I wasn't released. My husband is a thief."

Liberty's chin quivered. Did he dare question her troubling remark or let it go?

Leaning her head against his shoulder, she said, "He first stole my heart. Then, he went and stole me and our baby from the hospital."

JoElle laughed out loud. "I do believe she's right, Mr. McAlister. You're a thief for sure. A very fine, loving, courageous thief and you wound up with a real jewel."

CHAPTER 9

Saturday morning Cass sat at the breakfast table, listening to the gleeful laughter, and enjoying the delightful camaraderie. God had blessed him beyond measure. After his first wife faked her drowning to run off with another man, it appeared his chance at happiness had been destroyed. He'd wondered how he could possibly raise five little children, alone.

Then, low and behold, along came Rebekah. He chuckled to himself. Whether she was crazy to take on such a brood or he was the crazy one for expecting a sixteen-year-old to be mature enough to handle such responsibility was debatable. But, as God would have it, marrying Rebekah turned out to be one of the wisest decisions he'd ever made. He looked across the table at his father-in-law and recalled the first few unbearable months after the old man moved in with them. Yet, what a blessing he turned out to be. Cal recalled Helen Keller's amazing story and had no doubt that God had sent little Badger his own miracle worker. For the first time since Badger's diagnosis, Call was beginning to believe that his son could lead a happy, rewarding life despite his deafness, thanks to Rebekah's Papa. All his concerns turned out to be nothing more than vain imaginations. Why did he ever doubt? Hadn't God always made a way?

After helping Rebekah with the breakfast dishes, he hung the dish rag and said, "Hon, I need to run a little errand. It shouldn't take long."

"If you're going into town, please pick up a bottle of Carter's Little Liver Pills for Papa. He's not been up to par, lately."

"Sure. I can do that." Was it wrong not to tell her he was going to see Deacon Phillips to accept the Pastoral position? He chewed the inside of his cheek as he contemplated the best way to tell her. "Hon . . ." Then, pausing, he shrugged. "Never mind. I'll be back shortly."

Goat and the twins ran downstairs, and Rebekah handed them each a syrup bucket holding their lunch. Goose and Gander stopped briefly to kiss Rebekah and their father. Goat threw up his hand. "Have a good day, Rebekah. You too, Pops."

Cass chuckled at the new moniker his son had chosen for him. "Thank you, son. I think I shall, and I hope you do well on your Algebra test."

Goat ran back to the bottom of the stairs and yelled, "Gazelle, if you're gonna walk with us, you'd better come on or we're gonna miss the bell."

Gazelle came rushing down the stairs, passed her father and

ran out the front door. Cass followed her. "Come back, young lady. Where did you get that dress?"

"Tell him, Rebekah. I need to go. We're running late."

Cass's gaze locked with his wife's. "Please tell me you didn't approve of that . . . that—"

She smiled. "Dress? It's a dress, dear."

"It's three-fourths of a dress. To be a dress, the hem needs to drop at least six inches."

Gazelle shifted from one foot to the other. "Can we please discuss my attire this afternoon? I have a test first thing this morning."

Rebekah looked at her husband and lifted a brow. "Is she free to go?"

Rolling his eyes, he said, "Go ahead. It isn't fair for you to be the cause of your siblings getting into trouble for being late, but young lady, I want you to come directly home from school. We need to have a long talk."

"Yessir." And with that, she hurried out the door.

"Rebekah, I must say, I'm extremely disappointed. You knew I wouldn't approve of her wearing a dress exposing herself in such a shameful way."

"Cass, sweetheart, the dress looks darling on her. All the young girls are wearing them a bit shorter, now. It's the latest style."

"But don't you see where it's leading, Rebekah? Next thing you know, women will be brazenly displaying their knees."

"Oh, honey, you're being overly dramatic. Frankly, I don't know why the dresses weren't shortened years ago. It would've made it much easier for a woman to get in and out of a buggy. Those long dresses were cumbersome and difficult to keep the hems from dragging the ground."

"I'll tell you why. For centuries, we've been a nation of Christian principles, but we are entering an era of moral decay and it's so subtle, the masses are unwittingly falling prey." He clamped his lips together. Why argue? It wasn't as if this was the first time he and Rebekah had been down this road. There were some arguments he apparently couldn't win. Gazelle's wardrobe was one of them. He kissed her and grabbed his hat from off the hall hat rack. "I'll be back shortly."

"Bye, and don't forget the pills for Papa."

Cass was greeted with enthusiasm by Deacon Phillips and in less than ten minutes after arriving, Friendship Community Church had hired a new Pastor.

He would continue to use his talents to sketch out his sermons to the local congregation and he'd now have more time to spend with his family and start the book of Sermon Sketches, which he'd had on the back burner for several years.

****

Saturday, Aunt Nan handed two sack lunches to Liberty and one to JoElle. "You'll be hungry by the time you reach Vinegar Bend. I've packed chicken, boiled eggs, sweet potatoes, corn pones, and fresh tea cakes."

Liberty said, "That was very kind of you. Thank you, Aunt Nan."

She reached up and gave him a hug. "I can tell you're leery of the arrangement, but I can promise you, my cousin can be trusted. She'd never lie to you, and she'd certainly never lie to me."

He feigned a smile. "Thank you." He believed Aunt Nan was being truthful and he desired to assure her he had no misgivings about the woman, but that was not the case. He could only wish it were true.

The trip was long, but after several hours on bumpy roads, Liberty pulled up in front of a lovely old home on Main Street.

JoElle's eyes watered. Many years ago, she fantasized of living in such a palatial setting.

How naïve she was to think the esteemed Dr. Theodore McDuffie ever had plans to make her his wife. She'd only worked at the hospital three months when she was offered a job at the shirt factory, making more money. However, the doctor, claiming to love her, pleaded with her to keep her night shift at the asylum. It made it convenient for them to be together, since they were the only two employees on the ground floor.

For thirty plus years, she lived in a tiny room in a Boarding House, which was all she could afford on her meager income. Like a horse with a carrot held in front of it, JoElle continued down a path with blinders on, seeing nothing but the promise of a wedding in front of her eyes. Her throat ached as she considered the years wasted for a man whom she foolishly allowed to use her.

Liberty opened the door and followed Elsie and JoElle into Elsie's beautiful childhood home. Elsie eagerly took her by the hand and said, "Come, and I'll show you two rooms and you can have your pick. Please excuse the musky odor. It's been shut up for—" She stopped. "I don't know how long."

Liberty could hardly contain the joy in his heart. His wife was making great progress. "Elsie is right. It's been shut up way too long. The first thing I need to do is open all the windows and let it air out."

JoElle's eyes glanced to and fro. "Oh, everything is so lovely. Please . . . you pick the room for me."

"Well, I suppose it would be good to place you directly across the hall from the nursery so you can hear Rebekah Lou if she should wake in the night." Then looking to her husband for confirmation, she said, "What do you think, darling?"

"That's a great idea, sweetheart."

"Then it's settled. Mine and Liberty's room is next to the nursery, but the baby has colic, so we might need to take shifts rocking her. That always makes her tummy feel better."

JoElle said, "I shall be happy to rock her all night if need be. After working the midnight shift for years, I'm accustomed to staying awake nights. However, when I do sleep, I'm a sound sleeper. So, if I fail to hear her crying, please knock on my door, and I'll be happy to tend to her until she feels better."

Elsie hugged her husband. "Didn't I tell you she'd be perfect?"

"Yes, you did. Why don't you ladies get settled and I'll bring in the luggage." He wanted to believe the woman was as sincere about wanting to help his wife as she pretended to be. He couldn't imagine what a set-back it would be for Elsie if JoElle turned out to be a plant from the hospital. What if her goal was to kidnap Elsie and take her back? He attempted to put such suspicious thoughts out of his mind. After all, the woman was most accommodating the night he asked for keys. She trusted him and he betrayed her. If either of them had a right to mistrust the other, wouldn't she have more reason to be suspicious of his motives than he of hers? Just as he would be convinced he was blessed to have her helping him, the doubts would find their way back into his thoughts.

Maybe she'd been offered a bonus for Elsie's return. He rubbed his hand across the back of his neck. But why would the hospital go to such lengths to have a patient returned to their care? Money? Of course. They possibly received a decent stipend from the State for each patient admitted. Liberty grimaced. He was becoming as paranoid as Elsie. If he didn't stop imagining the worst, JoElle would have two patients to care for instead of one.

He went back into the house and found Elsie in bed and JoElle rocking the doll in the nursery.

She said, "Elsie was exhausted from the trip, so after we ate our sack lunch, I helped her dress for bed and encouraged her to get some rest. She felt the baby needed to be rocked to sleep, so I promised I'd tend to it. I think it's about time—"

Liberty bit his lip. "Yes. I think I know what you're about to say—I suppose you think it's time I told her the truth."

She thrust her palm in the air. "Goodness, no. I was going to say I think it's time to lay Rebekah Lou in her crib. Mr. McAlister, I think you're doing everything right. Elsie has had a lot of changes in the past few days. Why don't we let her tell us when it's time?"

"But do you really think she'll come to realize on her own that her beloved Rebekah Lou is nothing more than wood and cotton stuffing?"

"I'm sure of it. She's making great strides. I've seen such a change in her. She's your wife, sir, but if you'd like my opinion, I can't see what it hurts for her to love that baby doll."

"It frightens me to think what she might do when she realizes Rebekah Lou is not real and then remembers how this all began." He explained to JoElle about Elsie's false pregnancy that sent her into a spiral, causing the delusions. "I foolishly had her committed, thinking she'd get the help she needed in the hospital. As it turned out, she was treated worse than an animal. They even suggested sterilizing her. Can you imagine? Suggesting sterilization when the reason she lost all sense of reality was because she wanted a child so badly and couldn't conceive? What was the point?"

"You were wise not to agree. Who knows, maybe in time she can have a baby."

He shook his head. "Sadly, that's not a possibility, but it's even more reason for them not to mutilate her." His face blushed. "Forgive me for bringing up such a sensitive subject. I pray I didn't embarrass you."

She smiled. "After having worked in an asylum for years, there isn't much that can embarrass me. I've seen and heard it all. Sterilization is becoming far too common, I'm afraid."

CHAPTER 10

Cass could hardly wait to get home to give Rebekah the news. Seeing her outside hanging clothes, he sneaked up behind her and wrapped his arms around her waist. When she turned her head, he kissed her on the cheek.

"You stayed gone a long time. Did you get Papa's pills?"

Slapping his palm across his forehead, he said, "Oh my lands, I knew there was something else I was supposed to do. I'll go back into town."

"Never mind. He seems to be feeling better. He's stayed in his room so much lately, I was worried that he was sick and wouldn't admit it. He assured me this morning he's been working on a project that's required him to stay shut up in his room."

"A project?"

Rebekah giggled. "You know, Papa. He was very secretive. There's no telling what he's up to."

Cass said, "Let's go in the house and sit down with a cup of coffee. I have something to tell you that I think will make you very happy."

After going inside, Rebekah cut her husband a slice of pound cake and poured two cups of coffee. "Now, what is this big surprise you have for me?"

He laid his hand on top of hers. "You now have a full-time husband."

Her brow creased. "What are you saying?"

"I won't be traveling the circuit any longer. I've already called and cancelled the schools on my schedule."

When she burst into tears, Cass was unprepared for her reaction. "I thought you'd be happy."

"Why would you think that? Have I ever even suggested that you give up your ministry?"

"No, but I know how difficult it's been for you with me away so much."

"Cass, you can't do this. It's not right."

Her attitude took him aback. "I don't get it. Don't you want me around?"

"It isn't that. God has put a calling on your life and to turn your back on it could be disastrous."

"I agree. And at this point in my life, I feel that calling is to be the Pastor of Friendship Community Church, to be available twenty-four-hours a day for my family—and to begin working on a book of Sermon Sketches."

Her nose crinkled. "But that's not possible. We have a Pastor at Friendship."

He grinned. "Yes, and you're looking at him. I didn't want to tell you until I knew for certain it was God's plan and not mine, but the deacons approached me weeks ago with the news that the preacher and his wife want to move to Georgia to be near their children. They asked if I'd consider taking over the Pastorate. It isn't something I took lightly, but I've been in constant prayer. I know God is leading in this direction."

He was relieved to see her frown turn upside down. "So, you're okay with it?"

"Okay? Oh, Cass, I'm delighted. I can hardly wait to tell the children. They love it when you're home and to think you'll be home every day and still be doing God's work will thrill them for sure."

Cass pushed back from the table to answer the telephone. It was Liberty letting him know he and Elsie had made it home.

Rebekah had so many questions when he hung up. "How's Elsie? Does she still have the doll? That's wonderful that he has a dependable lady to help nurse her back to health. But what will happen to Liberty for breaking into the hospital and kidnapping Elsie? Will they make her go back?"

"I don't have all the answers, sweetheart. I only know they're home and they have help. Let's be grateful for the good things in the here and now, instead of worrying about what tomorrow might hold. He invited us to visit, but I think we should give Elsie time to get settled. I can only imagine the stress these changes have had on her."

****

Liberty, Elsie, Rebekah Lou, and JoElle were sitting around the fire in the Parlor when someone knocked on the door. Liberty jumped up. "That must be Cass and Rebekah. I called to let them know we were home and invited them to drop by, but I didn't expect them so soon."

When he opened the door, his throat tightened, seeing the sheriff. Masking his fear, he said, "Afternoon, Lloyd. What can I do for you?"

When JoElle realized it was the law, she escorted Elsie to the bedroom, suggesting she lie down with Rebekah Lou. Then, easing back into the hall, her pulse raced as she listened to the conversation.

"Liberty, don't make this any harder than it has to be. Trust me, I don't want to be here, but I've been sent to do my job."

"Your job? I'm afraid I can't help you, Lloyd. I'm a farmer, not a lawman."

"Let's don't play games. I received a call from Bryce Hospital last Friday morning to be on the lookout for you and your wife. While having coffee at Maude's I heard someone say they spotted you driving into town. I'm afraid I need to take you in."

"You're arresting me? And what's the charge?"

"Breaking and entering. They say you broke into the hospital in the middle of the night and kidnapped your wife. I've had instructions to arrest you and to return Elsie to the institution."

Liberty broke down. "Please, Lloyd. Give me a chance to leave town with her. I'll go where you can't find me, and you don't have to let them know you found me here."

"I wish it were that easy, but I took an oath to uphold the law. Breaking and entering is a criminal offense, as is kidnapping. Don't make this any harder than it has to be, Liberty. I'm sorry. I really am."

"Then take me and do what you will. But I can't let you take Elsie. You have no idea what she went through in that place. She didn't commit a crime and there's no reason she should be required to go back. If I had known then what I know now, I would never have taken her there. I thought she'd get help, but I was wrong."

JoElle ran into the parlor and with her hands planted firmly on her hips, she boldly announced, "Sheriff, I'm afraid you've made a trip in vain."

"I'm sorry? And who are you?"

"My name is JoElle Jernigan. I'm the hospital employee who gave Liberty the keys to the patient's room Wednesday night, allowing him to leave the asylum with his wife. So, you see, he can't be charged because no crime took place. The patient was released to her husband's care by an employee."

"I'm confused."

She shrugged. "Well, sir, I didn't have the authority to release her. I broke hospital rules, but I didn't break the law. I was fired and for just reason. But there was no breaking and entering and no kidnapping."

"I understand you want to help your friends, ma'am, but there's a hole in your story. You aren't even aware when the kidnapping took place. You said, Wednesday night and according to the hospital, she went missing Thursday night."

"I can't explain why she wasn't reported missing Thursday, but I have a sneaky idea that Nurse Whitaker had something to do with it. Dr. Manley had placed her in charge, and it's possible she may have waited until after the new doctor arrived Thursday night to report it, so it would appear to have taken place on his watch. It certainly sounds like her mode of operation."

Lloyd listened intently to her story, then said, "May I use your phone?" After making a call to the hospital and verifying that the bookkeeper, a woman by the name of JoElle Jernigan was fired Thursday night, he made an apology to Liberty. "I'm sorry, man. I was only doing my job."

"I understand. No hard feelings."

After the sheriff left, Liberty's gaze locked with JoElle's. His eyes filled with tears. "Would it be inappropriate if I hugged you?"

She snickered. "I could use a hug about now. I was scared. I thought he might throw us both in the hoosegow!"

Liberty fell back into his chair. "I can hardly believe it. I'm free and I have my Elsie. Thank you, JoElle. I hate to admit it, but until you stood up to the sheriff, I had reservations about you. I didn't like having the doubts, but it seemed too much of a coincidence that you showed up at Aunt Nan's shortly after we did."

"Coincidence? Or an act of God?"

"You're right. It *was* too miraculous to be a coincidence. It was divinely orchestrated. God knew that Elsie and I would need you."

"And I needed a family, Mr. McAlister. For weeks, I watched Elsie when Nurse Whitaker would take her into the courtyard, and I could see the fear and confusion in her eyes as she clung to her Rebekah Lou. I ached to hold her in my arms to comfort her. I'm determined to see her well. When I do, I'll feel my life wasn't completely wasted. I've made so many mistakes in my lifetime. I'm not a young woman and I don't want to die, feeling as if my time on earth was spent accomplishing nothing worthwhile."

"You have a home here for as long as you wish to stay. We haven't discussed a salary, but you name it and I'll be in agreement."

"Thank you, but all I want is to help Elsie, and to cook and run the household until she is well and wishes to do it on her own. For years, I've lived in a Rooming House and worked nights. After work, I'd go to my room, sleep until three o'clock, then go downstairs to the dining hall and eat a cold plate left over from lunch. Supper was served at five o'clock, and after eating mid-afternoon, I wasn't hungry. Therefore, I had no interaction with the other boarders. It's been a very lonely life. Growing up, I was a fairly good cook. I hope I can please you and Elsie."

Liberty reached in his pocket and pulled out a money clip. He placed several folded bills into JoElle's hands. She looked down and shook her head. "I can't take this, sir. It's far too much. I wouldn't know what to do with so much money."

"Perhaps you'd like to go into town and buy you some nice clothes. I've been told there's nothing to lift a woman's spirits like a new wardrobe."

Her eyes lit up. "I know I should object, but it's been a long time since I've had a new dress. Thank you, Mr. McAlister. If it's alright with you, Elsie and I will go shopping in the morning."

He glanced down. "Perhaps it would be better for Elsie to remain here."

"I don't understand. Why, if you don't mind me asking."

He hesitated, then said, "It's . . . it's the doll. She would insist on taking it. I must do everything possible to help her retain her dignity. I can't stand the thought of people making fun of her."

"But I won't allow that to happen, sir, and I think the outing would be good for her."

"I know you mean well, but how could you prevent it?"

"I'll help Elsie understand that as Rebekah Lou's nurse, I should be the one to tend to the baby as we shop. She likes for me to hold her. If folks laugh at me, so be it. Keeping Elsie hid in this house will do more damage than she'd incur by getting out and mingling."

CHAPTER 11

Wednesday night the Marlowe family dressed to go to Prayer Meeting at Friendship Community Church. Cass and Rebekah agreed not to tell the children about his decision to accept the Pastorate, thinking it would be a fun surprise for them to hear the announcement. Naturally, they'd be overjoyed to learn their father would be spending more time at home. Rebekah had prepared refreshments to serve to friends after the service, to celebrate the good news.

The surprised look on the children's faces was a sight to behold when Deacon Phillips called Cass to the pulpit and presented him to the church. The twins squealed with delight and Goat ran up and wrapped his arms around his father, exclaiming they'd now have more time to spend together to fix up the fishing boat. Papa stayed home with Badger, and Rebekah held MyEwe in one arm and accepted congratulatory hugs from the excited church members with the other arm.

Everyone seemed thrilled—everyone but Gazelle. She glanced toward the back of the church at her beau, Ryker Adams, and saw him walking out the door. She whispered to Goat, "Tell Rebekah I needed to leave, but for her and Father not to worry about me. I'll be okay."

"Sure, sis. Another one of your headaches?"

Without responding, she slipped out without being noticed.

Ryker was driving away when she ran and jumped on the running board. He stopped and waited for her to get in. "It's no use, Gazelle. We can't do it."

"Of course, we can. My bag is packed. Nothing has changed."

"Maybe it has. Maybe I've changed."

"Are you saying you don't love me?"

"I'm saying I love you too much to cause problems between you and your father. You saw how happy he was tonight. These people love him, and he loves them. For us to proceed could cause big problems for him."

"I don't see how."

"Don't you get it? There'll be some who will say a preacher should be able to control his household and such talk could get him fired. I've just recently begun to feel he trusts me. I don't want to be the cause of him losing confidence in me, nor being disappointed in you."

"Oh, Ryker. He'll get over it. If you love me, you'll go through with it."

He drove her home, then walked around and opened the car door for her to get out.

She stood on her tiptoes, with her head held back, waiting for him to kiss her.

Instead, he brushed his fingers across her lips and said, "I'm sorry. It won't work, Gazelle. I wish it could, but it's no good."

When he turned to walk back around the car, she said, "Aren't you coming in? I heard Rebekah inviting everyone to come over for refreshments after church."

"I don't think it's a good idea. I need time to think."

"You're breaking up with me, aren't you?" Gazelle burst into tears and ran into the house. She didn't stop until she reached her bedroom.

Half-an-hour later, she heard the front door open and the sound of loud voices and laughter as people from church poured into the house.

Rebekah and two ladies went to the kitchen to brew coffee and pull out refreshments. Cass and the men stayed on the front porch. Goat came through the kitchen and yelped when Rebekah rapped his knuckles after he snuck a chunk of peanut brittle.

With her flattened hand on his back, she gave him a push. "Out of the kitchen until you're called—and go upstairs and check on Gazelle. Ask her if she feels like coming down to eat, but if she doesn't, you can take a plate up to her."

He came back down, minutes later. "Her door was closed. I

knocked, but she didn't answer."

"She probably took a powder and it's put her to sleep. I can't imagine what's causing these horrible, frequent headaches."

Goat chuckled. "You should send her to see Dr. Ryker. I'm sure he could cure anything that ails her."

Mrs. Thelma Redding heard the conversation and remarked, "I think all the young girls in Vinegar Bend have a crush on young Dr. Ryker. He is a handsome young fellow. But if you ask me, they'd be better off looking in their own backyard, rather than falling for someone they know so little about. Not meaning to gossip, but I've heard things."

Falling into the trap, Myrtie Booker asked the question Thelma appeared to be anticipating. "What things, Thelma?"

She gave her corset a yank, then peeking around, as if she were about to divulge a top secret, she said, "Well . . . Perhaps I shouldn't say anything. But since you've asked—my sister's husband's first cousin lives in Tallahassee, Florida, where Ryker grew up and she said he has a sweetheart there, waiting for him to make enough money to come back for her. I'm afraid there'll be a lot of broken hearts when all the young hopefuls in Vinegar Bend discover he's off limits."

Goat said, "That's not true."

Rebekah's jaw dropped. "Goat Marlowe, you apologize this instant."

He lowered his head. "Sorry, Miz Redding. I didn't mean for it to come out the way it sounded."

"Then how did you mean it, young man?"

"I don't know. Please excuse me."

Rebekah attempted an apology in his behalf. "I don't think he understood, but even so, he shouldn't have blurted out the way he did. It was completely out of character for Goat. He's really a good kid."

"Don't bother making excuses for him, sugar. Take a little advice from someone older and wiser. You and Preacher Marlowe need to clamp down on that young'un before he gets out of hand. Take my word for it, he's gonna be a handful in a year or two if sump'n ain't done about that mouth of his. It behooves me to think about what our world is gonna look like in a few years when all these smart-alecky young'uns take the reins." She threw up her hands and rolled her eyes. "Lord, help us."

The excitement of having her husband pastor a local church suddenly began to lose its glamour. Rebekah had never had anyone speak ill of the children and she had no intention of putting up with it, even if she was a Preacher's wife. She had a cutting remark on the tip of her tongue, when she tightened her lips. Was it worth risking getting her husband fired from a position he apparently wanted, for the satisfaction of putting Thelma Redding in her place? It was a difficult question to answer.

Cass helped Rebekah clean the kitchen after everyone left. Teasingly, he said, "Well, how does it feel to be the wife of a full-time local Pastor?"

"Scary."

He drew back. "Scary? That wasn't the answer I expected. What reason would you have to be afraid?"

She shared with him the conversation with Mrs. Redding. "Cass, I'm sure I handled it wrong." Her lips twisted in a wry smile, "However, if I had it to do over again, I'm afraid I'd be even more abrasive because the more I think about it, the angrier I become. The gall of the nosey old bird to question how we raise the children."

He laughed out loud. "My, she did get your goat, didn't she? I've never heard you speak so begrudgingly toward another human being."

"I've never had anyone speak ill of the kids. They can say what they will about me. . . but I won't tolerate them belittling the children."

"I think you're tired, and rightly so. You worked extremely hard to make this a special occasion and you pulled it off beautifully. To be honest, I had reservations about taking the position at the church, but you saw how they showered us with love. I'm sure things will look much brighter tomorrow, after a good night's rest."

Goat lay on his bed reading a Zane Grey novel. Realizing he'd reached the end of the chapter without having a clue what he'd read, he slammed it shut. Wouldn't it be wrong not to tell Gazelle what he'd heard? Though he hadn't wanted to believe it, what reason would the old lady have for making up such a story? To tell Gazelle would break her heart, especially after she admitted to letting him kiss her. The more he thought about it, the more convinced he became that Ryker Adams was toying with his sister's feelings. He had to put a stop to it before things went any further. Naturally, she wouldn't want to believe it, but perhaps when she confronted Ryker with the allegations, he'd confess. Goat felt as if he'd swallowed a hacksaw when sharp pains sped back and forth between his heart and his stomach. He had no choice. The sooner she found out, the quicker she'd be able to put him out of her mind.

He knocked lightly on her door. "Sissy, it's me."

"What do you want, Goat?"

"May I come in? I have something to tell you."

"Sure."

He walked over and sat on the side of her bed. "Rebekah said you had a headache. Feeling better?"

"It's late, Goat. What is it you wanted to tell me?"

He bit his lip. "I don't know how to tell you this—and of course, there may not be a word of truth to it—but I think it only fair that you know so you and Ryker can put the rumors to rest."

She rolled her blood-shot eyes. "There is no Ryker and me. It's over."

Goat blew out a heavy breath. "So, he told you? That's a relief! I dreaded breaking the news to you, Sis, because I knew you were crazy about him. It must've made you really angry to find out he has a sweetheart waiting for him in Florida. He's a real cad. Consider him good riddance."

She threw her legs off the side of the bed and sat up. "What are you talking about, Goat?"

"You said you broke up, right?"

"Right. But who told you he had a girlfriend?"

Goat went through the conversation he heard downstairs. "When you said you broke up, I naturally assumed it was because of the other girl. If you didn't know about her, then why *did* you break up?"

Her chin quivered. "It doesn't matter. It's over, so he can have a dozen girlfriends, for all I care."

His lip curled. "I'm glad you feel that way, because after listening to Mrs. Redding, I wouldn't be surprised if he doesn't. She made Ryker sound like a real Romeo, running around breaking hearts."

She rubbed her temples. "Goat, I'm feeling tired. Would you mind?"

He stood. "Of course not. I only came to let you know what was going on behind your back. Since you already knew, we both should get to sleep. Nite-nite, Sis."

The knot in her throat prevented her from speaking. She fell back into the bed and pulled the covers over her face to keep her brother from seeing the tears flowing from her eyes. After he walked out, she reached in the drawer of her bedside table and scribbled a note.

Dear Ryker,

I thought you loved me, but when you ran to your car and drove away, it should've been proof to me that I was wrong. I now know the truth. I hope you and your Tallahassee girlfriend will be very happy.

I will never forget you, but it doesn't mean I won't try.

Gazelle

Then, tearing it up, she tossed the pieces into her memory box. Why should she trust old lady Redding over Ryker?

CHAPTER 12

As Elsie's caregiver, JoElle insisted it was imperative that Liberty trust her to make sound judgments, else she was nothing more than a housekeeper. "I know I can help her, Mr. McAlister, but I need you to have confidence in me. I'll make mistakes, but I'll learn from them. I can't explain it, but I feel such a strong connection with Elsie, I sometimes feel I can read her mind."

He threw up his hands and smiled. "You've convinced me. I need to stop worrying and trust her into your care. If you feel shopping would be therapy, you have my blessings."

Thirty minutes later, JoElle and Elsie walked into the Parlor. Elsie said, "Honey, JoElle and I are going shopping. Can we bring you back anything?"

"I'm fine. But I'll be happy to watch Rebekah Lou while

you're gone."

"We'll be taking her, but JoElle said as her nurse, she should be the one to carry her. Isn't that sweet?"

Liberty's eyes blurred with tears, seeing JoElle cuddling the doll. Kissing his wife on the cheek, he said, "You look beautiful, dear. Is that a new hat?"

"I . . .I don't . . . uh, yes. This is a new hat."

JoElle shook her head. "I think Elsie meant to say she hasn't worn it in a long time. We found it in her closet. Right, Elsie?"

Elsie's eyes squinted, the way they always did when she struggled to remember. "I haven't worn it in a long time."

"Well, I've never seen you looking more beautiful. You ladies have a good day and I hope you find everything you're looking for. I'd suggest riding over to Mobile to shop. You'll have lots more choices there."

****

JoElle thought it was true when she told Liberty she didn't care if people laughed at her. She wanted it to be the truth. But if she didn't care, why was it so hard for her to make eye contact as they passed people on the street. Yet, she'd made Liberty a promise and she intended to keep it.

After a couple of hours shopping in Mobile, JoElle had bought three new dresses, a pair of shoes and two hats. Elsie bought a bottle of perfume and a bathrobe for Liberty.

"Elsie, how would you like to go into the drug store for a chocolate malt? Doesn't that sound good?"

"I don't know. What's a malt?"

"You'll see. I think you'll like it."

"JoElle, I'll take Rebekah Lou. I'm sure your arms are tired."

"Not at all. Besides, as her nursemaid, it's my job to take care of her. If I didn't, I wouldn't feel needed and I'd have to find another place to work."

Elsie's face scrunched into a frown. "No. Don't leave. Please don't leave."

"Relax, honey. I'm not leaving. I plan to stay and take good care of little Rebekah Lou."

They were finishing their malts when a little girl ran up to JoElle and squealed. "I have a baby doll just like yours."

Her mother ran over, snatched her by the hand and said, "Come with me, dear."

Elsie glared at JoElle. "Why did that little girl call Rebekah Lou a baby doll?"

JoElle bit the inside of her cheek, contemplating her answer. Perhaps, this was the opportunity she'd been waiting for. But was Elsie ready to face the truth? Drawing a deep breath, she said, "Could it be because she looks exactly like a baby doll?"

Elsie's face lit up and there were no more questions. After several hours in Mobile, they drove back to Vinegar Bend. Riding through town, Elsie pointed to a shop across the street. "Stop! That store looks familiar. I'd like to go inside." As they approached the store, Elsie pointed to the sign painted on the window. "E-L-S-I-E. That's my name." Elsie walked toward the back.

The salesclerk said, "Ma'am, the dresses and hats are all up front. The back room is off-limits to the public."

Elsie didn't respond but kept walking.

Again, the clerk pleaded. "Ma'am, there's nothing to see in the back."

"Yes, there is." She pushed back the curtain over the entrance and ran inside, leaving JoElle and the clerk behind.

JoElle whispered to the clerk, "I'm sorry. I don't think my friend understood. Are you the owner?"

"Yes. I have it leased by the month, but I don't plan to renew. I was led to believe it was a thriving business, but to be honest, I made more money picking cotton."

"So you don't own it. Do you know the owner?"

The salesgirl pointed to the sign. "Some woman named Elsie. I've never met her."

JoElle smiled. "I think you just did."

The woman's brows met in the middle. "Her? I'm sorry. I hope I didn't offend her. I didn't mean no harm. It's just women sometimes go back to the sewing room and start pulling down bolts of material that have been specially ordered. They become irate when I try to tell them it was purchased for someone else and it's not for sale."

JoElle said, "Would you mind if I go back there with her? I promise we won't bother anything. I think she needs to look around."

"Yes ma'am. I've tried to keep things in order. I was told the owner was away on a Sabbatical. Not sure what that means, but my lease doesn't run out until the end of the month. I hope she won't make me leave before I have an opportunity to finish my orders."

JoElle smiled. "You have nothing to worry about. Now, if you'll excuse me."

"Sure. Ya'll make yourself at home." She blushed. "I reckon she is home. That's a beautiful doll. I suppose you bought it for your granddaughter?"

JoElle looked up to see Elsie standing there staring at them.

The bell on the front door rang, and the clerk excused herself to wait on the customer.

"Ah, Elsie, Rebekah Lou and I were just about to go to the sewing room to see what you found back there."

"I want to go home. Please, take me home."

"There are some lovely dresses on the rack up front. Would you like to browse through them?"

"No. I want to see Liberty."

Entering the car, JoElle handed her Rebekah Lou, but it was apparent her mind was not on her baby. Tears welled in her eyes.

Driving back to the big house on Main Street, Elsie appeared to be in deep thought, and JoElle thought it best not to question her. As they drove into the yard, Liberty was driving off. He stopped, and leaning his head out the window, said, "You girls are back sooner than I expected. I hope you found what you were looking for."

Elsie yelled, "Liberty, we need to talk."

He glanced at JoElle, who lifted her shoulders in a shrug, indicating she had no idea what was going on.

"Sure, hon. I'm on my way to see a fellow. I won't be gone long."

"No. Please. Now!"

He got out of his vehicle and opened her door. "What's wrong?"

"That's what I want to find out. I'm so confused."

JoElle said, "If you two will excuse me, I'll so get supper started."

Liberty held his hand out to help Elsie from the car. She turned around, laid Rebekah Lou on the car seat and closed the door.

"Honey, aren't you going to get the baby?"

"No."

"Okay. I suppose we can let her sleep. She looks comfortable, doesn't she?" Puzzled, he walked his wife up the steps to the porch. "Would you like to sit out here and tell me what's bothering you?"

Elsie burst into sobs. "Liberty, I don't have a baby."

"Sure, you do, sweetheart. She's sleeping in the car. Shall I get her, now?"

"No. There is no Rebekah Lou. It's a doll. I know that now. I remember. I remember everything. I went to my store, today, and all the painful memories flooded back all at once. At first, I had trouble separating the real from the unreal."

Liberty wrapped her in his arms and let her cry as she recalled all the events that happened prior to being hospitalized. Then drying her tears with his handkerchief, he said, "Honey, I know this is very painful for you to relive the past few months, but it's wonderful at the same time. Don't you see? This is what we've been praying for and it's happening much sooner than I could've hoped or dreamed."

She leaned her head back and smiled through her tears. "Well, now you're crying."

"But they're happy tears. My wife is back. Thank you, Lord, thank you."

She said, "When JoElle and I drove up, you were about to leave. Where were you going?"

He chuckled. "I'm glad you reminded me. I almost forgot. I have an appointment with a fellow at the farm."

"Maybe I imagined it, since I still have a problem separating real events from the unreal, but I was thinking you sold the farm."

"I did."

"Then I wasn't hallucinating."

"There was a clause drawn in the contract, saying I had until the eighteenth to sign the papers making the sale final.

Barlow Abrams agreed to buy it, since it joins his daddy's place, but he knew how hard it was for me to part with it. So, he insisted we put in a stipulation that if either of us changed our minds, the sale would be null and void. Since this was the last day,

I was on my way to sign it, but I've just changed my mind. I'm keeping it."

She popped her palms on either side of her rosy cheeks. "Oh, Liberty, that makes me very happy. But won't Barlowe be terribly disappointed when he learns you won't be selling?"

"Not at all. I knew he didn't need it. The only reason he agreed to buy it was to keep someone else from getting it. The Abrams are great neighbors and pleaded with me not to sell."

Liberty could hardly believe he was sitting there having a sensible conversation with his wife.

JoElle walked out to the porch to let them know supper was ready. "Where's Rebekah Lou?"

Elsie stood and hugged her. "There is no Rebekah Lou."

JoElle swallowed the lump in his throat. "No Rebekah Lou? Are you saying—?"

Nodding, she said, "I can't say it was a sudden revelation. For a couple of weeks, I've been having flashbacks. For a split second, I would realize I was holding a doll, but the next minute, I'd go into denial, not wanting to give up my beloved Rebekah Lou."

JoElle wrapped her arms around Elsie's neck. "Hon, we'll both miss her, but this is a happy moment. It's proof that you're being healed."

"I know. Liberty, I'd like for you to take the doll down to Dorie Granger's shanty and give it to her little girl. When I ran the Millinery, I'd catch Dorie staring in the window on occasions, and my heart would break for her because I knew she longed for a new dress. I even tried to convince her once that I had a dress I couldn't sell, and I'd like for her to have it. She thanked me but said Harlan wouldn't allow her to accept charity. She had a hard time when they were together, but since he took off with that other woman, I don't know how she and the child are making ends meet. I doubt the little girl has ever had a doll of her own and I'm sure she'd love our little Rebekah Lou."

"That's a great idea, sweetheart. I'll take her with me on the way to see Barlowe."

JoElle hugged her. "You're very kind, sugar. I became attached to Rebekah Lou, too, so I'm glad she'll be going to someone who will love her as much as we did."

"Thank you, JoElle. It's the only way I could let her go. I'll never forget how my heart melted when that little girl's big green eyes gazed up at me the day I offered to give her mother a new dress. I wanted to pick her up and squeeze her. I'd never felt such affection for a child—any child. She was barefoot and her hair was matted. One sash was missing from her tattered dress and the other hung down, dragging the sidewalk. Yet, she was the most beautiful little creature I had ever seen. If I had a little girl, I like to pretend she'd look exactly like that precious child."

JoElle said, "I know exactly how you feel, Mrs. McAlister."

"You do?"

"Yes. If I had been so blessed to have had a daughter, I like to pretend she would've been exactly like you."

Elsie's eyes glistened with moisture. "That's the nicest thing anyone has ever said to me.

I realize I'm not as well as I need to be, but I'm much closer than I've been in a long time, thanks to you. I know in my heart God sent you to me to aid in my recovery."

Liberty said, "I agree with Elsie." He paused. "Hey, there've already been enough tears shed here today to fill a #2 washtub. Why are you crying, JoElle?"

"These are happy tears." Her voice cracked. "I've never felt part of a family until I came here. To tell the truth, I'll even miss rocking sweet Rebekah Lou. I'll never forget you Mr. and Mrs. McAlister, and if you could please allow me a couple of days to find another job, I'll be moving on."

Elsie's brow furrowed. "Moving? Must you go?"

"I'll miss you, terribly, but you no longer need my services."

"Are you serious? I need you more than ever. I have a shop to run. I can't wait to start sewing again and Liberty has a farm to tend. I'll be needing a cook and housekeeper. However, I realize you're an experienced bookkeeper and probably prefer a job in your field."

"Oh, Mrs. McAlister, You're wrong. I'd much rather stay here and work for you and Mr. McAlister. It doesn't feel like work."

"Then it's settled. I'll admit you tend to spoil us a bit the way you fuss over us but now that I'm doing better, we'll try not to take advantage of your good nature."

"Oh, but don't you see? I love it. It's a joy making over you and your husband. For the first time in my life, I feel as if I've found a home. Like I'm taking care of my own children and that's a really good feeling.

"Children?" Liberty chuckled.

"Oh, I understand that you and Mrs. McAlister don't consider yourselves children. But if I had been so blessed to mother little ones, I suppose by now, they'd be about the age of your wife."

Liberty chuckled. "Then it's final. You've got a home here. I once dreamed of adopting. However, I never expected to be adopting a mama, but I couldn't have picked a better one."

Elsie wrapped her arm around her husband's waist. "I agree, darling." A smile crept across her lips as she held out her hand. "Welcome home, Mother Jo."

JoElle's eyes opened wide. "Mother Jo?"

Liberty's gaze locked with his wife's, signaling his approval. "I like it. Mother Jo. Yes . . . It's perfect. But if we're to be family, there'll be no Mr. and Mrs. McAlister. From now on, it's Liberty and Elsie."

JoElle's chin quivered. "Bless your heart, do you mean it?"

"Of course, we mean it."

"For years, I've prayed for a family, but I felt God was punishing me for a sin I committed years ago. Truly, the Lord has answered my prayer."

Liberty rubbed his hand across the back of his neck. "Mother Jo, we all have regrets of things we've done in the past, but we have a loving, forgiving God, who says He tosses our sins as far as the East is from the West and remembers them no more. Isn't that wonderful? We're the ones who keep digging them back up, continually pleading for forgiveness. I know how much you love the Lord, Mother Jo, so it's time for you to accept with gratitude that your sin debt has been paid." He pecked her on the side of the cheek. "Now, if you ladies will excuse me, I should be on my way to let Barlowe know the farm is no longer for sale."

CHAPTER 13

January 22, 1920

Gazelle tossed and turned, unable to sleep. Did Ryker really break up with her? He didn't answer her question when she asked. Did he really have a girlfriend waiting for him in Tallahassee, Florida? She didn't want to believe it, but why would anyone make up such a story? Tears soaked her pillow. She couldn't imagine living without him.

Reaching for her Bible on the bedside table, she decided to seek an answer from the Lord by letting it fall open and reading whatever popped up. But after a couple of chapters of Lamentations, she decided that wasn't a good idea. Then, turning to Ruth, her favorite chapter, she read the whole book and between those pages it became crystal clear what God would have her do. The thought that Satan could've tricked her into giving up and losing the best thing that ever happened to her, made her shudder. So, what if some girl in Tallahassee claimed she loved him? There were probably a dozen others who made the same claim. Was it his fault he was so handsome?

She crawled out of bed and quietly dressed. It was a superb plan and sure to work. After all, it was tried and true. God had used it before, and it worked so well it was recorded in the Bible. Recalling her father's words that the scripture was given to us for our instruction, these were definitely instructions she could abide by.

Waiting until 2:30 a.m., she quietly reached under her bed and pulled out her packed bag. Tiptoeing out of the house, she eased the door shut, then walked the four miles to the little cottage where Ryker lived. At least a dozen times on the way, she changed her mind. Her father would be furious when he discovered what she'd done, but she'd point him to the book of Ruth and he'd have no defense, since her actions were scripturally based.

Walking up the creaky steps, she slowly eased the front door open and squinted her eyes, trying to see in the darkness. It didn't take long before she could focus. She saw a bed in the far corner and the silhouette of a body.

She'd read Ruth's account over and over and each time she read it, her heart would melt at such a romantic story. With her instructions tucked under her arm—just in case she needed to read them to Ryker to convince him she was simply following God's will—she eased over to his bed. Then, very quietly she eased down and uncovered his feet, although she didn't understand the purpose. But it's what Ruth did, and it wasn't up to her to alter a jot nor tittle of the Lord's word.

He changed positions and her heart pumped so hard she could feel it pounding against her chest. She relaxed when he didn't wake up, since it was important that everything be carried out, scripturally.

At four-thirty, she jumped when she heard him holler. "Who are you and what are you . . ." He stopped. "Gazelle? What do you think you're doing here?"

She squealed. "We did it, my love. It worked!"

"We did what? Oh, Gazelle, what are you saying? Lord, please tell me this is a nightmare."

He sat up rubbing his eyes as she rattled off her interpretation of the third chapter of Ruth. "And then, Boaz awoke and, not recognizing her at first he asked who she was. Just as you did. Then he told her in verse eleven that she shouldn't be afraid because he would do all that she required, and of course that meant a wedding was about to take place." She snickered. "In case you're wondering, I require the same thing."

Ryker ran his fingers through his hair. "Oh, Gazelle, this is crazy. You're taking the story out of context and making it say what you want it to say. You have no business in my bed. Oh my lands, if your father finds out—" He groaned. "I've got to get you home. Go in the other room while I dress, but it'll be up to you to explain to Reverend Marlowe. He'll probably want to have me tarred and feathered and driven out of town, and who could blame him?"

She smiled. "Father's a reasonable man and not given to violence, but I'm sure he'll want to know why you waited until almost daylight to take me home."

"I'll tell him . . . I'll just tell him the truth. That you sneaked into my house in the wee hours of the night and when I awoke, you were curled up at my feet."

"That's exactly what you should tell him. I think Father will be impressed that our actions followed the instructions in the Bible—at least to the best of our knowledge."

"*Our* actions? Best of *our* knowledge? I had nothing to do with it."

"Neither did Boaz, but he knew what he was required to do, and he married her." Giggling, she stood and sashayed out of the room to wait for him in the tiny kitchen.

Ryker sat on the edge of the bed with his face buried in his hands, contemplating what he should do versus what he wanted to do. He'd wanted to marry Gazelle from the moment he first met her. His heart raced at the thought of coming home to her every night.

When the positives of marrying began to outweigh the negatives, he attempted to refocus. Was he insane? He'd lived in Vinegar Bend long enough to realize all it would take to ruin the Reverend would be for a few nosey women to hear that his daughter ran off to get married without his blessings. It would provide sufficient fodder for a scandal since no one even knew they were dating. If Doc Brunson received too many complaints about his assistant, he might be compelled to fire him. It was something he had to consider. Without a job, he wouldn't be able to support himself and he certainly couldn't support a wife. Ryker clenched his eyes shut. The fact that he was even contemplating the ramifications frightened him. He had to get the absurd notion out of his head.

Hearing the rattle of pots and pans in the kitchen, he hurried in to find Gazelle with her hands in a bowl of dough. "What do you think you're doing?"

"Making breakfast. You do eat breakfast, don't you?"

"Gazelle, you know if we had your father's blessings, nothing would make me happier than to call you my wife. But that's not likely to happen, not for at least another year, and even that may be false hope."

"You're right, sweetheart. If we waited for my overly protective Father's approval, I could be past child-bearing age by the time he came around. That's why we need to do it Naomi's way. Look how well it turned out for Ruth and Boaz."

"I think you should go back and read the chapter again. You aren't Ruth and I'm not Boaz. It would never work." Seeing a spot of flour on her nose, he walked over and with his forefinger, brushed it off. Though it was the farthest thing from his mind, he leaned over and kissed her.

Smiling, she stuck the biscuits in the oven. "I knew you loved me."

"I never said I didn't love you. I love you so much it hurts, but you're fifteen, Gazelle, and I'm twenty-two. Your father would have every right to come after me with a shotgun."

"Almost sixteen, thank you, and he'd have no such right since Rebekah was only fifteen when she and Father married." Pouring two cups of coffee, she added, "He was much older than you when they tied the knot and they're a perfect match."

"Are you serious? She was fifteen? I knew she looked young, but I had no idea." He murmured, "Fifteen? Well, what d'ya know. I never suspected there was that much difference in their ages. They look like the ideal couple."

"That's my point. They are the ideal couple, and my father would be the last person to object because of age."

"Then let's go ask him, and if he gives us his blessings, then . . . "

Taking the biscuits from the oven, she buttered a couple and placed on his plate. "He couldn't possibly give us his blessings."

"But you just said he wouldn't object."

"No, that's what you thought I said. I said age wouldn't be a factor. But don't you get it? He'd feel it his fatherly duty to object, even though he didn't ask Rebekah's father for his blessings."

"Are you sure? About him not asking her father for his blessings?"

"Yes, I'm sure. Rebekah ran away to get married. We can do the same."

"But my family . . . I know they'd expect to be invited to the wedding. I've told them all about you and they're dying to meet you—especially my mother."

"And I want to meet them, but there'll be plenty of time later."

He ate in silence as he weighed the negatives against the positives. He loved Gazelle and she loved him. The mere thought of coming home every night to the beautiful girl sitting across the table from him made his heart palpitate. So, she was only fifteen. She was mature for her age and certainly two people had never been more in love. The Reverend's ministry didn't suffer when he chose to marry a fifteen-year-old, so why should he think it would be jeopardized by his daughter following in his footsteps? He shoved his chair back, then reached for her hand. "What are we waiting for?"

She jumped up and threw her arms around his neck. "Let's go!"

Ryker called Doc Brunson and without lying, yet not telling the whole truth, he mumbled something about having something to attend to and he'd be late coming in.

Gazelle said, "Take me home."

"Home? You've changed your mind?"

"No, silly. I won't go in the house. I'll stay outside in the swing. I'll go inside when I hear Rebekah calling us for breakfast and she and Father will assume I woke early and dressed. After breakfast, I'll walk with the kids to school, but I won't go in the building. I'll be waiting for you at the big oak behind the schoolhouse."

Ryker stopped the car at the gate, instead of pulling up into the yard. "Gazelle, are you sure we're doing the right thing?"

Her brow furrowed. "You aren't getting cold feet, are you?"

"No. I just want to make sure this is what you want."

"I've never wanted anything more." She bent over and pecked him on the cheek. "Gotta run. Rebekah will be calling everyone to breakfast soon."

Gazelle was pleased when everything seemed to be falling in place, according to plan. Goat was full of talk, giving her very little time to add to the conversation, which suited her fine. She had one thing and one thing only on her mind.

When they reached the school, the twins ran on inside.

Goat stopped and said, "Sissy, are you all right?"

"Why do you ask?"

"You don't seem like yourself. Reckon you might be coming down with something? If you are, I sure hope you don't give it to me. I'm supposed to go over to Belle's tonight to study."

"Belle? What about Katie?"

"Didn't I tell you? I broke it off with Katie."

"Why? I thought you were crazy about her."

"I thought I was, too, until Belle moved here. She slipped me a note in class and asked if I'd go over to her house and help her study for the semester tests."

"Goat, I really like Katie. I hope you know what you're doing."

"I do. I suppose we should go in. It's almost time for the bell."

"You go on. I don't think I'm going to school today."

"So, I was right. Sorry you don't feel well. Go home and gargle with salt water and maybe it'll kill any germs lurking in your body. Hope you get to feeling better."

"Thanks, Goat."

She couldn't have planned it more perfectly. After the bell rang, Gazelle hurried behind the schoolhouse and saw Ryker's car, waiting for her. She jumped in and squealed. "Let's go."

"Does anyone know?"

"Of course not. I had a hard time keeping it from Goat. We tell one another everything. Not that I can't trust him, but I didn't want to put him in a precarious situation of having to decide between lying or ratting on me."

"My mother's brother is a preacher over in the Beulah Community. I contacted him and he's agreed to marry us." He gripped the steering wheel. "Gazelle, are you positive this is what you want?"

"How many ways can I say it, Ryker?"

"Okay, I just need to know that after having time to think about, you still feel the same way. After we're married, we'll go break the news to your father."

Her eyes widened. "Oh, no. We can't do that."

"Why not?"

"Don't you see? He'd feel it his fatherly duty to have it annulled."

"So, what do you propose we do?"

"We'll get married, and afterward you can let me off near the house and I'll walk home. Rebekah will assume I'm sick, so when Goat and the twins get home and ask how I'm feeling, there'll be no reason for her to suspect anything."

"But I thought you'd be moving in the house with me."

"That will come later."

"So why are we rushing to get married?"

"Why should we have to wait? There'll be times I can sneak away to be with my husband." She rolled her eyes toward the top of her head and clasped her hands over her heart. "My husband! Doesn't that sound divine, sweetheart? I love saying 'my husband.'"

Ryker agreed it seemed to be the best decision. All the negatives that concerned him suddenly seemed insignificant, especially after learning that Rebekah ran away to marry a stranger much older than her, when she was Gazelle's age. When the time was right, they'd announce their marriage.

They arrived at his Uncle Wilbur's little log cabin at 8:30. The preacher and his wife met them at the door. He was a tall, thin man who looked a lot like pictures she'd seen of President Lincoln. His wife was short and pudgy, and her twinkling eyes turned into tiny slits when she smiled.

Gazelle took an immediate liking to the sweet, elderly couple. The woman threw her arms around her and said, "Law, Ryker, shug you sure picked a beauty. Ain't she a beauty, Pa?"

The preacher pulled his coat together and nodded. "You right about that. She's a purty little thing."

Ryker said, "Gazelle, this is my Uncle Wilbur and Aunt Wynelle."

The woman reached for Gazelle's hand. "And now, we'll be *your* Uncle Wilbur and Aunt Wynelle."

The preacher said, "Ma, these young folks got places to go, so let's don't hold 'em up no longer." When he asked Ryker if he had a ring, he covered his face and groaned. "I forgot I'd need a ring." Aunt Wynelle smiled and pulled hers off. "Here, you can borrow mine for the ceremony."

The wedding took less than two minutes and Gazelle felt a blush rush to her face when Uncle Wilbur said, "You may now kiss your bride." She'd never kissed a boy with someone watching. But then, she'd never kissed a boy. Ryker was a man and he was the only man she'd ever kissed or ever wanted to kiss. Rebekah kept rolling the wedding band around on her finger. She didn't get to wear it long, but it was fun seeing it on her hand.

After getting in the car, Ryker handed her the Marriage Certificate. She read it, smiled, then handed it back to him. "You keep it. I'm afraid Father or Rebekah would find it if I took it with me."

They rode to Ryker's cottage and he carried her over the threshold. They celebrated with a cup of sassafras tea. After an hour and forty-five minutes, in what Gazelle declared to be the shortest honeymoon in history, Ryker said, "I hate to say goodbye, my beautiful bride, but I promised Dr. Brunson I'd go by and check on the Widow Harris before going to the clinic. I want to be with you, forever, Gazelle. I want to come home to you every night and feel you jumping into my arms, the way you did a few minutes ago."

"I want that too, Ryker, but I've explained to you that it's not possible yet. I'll soon be sixteen and you can ask Father for my hand on my birthday. He'd never agree as long as I'm only fifteen."

"But what will he say when he finds out we're already married?"

"Fiddle-Faddle. He won't find out."

"How can he not find out?"

"We'll go through the motions of having a church wedding and allowing him to perform the ceremony."

"There's one little matter you seem to have forgotten. He'll need to sign the Marriage Certificate . . . and it's already signed."

She giggled. "Oops. Oh well, we'll cross that bridge when we get to it. I'll think of something. I'm too happy right now to worry over problems that might never come to pass."

He stopped for her to get out of the car, a half-mile from her house. He slid over and with his thumb, he lifted her chin and kissed her. "Good-bye, sweetheart. One day, there'll be no more goodbyes."

Gazelle walked into the house shortly before noon. And just as she'd imagined, without having to give an explanation, Rebekah made the assumption she left school early because she wasn't feeling well.

"Gazelle, you didn't seem to be yourself when you left for school. I should've known you were sick. Why don't you go upstairs, get on something comfortable and rest until suppertime?"

"Thanks, Rebekah. That sounds great."

"Would you like a cup of hot tea before you go?"

"No thank you. I just had a . . . uh . . . I mean I just need to lie down." Her words trailed off as she hurried up the stairs. Grateful for time to be alone to bask in the memories of the past few hours, she closed the door to her room and sailed across her bed, hugging her pillow. "Oh, Ryker, I love you so much I hurt inside. I wish we could be together."

CHAPTER 14

Liberty pushed back from the table. "That was a delicious lunch, ladies. Thank you. I need to get back to the farm, but I'll be back in time for the birthday party."

Elsie blinked. "Party?"

"Yes, remember, sweetheart, I told you yesterday we were all invited to Gazelle's sixteenth birthday party?"

Sensing her desperation, JoElle reached for Elsie's hand. "We went shopping together, dear and we bought Gazelle a present. Can you remember what we bought?"

Suddenly, her eyes lit up and her mouth opened wide. "Oh, of course. I remember. We went to the drug store and bought her a bracelet with a charm on it."

"That's right."

"Oh, Mother Jo, I panicked when my mind went blank. It was frightening."

"We all forget things at times, dear. You are well. You need to believe it. Fear is a tool of the devil. If you allow it, it will hinder your faith and keep you from accepting the truth about yourself. Now, you and I need to decide what we shall wear to the party, although I'm still not sure I should go. I'm not really acquainted with these friends of yours, except for Preacher Cass, of course."

"More reason for you to go. You need to know them, and they need to know you."

****

Gazelle, Goat and the twins were walking home from school, when they saw the Happy Birthday posters, which Rebekah had placed along the route leading to the house.

Goose squealed, "It's your birthday, Gazelle, and I made you a present. I think you'll like it."

"I'm sure I will, Goosey girl."

Goat read a large poster nailed to a tree. "Happy Sweet Sixteen, Gazelle." He whispered, "She put your age on it. Do you want me to take it down?"

"Why would you do that?"

"I didn't think you wanted you-know-who to know how old you are. Or should I say, how young you are?"

"Ryker knows. I told him already."

Chuckling, he said, "I suppose you told him just before he ran out of the church the night Father was voted in as the new Pastor. I wondered what scared him."

When she didn't respond, he prodded. "Well? Was that when

he found out?"

"What difference does it make? I said he knows, didn't I? I don't know why you're so obsessed with my age." Tears welled in her eyes.

"Jeepers, Sissy, I didn't mean to upset you. Please don't cry. I was just picking at you. I'm sure he doesn't care. You're about the prettiest girl in the whole county. Did Rebekah invite him to the party?"

"Why should she?"

"Why? Because he's your beau. Isn't that reason enough?"

"But she doesn't know that."

"Shucks, I don't know what you're afraid of. Why don't you tell them how you feel?"

"I plan to. I wanted to wait until after my birthday, so I could remind Father that I'm older than Rebekah was when he took her for a wife, but I'm getting worried."

"Afraid of what Father might say to him?"

"No. Remember when you told me Ryker had a girl in Tallahassee?"

"Yeah but look at the source. Thelma Redding. I wouldn't believe anything that woman says."

"You're right. It wasn't true."

"Then why did you bring it up?"

"I don't know. It's just that—well, he's been driving by the house every day on his way to work and on his way home. He hasn't driven by in four days. I don't understand why he stopped coming by."

"Is that what's got you so moody?"

"It's not as easy for us to get together, since Father is home so much, but I always look forward to seeing him pass by on his way to the clinic. Sometimes I'd run out and stuff a note in his hand and he'd have one for me before he'd drive away. I looked forward to getting his love notes. Something must be wrong."

"I wouldn't worry about it, Sissy. I'm sure he'll have a good explanation when you see him. Maybe he's been spending a lot of time at the hospital, lately."

"Do you think maybe he's sick? I hadn't thought about that. I hope not."

"That's not what I meant. He's a doctor, Sissy. He probably has a patient, or patients who are taking up a lot of his time. If you have thoughts of ever marrying him, you'll have to get used to sharing your time with his patients. Frankly, I think you should go ahead and tell Rebekah and Father that you're in love and that you want their permission to court him. If they knew you'd been sneaking around for months to be with him, I'm sure they'd be disappointed. Don't you think they'd much prefer that you be honest with them?"

"He knows it's my birthday and we plan to tell them tonight."

"I promise you, you'll be glad you did. I told them I'm courting Belle and they hardly blinked. I decided they already knew."

"That's different. You're a boy."

"But Belle's a girl. I don't see anything different about it."

Gazelle rolled her eyes. "The Reverend Marlowe, Pastor of Friendship Community Church, is not her father and you and Belle are the same age."

"So?"

"People talk. Specifically, Mrs. Thelma Redding."

"Let her talk. Nosey old biddy."

Gazelle stopped. "Go ahead to the house and tell Rebekah I'll be there shortly."

His brow furrowed. "What's wrong?"

"Nothing. Go on."

"You're white as a sheet. Are you okay?"

"Please, Goat. Leave me—" She bent over and threw up.

"Why didn't you tell me you were sick?"

"I'll be fine. Please don't tell. I wouldn't want to ruin Rebekah's plans for my party."

"That's ridiculous. She'd understand and we could postpone it a day or two until you're feeling better. Are you fevered?"

"No. I'm sure it's something I ate. I'm feeling better already. Now, please. Not a word."

"Okay, but what if you need to see a doctor?" Half-grinning, he bit the corner of his bottom lip. "Maybe Doc Brunson will send his good-looking assistant."

Her face pinched into a frown. "I don't need a doctor. Just leave me alone."

"Hey, I didn't mean to make you angry. I was just fooling

with you."

"I'm sorry. I know you were. Let's just forget it, okay?"

Rebekah greeted them at the door. "Gazelle, go look in the dining room. I hope you like it."

Goat ran ahead of her. "Wow! Come look, Sissy. It's chocolate. How many layers, Rebekah?"

"Twelve and yes, it's chocolate."

Gazelle ambled in and stood at the door. "Thank you, Rebekah. It looks delicious. Now, if you'll excuse me, I think I'll go to my room and take a short nap before our guests come."

Rebekah's brow creased. "You look pale, dear. Do you feel okay?"

"I'm tired. I've been staying up late at night studying. Do you mind?"

"I think a nap is a great idea. You've been pushing yourself too hard lately, but looking at your grades, it seems to have paid off for you. You'll have a couple of hours before the guests arrive. Sweet Sixteen. Aren't you excited?"

She glanced at Goat and feigned a smile. "I am. It's what I've been waiting for."

****

Liberty arrived home and the ladies were dressed in their finery and waiting on the porch. "Sorry, it took longer than I expected. The cows got out of the fence out and I had to go look for them. By the time I rounded them all up, I realized how late it was getting. I can be ready in twenty minutes." Gazing at his wife, he smiled, then said, "Turn around, beautiful, and let me look at you. Is that a new frock?"

"Yes. Do you like it?"

"Like it? You look ravishing."

Seeing the blush rush to her cheeks, he wondered if he'd said anything improper, but it was the first word that came to mind. Then turning to JoElle, he said, "And you look right spiffy, yourself, Mother Jo. Yes ma'am, right spiffy. If I wasn't already betrothed to a very special lovely lady, you could certainly turn my head."

JoElle blushed, "Oh my goodness, you silly man, how you do go on."

"Well, it'll be a privilege to escort two such lovely ladies tonight."

"You're very kind, Liberty. It's been a long time since anyone has complimented me. I'll admit it was fun picking out a new frock and having my hair curled, but after thinking it over, I think it best to let you two go without me."

Liberty's eyes widened. "Absolutely not. It's not every man who has the privilege of adopting such a beautiful mother and I insist on showing you off."

Elsie reached for her hand. "I agree with my husband. You look lovely and we want our friends to get to know you as we do."

"Are you sure? It's been so long since I've socialized, I'm afraid I'll be a wallflower and I shan't want you two to feel the need to babysit me while everyone else is having a gay time." Wringing her hands, she pleaded, "Please go without me."

Liberty winked, "Not a chance. Whither we goest, thou shalt go. It's Biblical."

His comment caused her to smile. "I think that only applies to brides."

"I assume you haven't read that part." Laughing, he gave a shrug, picked up her shawl from the back of a chair and draped it around her shoulders.

JoElle stood on one side and Elsie on the other and the three walked arm-in-arm to the car.

CHAPTER 15

Upon arriving at the Marlowe home, Liberty, Elsie, and JoElle were greeted by Cass and Doc Brunson. The men were standing in the yard and appeared to have been involved in a serious conversation.

Rebekah opened the front door and ushered the ladies inside. "You fellows don't linger out there too long. We'll be ready to eat, shortly."

Liberty shook hands with the men, then seeing the lines on Cass's face, he said, "Is something wrong?"

Doc Brunson bit the corner of his lower lip. "I'm afraid I'm the bearer of bad news."

"Oh?" Liberty pulled out his pipe and packed the tobacco.

The doctor's face twisted into a frown. "I don't know if you were privileged to meet my young assistant, but—"

Liberty took a puff on his pipe, while nodding. "Ryker? Yes.

Fine young man. We're blessed to have him here. What about him?"

Cass hung his head. "He died this evening of Diphtheria. Doc says it's just happened. The women haven't been told, yet."

Liberty covered his face with his hands and moaned. "Nooo. I am so sorry. He was such a personable young man with a bright future ahead of him."

Three ladies from the church walked up, and Doc Brunson quickly changed the subject.

Cass said, "Go on in, ladies. We'll be joining you shortly."

Thelma Redding sniffed. "I suppose you men are out here to suck on the devil's weed. That's all tobacco is good for. If I were your wife, I wouldn't put up with that stinking habit for a minute. All that smoke makes you smell like you've been to a hog-killing. Yessir, I'd pack my bags and walk straight out the door, if I were married to you."

Liberty tipped his hat. "And if I were your husband, ma'am, I'd help you pack."

With her nose in the air, she strutted into the house, looking as if she thought she had the upper hand in the conversation.

Cass chuckled, "I believe she thought you were in agreement with her, Liberty."

Liberty rolled his eyes. "If she were my wife, she'd have to be fast to beat me out the door."

The doctor said, "Cass, Liberty goes to church in Citronelle, so it's easy for him to say what he will. But I feel I should warn you, since you're the new pastor at Friendship. Be careful how you deal with her. Thelma has a lot of influence in the church. Folks are afraid to speak out against her, so any recommendation she makes, passes. If it weren't for the Redding money, I'm afraid we wouldn't be able to pay you. I'm just saying tread softly in her presence."

"Thanks, for the warning, doc, but I can handle Thelma. Perhaps we should go inside and join the ladies."

"Hold on a minute, Cass. Before the women walked up, I was about to tell you that I came here as soon as I could, since I've known for some time that Ryker was fond of your daughter. I felt she should hear the sad news from you, rather than getting it through other sources. I know it will be devastating to her. I'm prepared to give her something to calm her, should she need it."

"I appreciate your thoughtfulness, doc, but actually, the kids didn't have much occasion to be around him, since he was a good bit older. I suppose you assumed they were closer than they were because he took them to see you the day Gander was stung by the wasp. Ryker happened to pass by the house that day, shortly after it happened. I was on the road at the time and—"

Doc Brunson interrupted. "Yes, I remember the incident well. He brought them to the office and little Gander's eyes were almost swollen shut."

"So, they said. If I remember correctly, Ryker took the kids to dinner at Maude's after you finished treating Gander. I don't know what he did or said, but he sure made an impression on Goose. I think she's been in love with him since that day."

Doc Brunson's brows meshed together. "You mean Gazelle, don't you?"

Cass shook his head. "No, Goose. My eight-year-old." Strange the doc seemed to keep confusing Gazelle and her little sister. He'd never known him to seem so addled before. "Gazelle has had eyes for the Tyler boy—Jeremiah—since they were little tots."

"So, you're saying Gazelle wasn't being wooed by my popular apprentice?"

"Of course not." Then seeing the peculiar expression on the doctor's face, as if he questioned Cass's statement, he added, "Well, now that you mention it, there was one time after he first got into town when I mistakenly suspected she might've been somewhat enamored with him."

"Oh? What made you think so?"

"It was silly. I had absolutely no reason to jump to such a conclusion and I later apologized. But he was a nice-looking chap with a charming personality, so when I saw him sitting beside Gazelle in the swing and knowing how young girls can get carried away by a smooth-talker, I lashed out, thinking he might be leading her on." He chuckled as he related the episode.

Liberty smiled. "Are you saying just because they both happened to be in the swing at the same time, it caused you to want to pull out the shotgun? That's hilarious."

He rubbed his chin. "Okay, I'll admit, I overreacted. But there was that muscular guy, six feet or taller, rubbed up against my innocent, unsuspecting fifteen-year-old. To make matters worse, his shirt was thrown across a chair, and he was sitting there beside her in his undershirt."

Liberty chuckled. "Hey, as hot and humid as it is here in South Alabama, I often pull off my shirt and leave on my undershirt. I'm sure we all do. Are you saying you found it offensive?"

Cass felt hot around the collar. "Maybe you aren't getting the picture. I'd never seen such enormous biceps, even on the strong man at the circus. His broad arm was draped around the back of the swing in what I now understand was a perfectly harmless gesture. But before I had an opportunity to assess the situation, my fatherly instincts took over."

"What did you do?"

"I lashed out and one thing led to another. We wound up exchanging some rather harsh words that neither of us meant."

The doc's brow raised. "Such as?"

Cass tried to wave it off with his hand. Then, seeing the fellows waiting for him to finish the story, he saw no option but to conclude what he started. "I foolishly went into a tirade, seeing that man sitting next to my little girl and . . . " His voice trailed off. "And I accused him of enticing a minor."

Doc said, "Hold on. I thought you said he was sitting with Gazelle."

"That's right."

Liberty said, "I'm confused, also. I thought you first said Gazelle, but just now, you said he was sitting next to Goose."

"Did I? I didn't mean to."

Doc rolled his eyes. "When you said he was sitting by your *little* girl, I suppose Liberty and I both assumed you were referring to Goose."

Cass's lip curled in a smile. "They're both my little girls. Not that I'm making excuses for jumping to conclusions, but if you fellows had a daughter, you'd understand that sometimes daddies can become complete idiots when it comes to their little girls."

Liberty said, "What was Ryker's reaction after you made such a serious accusation?"

"What you'd expect from any rational man accused falsely of such a grave offense. His tanned face turned blood red and the veins in his neck protruded like thick ropes. I though he was gonna wallop me one and he had every right to do so. He got in my face and advised me he'd see whomever he chose, whenever he chose and then he blurted out that he was in love with Gazelle."

Doc Brunson nodded. "Yep! That was the impression I had."

"But don't you see? He didn't mean it. It was his way of getting back at me for being such a jerk. I'll admit it threw me for a loop for a minute or so, but then I realized he wasn't serious. She was fifteen, for crying out loud. After a tongue-lashing from my sane wife, I realized how foolishly I had acted. A young man his age and of his caliber wouldn't be interested in a fifteen-year-old kid, when every available young woman in town was drooling over him."

Seeing Doc Brunson's staunch glare, he pulled at the neck of his shirt collar, "I know what you're thinking. Rebekah was no older than Gazelle, but that was different." As if his statement required the added emphasis, his voice elevated. "*Much* different."

"Are you sure?"

"Of course, I'm sure. Rebekah had to grow up quickly. She was much more mature at fifteen. She could outwork any woman twice her age and her maturity level astounded me." He waited for the doctor to agree, but when he didn't respond, Cass felt the need to expound. "I suppose when Ryker first moved to town, girls of every age for miles around were hoping he'd have eyes for them." He smiled. "Even my eight-year-old thought she was in love with him." Although I'm not so naïve that I can't imagine that Gazelle might've been a bit infatuated with his good looks, it was nothing more serious than that. But the news will hit little Goose hard. My Goosey girl has been saying for months that she was planning to marry Ryker when she grows up." His smile faded. "Yep, it's gonna be hard to explain his death to my baby girl."

Doc Brunson pulled at his mustache. "But according to my understanding—" He stopped. "Nevermind." Lowering his head, he said, "I'll sure miss him. He was a quick study and a perfect gentleman. He had a boyish charm about him that seemed to draw folks to him. To tell the truth, business picked up after he joined me at the clinic." Then with a crooked smile, he added, "But his gentle manner didn't mean he was a milksop. No sirree. If someone crossed the line with him, he could become tough as nails."

Cass gave a hearty nod. "I can vouch for that. I didn't know him very well, but I did discover that much about him." Then changing the subject, he turned to Liberty and said, "I thought Elsie looked fantastic when you all walked up tonight. How is she doing?"

"Much better, thanks to our angel of a caretaker. JoElle Jernigan was the answer to my prayer. Elsie wouldn't have made such tremendous progress without such excellent care."

"That's wonderful. She seems to genuinely love Elsie."

"And the feeling is mutual."

Goose came to the door and yelled, "Rebekah said it's time to come inside. She's about to cut the cake."

The fellows followed Cass up the steps. He strode over, held the door open and whispered, "Doc, I'll let you be the judge as to when you think it best to break the news to the ladies."

He nodded in agreement. "Although notifying loved ones of a tragic death has been part of my profession for these past thirty years, it's still difficult to do. There's no getting around it, so the sooner, the better, I suppose. I'm sure the events surrounding Ryker's death will be greatly exaggerated by the time the news travels the gossip circles.

CHAPTER 16

May 28, 1920

The laughter billowing from inside the house made Cass's stomach turn. In a few short minutes, all that joyful noise would come to a sudden, shocking halt. If only it hadn't happened on Gazelle's sixteenth birthday. The news would put a damper on the party and ruin it for her.

Guilt consumed him for allowing his thoughts to center on his daughter, when his grief should be directed solely on the young man with a promising future, who had just lost his life.

The women were gathered in the kitchen when the fellows entered. Rebekah said, "Cass, please call the children and tell everyone to go to the dining room. I think we're ready for the party to begin."

Goat was the first one down, followed by Gander. Then, as if the procession had been carefully orchestrated, Gazelle ambled slowly down the stairs looking quite regal in the pink dress and white pinafore Rebekah had bought for the occasion. Her long dark locks bounced in gentle waves with each step she took. Her eyes darted about the room, searching each face. As she descended, the guests clapped and yelled, "Speech, speech."

Cass couldn't have been prouder. "You have the floor, baby. What would you like to say to these wonderful friends who have come to share this special day with you?"

Her frightened glare locked with her brother's kind blue eyes. Goat gave her a slight nod, then quickly raising his hand high in the air, announced, "Please allow me to do the honors."

Cass scratched his head. Was this really his son? The same kid who had always shied away from the spotlight? His gaze shot from Gazelle to Goat, then back to Gazelle who remained on the third stair from the landing, looking like a Princess.

Goat hurried up the three steps to stand with his arm around his sister. Then boldly announced, "The family would like to thank you all, for coming here tonight to help celebrate this joyous occasion. It's a real privilege to call Gazelle my sister. Anyone who knows her will agree that I am truly blessed."

The crowd applauded once more. Cass assumed the whole thing must've been prearranged until he made eye contact with his wife who appeared equally stunned by the sudden chain of events.

Goat cleared his throat. "Not only are we siblings, but we're also best friends. Esther Jane Marlowe—known affectionately as Gazelle to her family and friends—is truly one of God's masterpieces—beautiful, sweet, smart, talented and trustworthy. But it's her compassionate heart that draws people to her." He picked up her hand and kissed it. "Happy Birthday, Sissy. I love you." The men cheered, the women cried.

Thrusting his hand into the air once more, Goat said, "Now, if I may, I'd like everyone to gather around the table and for my father to pray God's blessings on my beautiful sister as he blesses this delicious-looking food, lovingly prepared by my step-mother."

Goat glanced at Gazelle, who blinked back the tears. She mouthed, "Thank-you."

Whispers, of, "Well, wasn't that the sweetest thing? What a beautiful speech. It's wonderful to see such love between a brother and sister."

Cass kept his thoughts to himself as he rubbed the back of his neck. It seemed only yesterday they were seven and eight, fighting like cats and dogs. When did this amazing transformation take place?

The crowd edged up to the table. Rebekah said, "Goat, after your father blesses the food, please go knock on Papa's door and tell him it's time to eat."

Cass, still bewildered over the impromptu speech, offered the shortest prayer he'd perhaps ever prayed.

Grandpa rolled in, riding in his wheelchair and holding Badger, who squirmed out of his arms and toddled up to the table to get a closer look at the birthday cake. In a jovial voice, Grandpa said, "Did someone say it's time to eat? My daughter has been working her fingers to the bone getting ready for this and Badger and I can hardly wait to try that cake. Happy Birthday, Gazelle."

She lowered her head. "Thanks, Grandpa."

He reached for her hand. "You don't look so good, sugar. Aren't you feeling well?"

"I'm fine."

Rebekah said, "I said the same thing, Papa, when she got home from school." Placing the back of her hand to Gazelle's forehead, she said, "You don't seem to have a fever."

Gazelle shoved her hand away. "I said I'm fine."

Her father gave her a curt look. Perhaps she didn't feel up to par, but that was no reason for her to be so short with her answer. However, he knew Rebekah would not approve of him correcting Gazelle for her rudeness in front of company—especially on her birthday. He'd let it go for now, but as soon as she felt better, he'd let her know that such behavior would not be tolerated. Just because she'd turned sixteen didn't mean she was grown.

Elsie stood beside her husband and whispered, "Dear, I sense Mother Jo is uncomfortable. She's hardly said a word. Perhaps we should leave."

He kissed her on the cheek. "I'm sorry I should've been more sensitive." Then draping his arm around JoElle, he said, "Folks, I should've done this sooner, but I'd like to introduce you to my Mother. This beautiful lady is Miss JoElle Jernigan. Your life will be enriched by making her acquaintance."

JoElle blushed and muttered, "Nice to meet you all."

Only Thelma Redding questioned the relationship. "Your mother? Well, I do declare, Liberty. I never knew you had a mother," to which he quipped, "Sure. Everyone has a mother."

Rebekah realized she'd been so busy, she'd neglected her guest. She eased up beside her to initiate a conversation, but it was her Papa who took it upon himself to put JoElle at ease. The old man wheeled over and asked JoElle if she'd mind helping him manage his plate. Elsie was pleased, since it seemed to be exactly what JoElle needed.

After fixing his plate, JoElle handed it to him. He thanked her, then suggested it was a lovely night and asked if she'd like to join him on the front porch.

Liberty sat across from the window and peeked out a couple of times, amazed at how relaxed they both seemed in one another's company. Elsie giggled. "She'll be fine, sweetheart. You don't have to protect her."

He whispered, "So you don't think I need to ask the old fellow what his intentions are concerning Mother Jo?"

"He seems safe enough to me, dear."

Liberty recalled how difficult Lonnie Brewster made everyone's life when he first arrived at Vinegar Bend. To see and hear him now, it was hard to believe it could be the same man. Not that he should've been shocked that such a transformation could take place since he'd experienced a dynamic change in his own life. He recalled how lonely he'd been before Elsie came waltzing into his life. Love had opened a brand-new, beautiful world for him. One, which he'd never known existed. Perhaps that's how Lonnie felt after becoming a part of the Marlowe family. Liberty hoped Mother Jo would feel that same love and acceptance in their home. He couldn't remember his own mother, since she died when he was very young—but he wanted to believe she was as kind as JoElle Jernigan.

Elsie giggled. "Stop watching them. He's harmless."

"Yeah? You wouldn't have said that this time last year. The old coot was a real booger-bear when he first came to Vinegar Bend."

She laughed out loud. "He couldn't have been too bad. He complimented me on my recipe for cow tongue."

Liberty's heart swelled. How good it was to hear her laugh again.

After everyone had finished eating, Rebekah said, "Doc, I'm glad you were able to join us. I wish Mrs. Brunson could have come with you."

"She would've . . . except—" He sucked in a heavy breath, then slowly exhaled. "I'm sorry to say that we've had some bad news, and it's hit the missus especially hard. She asked that I make her apologies."

"Oh, I'm so sorry. Is there anything we can do?"

"I'm afraid not. I think most of you, if not all, have met my young intern."

Heads nodded.

"He was a brilliant student with potential of becoming an excellent physician."

Rebekah said, "He was there for me when MyEwe was born. I was very impressed with his knowledge. I couldn't have asked for better care. Are you saying he's ill?"

Cass assumed there was no easy way to convey such news, yet he shuddered when Doc blurted it out. "Ryker died this evening at a quarter past five. You folks are the first to know. He indicated to me that he was especially fond of the Marlowe family, so I felt he would've wanted me to share the news with them first, rather than have them read it in the morning paper."

Rebekah clasped her hands against her cheeks. "Oh, no. My goodness, that's terrible. He was so young and took his work very seriously. MyEwe probably wouldn't be alive today if it hadn't been for his excellent care."

Cass glanced at his little Goose, who seemed to be taking the news much better than he'd imagined. She looked up into Rebekah's eyes. "Can I still marry Ryker when I get to Heaven?"

Rebekah whispered, "We'll talk about it when I tuck you in tonight." Then addressing Dr. Brunson, she asked the question that was on everyone's mind. "What was the cause of death?"

"Diphtheria." Mouths gaped open and gasps could be heard around the room at the sound of the dreaded word. "I don't have to tell you folks, diphtheria is a very contagious disease, and we need to pray that we can keep it contained before losing anyone else."

Thelma Redding plopped her hands on her hips. "Well, I have

nothing against praying, but I want to know what you plan to do to keep us all safe? My third cousin removed, on my mother's side of the family told me of a town that was completely wiped out by this horrible disease. I know it's customary for the church women to prepare a corpse for burial, but I wouldn't touch him with a ten-foot pole, and if the other women care about themselves and their family, they won't either. I insist that you put his body in a metal drum and burn it tonight. It's the only way to keep our town safe."

Doc started to speak when Cass stepped up. "This is a sad day for our community. Let's join in prayer for comfort for the many friends, acquaintances and family members who will sorely miss young Ryker Adams." Cass had hardly begun the prayer when a loud thud caused everyone to open their eyes to find Gazelle passed out on the floor.

Rebekah's was the first to rush over and cradle her head in her hands. "Please, bring me a wet rag." Then looking into Doc Brunson's eyes, she whispered, "She's been having awful headaches. Please tell me it's not diphtheria."

He knelt down beside Gazelle, then looking up at Rebekah, he whispered, "Perhaps we should call an end to the party."

She nodded, and taking the cue, he said, "Folks, I'm sure the Marlowe's appreciate you all coming. Now, if everyone will be so kind as to exit the room, it will allow me an opportunity to examine this child."

Cass objected to leaving, but Rebekah took him by the arm and led him into the Parlor.

Gazelle opened her eyes and the doctor instructed her to open her mouth wide. "Sore throat?"

She shook her head as she sobbed.

"Well, you don't have a fever. Do you feel nauseated?"

"I want to go to my room." She was glad he didn't press her further.

"I'll tell your father to come help you up the stairs."

"Please don't. I want to be alone."

"Honey, until we can determine what caused you to pass out, it isn't safe for you to attempt the stairs alone. What if you should pass out on the stairs?"

"Then you help me, please."

"Very well." Lifting her from the floor, he wrapped his arm around her waist to keep her steady and guided her as she ascended the stairs, then saw her safely to her room.

When Dr. Brunson returned to the Parlor, he was surprised to see no one had left. Cass met him at the door. "How is she, doc? Are you taking her to the hospital?"

"No. I don't think that will be necessary."

Thelma Redding said, "It's diphtheria, ain't it doc? We're all gonna die, sure as the world."

He rolled his eyes. "Calm down, Thelma. She doesn't have diphtheria."

"How can you be sure?"

"Because I'm a doctor."

"Then what caused her to fall out?"

"It could've been a number of things. It was quite warm in the dining room and we were crowded together. Perhaps she got too warm." He pursed his lips, then continued. "But without further evidence leading me to believe otherwise, I think she was shocked upon hearing of Ryker's death."

His words seemed to satisfy Thelma and ease her mind. "If it ain't diphtheria, that sounds like a possible explanation. From what I understand, every teen-age girl in the county had a crush on him. Law, that boy was more famous in Vinegar Bend than Rudolph Valentino. It won't surprise me if we don't have a dozen young girls having the same reaction upon hearing the devastating news. From what I hear tell, he was engaged to a girl in Tallahassee. I think my sister knows her. I'll call and tell her to give her the news."

Goat shouted, "How many times are you gonna repeat that lie? Ryker wasn't engaged to anyone." He knew better than to look toward his father. He rushed out of the room, though the doctor called after him, saying, "Son, I think your sister wishes to be alone."

Ignoring the suggestion, he leaped up the stairs, skipping every other one.

Knocking on her door, he waited. When there was no answer, he gently pushed it open. "Sissy, it's me."

He sat on the side of her bed and hugged her tightly. "I'm so sorry. I know you loved him, and he loved you."

"Oh, Goat. I can't believe he's gone. I was angry because he stopped riding by. I had no idea he was sick. I want to die, too."

"No, Sissy. You don't mean that."

"I've never meant anything more. I don't want to live without him."

"Sissy, you know he wouldn't want you talking like this."

"He would if he knew—"

"You're wrong. He knew how much you loved him, but he wouldn't want you to take your life, just because he lost his."

"You don't understand."

"I understand how sad I'd be if anything happened to you. Besides, if you died, it might make me want to die. And if I died, the twins would be so lonely, they might choose to die. Then, Father might decide he couldn't go on without us. Then Rebekah, then Grandpa—do you see what I mean? Every death affects someone—but those of us left behind must think of the others who could be devastated by our death. We have to be strong. I can't imagine how much you hurt, but with the passing of time, it won't hurt so much."

"You're wrong, Goat. The pain I'm feeling won't ever go away. Ever. I loved him so much. You have no idea how much. Please go back downstairs and tell them I'm okay."

"But you're not okay."

"I don't want anyone fussing over me or asking questions. Please do as I say."

"Sure, Sissy. If that's what you really want, but I don't think you should be alone in this frame of mind."

"Please?"

He picked up her hand and kissed it. "Okay, I'm going."

Goat walked back into the Parlor, and everyone except Liberty, Elsie and her caretaker, Mrs. Jernigan, had left.

Cass said, "How is she?"

"She'll be fine."

"Good. I'll go check on her."

"No, father. She's asked to be alone. I think she may need to go to sleep."

"But I want to see—"

Rebekah reached for his hand. "Darling, if she's asked to be alone, I think you should honor her request."

Elsie said she'd had a wonderful time, but that she felt they shouldn't keep Mother Jo out too late. As they walked out to the porch, Liberty whispered, "I'm not sure we're doing her a favor by pulling her away. Seems to me she's enjoying herself. You don't think she's sweet on the old man, do you?"

Elsie grinned. "Don't be ridiculous. You know she's more at ease when she feels she's taking care of someone. I was glad Mr. Lonnie asked her to help him with his plate."

Liberty feigned a scowl. "Maybe he needed help, but then maybe it was a way to get her off to himself. The old codger better not take advantage of our sweet mother or he'll have me to answer to."

On the way home, Liberty said, "Mother Jo, I think your fear of being a wallflower was for naught. Seems to me you were the Belle of the Ball. Mr. Lonnie seemed to think so, too."

"Aww, pshaw, son, you're making me blush."

Elsie punched her husband. "Stop teasing her. I think it was sweet of her to help Mr. Lonnie and I'm sure he was grateful."

Liberty smiled. "Oh, I agree. I'm sure he was most grateful. If I were a single man in a wheelchair and wanted to get the attention of a beautiful woman, I suppose I would suddenly become very needy, also, if it would get her to spend time with me."

Elsie said, "Liberty is teasing you, Mother Jo. He knows better."

JoElle snickered. "I don't mind the teasing. It's true, Lonnie was perfectly capable of balancing his plate and I knew it. But he had such a beautiful smile and there was something about him that drew me to him as soon as I saw him. So, when he asked me to help him, I knew he felt the same connection with me that I felt toward him."

Liberty put on brakes.

Elsie said, "What are you stopping for?"

He glanced in the back seat. "Mother Jo, am I gonna have to ask the fellow what his intentions are?"

She giggled. "Don't be silly. I'm just saying I feel as if I made a dear friend tonight. We had such a delightful time on the porch and there was never a lull in the conversation. Thank you for inviting me to go with you."

Liberty cranked the car and there was no more talk of the party, or of Mr. Lonnie, or of the devastating news that a prominent young man in the community had just died of a dreadful disease. His thoughts centered on his wife who sat humming softly. He recognized the tune to "Love Lifted Me." He sang along as she hummed. "Love lifted me . . . love lifted me. When nothing else could help, love lifted me." She looked beautiful and appeared perfectly normal. Was it possible that the past months of the frightening insanity would dissipate into nothing more than a horrifying memory? But if a false pregnancy could've caused the nervous breakdown, would he be relegated to live in constant fear of the next horrible experience? And the next? Could he possibly protect her from every unpleasant encounter in life? He attempted to clear his thoughts. Why fear the unknown? Couldn't he just enjoy the moment, instead of conjuring up the 'what if's?'

CHAPTER 17

The children were up early, excited that it was the last day of school before summer break. They were all dressed and sitting around the breakfast table before being called—all except Gazelle.

Rebekah pulled the biscuits from the oven and asked Goat to call his sister to the table. Seconds later, he ran back down the stairs and called his father aside, not wanting to upset the younger kids. "She's gone."

Cass laid his hand on his son's shoulder. "Calm down. What do you mean, 'gone.'"

"Just what I said. Gone. Not in her room."

"Don't get so excited. I'm sure there's a logical explanation. Go look on the porch. She probably woke up early, excited over this being the last day of school."

Goat's breath came out in heavy spurts. "You don't understand, Father. She won't be on the porch. She. Is. Gone!"

Cass's eyes squinted. "Goat, is there something you need to tell me?"

His Adam's apple bobbed. "I don't know."

"What do you mean, you don't know. Either there is or there isn't."

"I know something but I'm not sure I need to tell it."

"Stop stalling, son and spit it out. Where is your sister?"

"I don't know and that's the truth."

"Then what were you babbling about?"

Goat ran his fingers through his hair. "She was very upset last night, but I didn't expect her to leave."

Cass rolled his eyes. "Upset? Why are you making this so difficult?"

"Father, the news of Ryker's death was a shock. She hadn't seen him in over a week and she had no idea he was even sick."

"I understand. It was a shock to all of us, but then teenage girls can get a bit emotional. Well, get to the table before the biscuits get cold."

Cass walked into the dining room and took his seat at the head of the table.

Goat stood in the doorway. "Aren't you even gonna look for her?"

"Please have a seat, Goat, while I ask God's blessings upon our food."

Goat's jaw dropped. "I don't get you. Don't you even care that your daughter's heart is breaking?"

Rebekah walked in from the kitchen and took her seat at the table. The front door slammed as Cass began to pray.

Rebekah looked at her husband. "What's wrong with Goat and why hasn't Gazelle come down?"

Cass related Goat's message and was unprepared for Rebekah's reaction.

"Cass Marlowe, I'm surprised at you. Your daughter is obviously devastated over the news of Ryker's death, and you sit here doing nothing to find her?"

"Hon, she's a teenager. According to doc, he was the heart throb of every young girl in the county. Let's leave her alone and let her have a good cry."

"Leave her alone? We don't even know where she is."

Hearing soft snubs at the other end of the table, he looked over at Goose. "What's wrong with you?"

"I don't know who I can marry. I wanted to marry Ryker."

He glanced at his wife with a wink. "I'm sorry Ryker died, sugar. He was a fine young man and the whole town will miss his presence, but he's now in a much better place. You know that don't you?"

"He is?"

"Of course."

"Then I know where Gazelle is."

Cass tucked her napkin at the neck of her dress. "Don't get anything on your pretty little school dress."

Rebekah's brow furrowed. "Cass Marlowe, Goose just told

you that she knows where Gazelle is. Aren't you even interested in listening to her?"

"I think I know, too." He picked up a bowl of grits and dipped them in his plate. "I figure she's down at the prayer stump and I think we'd be doing her a favor by allowing her to have a good cry to get it out of her system." Feeling Rebekah's glaring eyes, he let out a heavy sigh. "Sorry, Goosey girl. Where do you think your sister is?"

"At that better place."

"What better place, sweetie?"

"Where Ryker went."

"No. No, that can't be." Cass felt his heart beating against his chest. "Why would you think that?"

"I woke up last night and went to the kitchen to get a drink of water. Gazelle was walking out the door."

"So where did she say she was going?"

Tears streamed down her face. "I wasn't s'pose to tell nobody."

"But it's important that you do. Where was she going?"

"I told you already. She said she was going to be with Ryker. I don't think she believed me when I told her he was dead."

Cass glanced at Rebekah and though her back was turned toward the wall, he could hear her sobs. He jumped up and ran out the door. He yelled for Goat to wait for him. When he caught up, he said, "Goat, do you have any information on your sister, which you haven't shared?"

"No sir."

"Then let's go to the Prayer Stump first, and if she isn't there, maybe you can think of somewhere to look. Are you *sure* you don't know something you aren't telling?"

He wrung his hands together. "Well, only that she was in love with Ryker and you're wrong if you think it was just a crush. He loved her, too."

Gander sat at the table, whining. "Today is our last day of school and the teacher promised us a party. If Goat and Gazelle don't get back in time, there won't be anyone to walk us to school."

Rebekah said, "I'm afraid you won't be going to school today, Gander, but I promise to make your favorite cookies and you and Goose can take some to Grandpa and Badger. I'm sure they'd like to have a party with you."

"Can we have three cookies?"

"Sure."

"Can I have four?"

"We'll see. Finish your breakfast and run outside and play."

Rebekah left the kitchen dishes alone and hurried upstairs to Gazelle's room. She reached under her bed and pulled out a metal box, which held Gazelle's prized possessions. Was it wrong to plunder? Or wrong not to? Goose's words kept repeating in her head. "She went to be with Ryker in that better place."

Jerking the box open, she fumbled through award certificates, newspaper clippings—then, seeing a torn letter, she tried to piece it together, but there were missing pieces.

Dear Ryker,

. . . loved me. . . but when . . Tallahassee. I hope . . . doesn't mean I won't try.

Rebekah bit her lip. So, Gazelle was in love with Ryker. She supposed Ryker told her about the girlfriend when he realized Gazelle was falling for him.

Goose's words kept rolling around in her head. Surely, the child misunderstood her sister. Or more likely, she could've made it up. She had a vivid imagination that sometimes led to the telling of fibs. Rebekah had even talked to her recently about making up false stories and telling them as if they were true. Yes, that had to be it. Cass mentioned Ryker had gone to a better place, and Goose must have imagined that her sister would be happy if she could be with Ryker in a better place—not understanding that her father meant Heaven.

An hour later, Goat walked into the house.

Rebekah looked out the door. "Where's your father? Did you find her?" She put her arms around him in a hug when she saw the tears in his eyes. She'd never really thought about it until now, but she didn't remember ever having seen him cry. When he didn't respond, she swallowed the painful lump forming in her throat. "Oh, no. Is she—"

"If you're asking if she's dead, the answer is no. If you're asking if she's all right, the answer is still no. I'm not sure she'll ever be all right."

"I'm sure it seems that way, now, but—"

"You didn't see her, Rebekah. She went berserk because we found her. She pleaded with Father to leave her alone. It's all my fault." He ran upstairs to his room.

Rebekah followed him. "Tell me what's going on, Goat. I've been worried sick. Where was she?"

He flung his body onto his bed with his face buried in his pillow. "Father was right. She was at the Prayer Stump." Unable to hold back the sobs, he said, "She was writing a letter to each of us, telling us goodbye."

"Goodbye? Where was she going?"

He screamed, "Don't be so naïve, Rebekah. She was planning to kill herself."

She swallowed hard. "Oh, no!"

"I'm sorry. I shouldn't have said that. I'm upset."

"Of course, you are. I understand. We're all upset."

"But if I'd spent more time listening to her instead of obsessing over Belle, she might've shared her feelings with me. Sissy and I were so close until I started spending so much time with Belle. I neglected her when she needed me most."

"I doubt there's anything you could've done differently to change things, Did she talk to you about her feelings for him?"

He turned over in the bed and lifted his head. "Sissy and I have had a lot of private conversations about a lot of things, none of which I wish to divulge."

"Fair enough. You two have certainly been through a lot

together, especially going through the heartache of losing your mother . . . then learning the truth. That had to be very traumatic with lasting effects. Gazelle remained amazingly strong through it all, but perhaps, unknown to us, the strain has been festering inside. Hearing the sad news of Ryker's death, followed by Thelma Redding's brash comment concerning the disposing of Ryker's body was enough to send anyone over the edge, especially someone emotionally fragile. The remark was very crude and uncalled for. I heard Gazelle gasp and that's when she fainted."

His teeth ground together. "Mrs. Redding is a hateful, nosey old goat. I can't stand her."

Rebekah's neck stiffened. "Goat! I'll admit she's a pill to be around sometimes, but your Father would be very upset if he heard you say such things. It isn't Christian."

"And neither is she. She gossips." His bottom lip trembled. "I don't reckon I've got room to talk, though. I'm no better."

"You? I've never known you to gossip."

"Maybe you don't know me as well as you think you do, Rebekah. I repeated something the old goat said, and I had nothing to go on but her word. Shoot, everyone who knows Mrs. Redding, knows her word is about as useless as a three-legged mule. I'm sure the words I repeated hurt Gazelle, deeply."

Rebekah bit her lip, recalling the torn note. So, that's how Gazelle found out about the girlfriend in Tallahassee. No wonder Goat was feeling such remorse.

"There probably wasn't a word of truth to it. I don't know if

Sissy believed it or not, but she never seemed the same after I told her. She stayed in her room more and I didn't pay attention to the change in her because I was spending so much time with Belle. I wish I'd never told her."

"You're building things up in your head, Goat. You know your sister has those terrible headaches. There's a lot of pollen in the air this Spring, and that's why she spent so much time in her room. I don't think she felt like being around any of us. Gazelle loves you very much. Surely, you know that."

He sat up in bed. "Really? If you love someone, do you want to kill yourself to get away from them? I don't think so."

"Oh, my sweet Goat. People who become suicidal aren't thinking straight. They're going through a difficult time in their life and are seeking a way to stop the pain. It wasn't us that she wanted to escape from. It was herself. We need to thank the Lord that you and Cass found her in time. We've been given an opportunity to support her through this desperate episode of her life and help her to understand how much we all love her. For that, we should be grateful.

CHAPTER 18

The front door downstairs closed with a bang. Cass and Gazelle's voices could be heard in the hall. Rebekah looked at Goat and with her finger over her lips, whispered. "Shh!"

Gazelle was crying. "But I don't want to see the doctor, Father."

"Sweetheart, you aren't well. I insist."

"I know you think I didn't know what I was doing, but you're wrong. And if you send for Dr. Brunson, I'll do it again. I Suwannee, I will."

"Don't say that, sugar."

"But I will. The doctor will ask a bunch of questions, but he won't learn a thing because I don't want to talk about it—to him or to you. Where's Goat?"

Goat sailed off the bed and stood at the top of the stairs. "Up here, Sissy. Come on up."

Rebekah ran down the stairs, pausing briefly to hug Gazelle as they passed, then hurried over to her husband, wrapping her arms around him. "I'm glad you found her," she whispered.

They lifted their eyes to the top of the stairs and watched Goat and Gazelle heading for her room.

Cass sighed. "I pray he can get through to her. Apparently, I can't." He broke into sobs. "What am I going to do, Rebekah? She won't talk to me, and I'm so afraid to take my eyes off her, for fear she might try it again. What would make her feel so desperate that she'd want to kill herself? You don't suppose it had anything to do with Ryker's death, do you? Doc said all the young girls had a crush on him. But Gazelle?"

"I don't know, dear, but we can't smother her. I know you're frightened. I'm frightened, too. But what is that verse you quote to Goose when she thinks there are monsters in her room?"

He paused, then said, "What time I am afraid, I will trust in Thee."

"That's the one. We can lift her up to the Father and trust him to watch over her and to bring peace and comfort to her hurting heart."

****

By daylight Saturday, the town was buzzing with rumors laced with only a hint of truth. The switchboard was busy as folks called friends and neighbors with the dreadful news that the popular young intern had died with Diphtheria and that Cass Marlowe's daughter was dying with the same dreadful disease. Dr. Brunson removed his telephone from the hook after being bombarded with calls from a sudden influx of hypochondriacs who insisted they were having symptoms and demanded immediate treatment.

Other calls came from angry individuals demanding information concerning how he intended to dispose of the corpse. Every conversation began with, "Thelma said—"

Thelma Redding made calls all morning, informing citizens of Vinegar Bend that her husband was calling for a noon meeting in the town square to discuss the troublesome situation.

At precisely twelve o'clock, Horace stood in the center of the Gazebo, appearing delighted at the large turnout. With his thumbs tucked underneath the collar of his silk suit, he strutted across the stage with a megaphone. "Folks, we've got a problem in Vinegar Bend. A big problem. As you all have heard by now, Dr. Brunson's trusted assistant, Ryker Adams has succumbed to a very contagious disease."

Thelma wobbled up the steps and standing beside her husband, she grabbed the megaphone from his hands. "For those of you who are wondering where he contracted it, no one can say for sure, but he most likely brought it back from one of his visits to Tallahassee, where I understand his lady-friend lives."

Horace feigned a smile, though anyone who knew him was acutely aware that he didn't take to relinquishing his megaphone, even to his wife. He jerked it from her hands. "Thank you, dear. I believe I see an empty chair on the lawn. Perhaps you'd like to take a seat." Then motioning toward a group of fellows huddled together, smoking cigarettes, Horace called out, "Would one of you gentlemen be so kind as to help my wife down the steps and find her a place to sit?"

"Now, as I was saying, we're all deeply saddened by Ryker's death, but we can't let our sympathy keep us from taking every precaution to protect ourselves, even if we have to step on some toes to ensure our safety. I've spoken to Doc Brunson and he has informed me that the deceased's body is lying on a table in the back of his office. That's not acceptable folks. It's time for us to speak up and insist that doc do the right thing."

Manly Jones spoke up. "What are you getting at, Horace?"

Horace's thick brows meshed together. "I'd think it would be obvious to a thinking man. It's a known fact that the body of a diseased person omits poisonous gases, filling the atmosphere with a noxious vapor."

"Speak English," Rodolph Jackson yelled out.

"I'm simply saying that as Ryker's body decays, the disease wafts through the air we breathe, spreading Diphtheria to our lungs. If the corpse isn't disposed of properly, the whole town could be wiped out within weeks."

Moans and a few gasps could be heard. Horace pounded his fist on the stand in front of him. "Folks, that's just not acceptable. I've spoken with Dr. Brunson, who said Ryker's parents are coming to Vinegar Bend today expecting to bury their son in our city cemetery. But we can't permit that to happen, now can we?"

Maude yelled, "Lordy mercy, that's just crazy talk. Dogs die around here all the time with the mange and are buried in shallow graves. Ain't none of us ever caught the mange, have we?"

One of the fellows in the back, puffing on a cigarette, yelled out, "You mean other than you, Maude? Folks don't call you Mangy Maude for nothing."

The crowd snickered but Horace ignored the comment, while acknowledging a raised hand. "Rodolph, you have a question?"

"Yeah. They have a right to bury their son, don't they? I don't get what you think you can do about it."

"I'll be glad to answer your question, Rodolph. It's not what I can do. It's what we as a town can do. *We*, Rodolph. We need to demand that doc cremate the body immediately and not wait for Ryker's parents to arrive."

Rodolph scratched his head. "What's that mean?"

Maude yelled, "He wants to set him on fire." She stomped up the Gazebo steps and shaking her finger in Horace's face, she yelled, "Ain't no way you gonna burn that sweet boy. It's a heathen practice."

Rodolph yelled, "What's heathen about it, Maude?"

"Well, I wouldn't expect you to know, Rodolph Jackson. You ain't been to church since you was old enough to shave. But every good Christian knows there'll be no resurrection for them that've been insinuated." She stomped back down the steps after having her say.

Horace chuckled. "I think you mean incinerated, Maude, but that's a myth that's been laid to rest among intelligent people. If you want to talk about what's unchristian, I'll tell you. It would be sinful to bury him here, when science tells us it would be delivering a death sentence to our beloved town."

Sallie Horton mumbled something.

Horace said, "Mrs. Horton would you please repeat your question?"

"I don't reckon it was a question. More or less just pondering. Maybe you could suggest the boy's folks take him home on a train and bury him in a family plot in their hometown."

Horace shook his head. "For our protection as well as the folks in Tallahassee, we can't permit that to happen, Talk about being unchristian, don't you see how unchristian it would be for us to allow the body to be transported, knowing it would be the death of the good folks in that town. People, we have no choice."

Manly scratched his head. "Seems kinda cruel to me, not to let the poor boy have a decent funeral. After all, he was mighty good to all of us."

"Manly, don't you think if Ryker could tell us his preference today, whether to be buried and infect us all or be cremated to save the town, he would choose the latter?"

Rodolph's face twisted. "Ladder? What ladder?"

Manly said, "Rodolph, there's a picture in my mama's Bible of a ladder reaching up to Heaven. Underneath the picture, it says, Jacob's ladder. I reckon that's the one he's talking about."

Heads turned when Doc Brunson drove up. He ambled up the steps leading to the Gazebo. Standing next to Horace, he took the megaphone. "Okay, folks, you can all go home. Ryker's parents, his brother and his former pastor all arrived by train this morning. A private graveside funeral was held, and Ryker has been laid to rest in the city cemetery. Now, if any of you choose to go dig him up, you can bury me in his plot because you'll have to shoot me first."

Manly raised his hand. "But Horace said—"

"I know what Horace said, but he's wrong. This meeting is over."

Horace yelled, "Wait!" But the crowd disbursed, leaving him alone in the square.

****

Sunday morning Cass knocked on Grandpa's door. "You ready to go to church, Papa?"

"Ya'll go ahead. I won't be going with you this morning."

"It looks as if Goat and I are the only two going, so if you should need anything, Rebekah and the young'uns will be staying here. Gazelle has another one of her headache's, so we didn't want to leave her alone."

He went into the kitchen to kiss his wife goodbye. "You might want to check on your Papa a little later in the morning."

"He isn't going with you?"

"No, and it's not like him to miss church. I always look forward to his critiques of the sermon on the trip home. I can always count on him being honest with me." He pecked her on the cheek. "Gotta run."

"He must be feeling poorly if he's staying home. To have been such a hermit when he arrived, he's certainly made a dramatic change. Lately, if anyone mentions going anywhere, he grabs his hat before asking 'where to?' I hope he's not coming down with something. I'll check on him after I feed the babies."

Five minutes after Cass left, Rebekah was feeding Badger and MyEwe breakfast when Papa rolled into the kitchen dressed in his best suit and had his slicked back with Macassar oil.

"Oh, Papa, I'm terribly sorry, but Cass has left already, and you look so nice. He was under the impression you wouldn't be going with him."

"That's because I didn't plan to go with him." Badger slid down from the table and ran over with his arms held out for his Grandpa to pick him up.

Grandpa shook his head and pointed to the table, making signs for him to finish his breakfast.

Rebekah helped her son back up to the table, sat down beside him, and handed him a glass of milk. "Papa, you sure are dressed up, not to be going anywhere."

"Who said I wasn't going any—"

Rebekah jumped up. "Excuse me. I thought I heard someone at the door."

"It's for me. Tell him I'm coming."

Not waiting to ask questions, though she had plenty, Rebekah hurried to the front door. "Liberty?"

"Is your father ready?"

"Ready? Uh . . . yes, I suppose he is. Won't you come in?"

"No, the ladies will be waiting for us. We'd better be on our way."

Grandpa rolled out to the porch and down the ramp that Goat built for his wheelchair. Liberty helped him into his truck and placed the chair in the back.

Rebekah had so many questions on the tip of her tongue, but held them in. If her papa didn't want her to know why he chose to go to Liberty and Elsie's church, rather than to hear his son-in-law preach, he could exercise that privilege. It didn't mean it didn't sting a little.

Though Cass still had five minutes before time for services to begin, the churchyard was filled with automobiles, buggies and fancy carriages by the time he arrived. He hurried inside, and saw Horace Redding standing up front. Horace made a point to pull out his gold watch, glare at the time, then tuck it back into the fob pocket on his three-piece suit. "Preacher, I'd like to take a few minutes to address the church before we begin."

Cass walked up the three steps leading to the podium and Goat took a seat on the front row. Cass pulled out a handkerchief and swiped the sweat forming on his brow. Anytime Horace Redding had something to say, it meant a storm was brewing.

He began by lamenting how the town was deeply affected by the death of Dr. Brunson's fine assistant. Amens chimed out. He added, "Reverend Marlowe, we all think the world of you." Heads nodded and there were more amens. "Yet, it's with grief in my heart that I must say I have somewhat against you."

The church grew silent. No amens. No shuffling of feet. No coughs. Nothing but a sudden chilling silence. He continued, "I came prepared to lead the service this morning, since I was under the assumption that you'd make the sound decision to stay home."

Cass winced. "Stay home? Me?"

Horace shoved his flattened palm in the air. "Please, sir! Allow me to finish. The disturbing news has reached us that your teenage daughter contracted Diphtheria from her beau, the late Ryker Adams, so naturally, I expected you to remain home to keep from exposing the rest of us."

Cass jumped up. "I'm afraid you've been misinformed, Horace. First, let me assure you that Ryker Adams was a friend of the family, but in no way was he romantically involved with my daughter and such an accusation disturbs me greatly. Furthermore, the rumor that she has Diphtheria is absurd. How do such stories get started?"

"Well, I hope I'm wrong, my wife tells me that last night that she fainted at her own birthday party and had to be carried upstairs. I was told she had every symptom."

Cass rolled his eyes. "Really? And what are the symptoms of Diphtheria, Horace?"

The door to the back of the church opened and Doc Brunson eased in and took a seat on the back row.

Horace's voice lifted. "I'm glad you decided to show up, doc, because I have somewhat against you, also."

Doc glanced around, looking astonished. "Are you addressing me?"

"You're the doctor, aren't you?"

"What's on your mind, Horace?"

"Your failure to protect our community is in direct opposition to the 'hypocritic oath you took."

Goat jumped up from his seat and faced the short, pudgy man. "Mr. Redding, the hypocritic oath is apparently the one you've chosen to give allegiance to, since I've never met a bigger hypocrite. Allow me to educate you. Doc Brunson took the Hippocratic oath to treat the ill, protect the patient's privacy and to abstain from mischievous practices, and anyone who claims he's ever broken it is as ignorant as you."

Cass jumped off the podium, rushed over and clamped his hand on his son's shoulder. "That's enough. Sit down, Goat."

"Sorry, Father. But I can't sit and listen to that nonsense. No one will stand up to Mr. Redding because they're too afraid he'll withhold his money, which he uses as leverage to run the church."

The corner of Horace's lip lifted in a smirk. "You have no idea how much money anyone gives to this church, young man."

"Wrong. Everyone knows exactly how much you drop in the collection plate from week to week because you never miss an opportunity to remind us." Goat finagled from his father's grasp and ran out the door.

Horace glanced around the sanctuary and smirked. "Well,

folks, I'm sorry you had to be exposed to that impromptu hissyfit, but conduct, both good and bad, is taught by example. If you ask me, that little smarty pants would benefit from a trip behind the smoke house. If he were mine, I'd tear up his britches and I'm sure many of you are thinking the same thing." Then, with a sarcastic grin, he said, "But we've all heard the expression, 'As the twig is bent, so grows the tree.'" He took a seat and glanced all around, smiling, as if seeking approval for his performance.

Cass was pulled between running out the door to catch his son or sticking it out to perform the job he came there to do. His gaze darted back and forth across the congregation as he attempted to read the stoic expressions. *Get thee behind me Satan.* His deep baritone voice shattered the silence when he trekked back up the three steps leading to the podium, singing to the top of his voice, "When We Walk With the Lord."

Only a few voices joined in at first, but by the time he got to the second verse and stood behind the pulpit, the congregation was standing and belting out the words.

Horace and Thelma refused to stand. Cass led in prayer, then took a seat in one of majestic-looking mahogany chairs on the pulpit that reminded him of the pictures he'd seen of thrones. He never had liked those chairs. There was only one who deserved to be on the throne and it certainly wasn't him. But Horace Redding had picked them out and paid for them himself and never missed an opportunity to remind folks.

Cass sat with bowed head while the pianist played, as two

ushers ambled down the aisle, passing the collection plate.

Horace sat on the end of the pew with his arms crossed over his chest. He refused to take the plate and his wife took the cue from her husband. She remained stone-faced and unmoving as if unaware of what was taking place. Jasper Smith reached across the two stiff bodies and took the plate from the usher's hands. After placing a couple of folded bills into the offering plate, he passed it down the pew.

Cass's heart pounded. He had a strong urge to disregard the sermon he came prepared to preach and deliver a pointed message to two specific individuals, condemning them for their divisive ways. He could put up with someone saying evil or untrue things about himself, but when Horace told a vicious lie about Gazelle, followed by the malicious accusation directed toward Goat, he'd crossed the line.

After the ushers took their seat, Cass left the 'throne' and lumbered back up to the pulpit. He glanced around at the crowd, sizing them up as he fought against the tempest raging inside him. Horace's vile accusations rolled around in Cass's thoughts like loose buckshot, causing his head to throb.

Perplexed about how to begin a sermon he'd not prepared, he left the pulpit and paced back and forth across the podium with his hands locked behind him. He had an obligation to call out the evildoers.

Returning to stand behind the pulpit, he turned to Matthew 23, ready to lead in the reading of the scripture. His throat tightened as he gazed out at the congregation. With his forefinger, he swiped beads of sweat forming on his upper lip. He massaged the tense muscles in the back of his neck.

Then, with a groan, he murmured, I *hear you, Lord.* Quickly flipping through the pages, he said, "Please turn in your Bibles to Hebrews 13:8 and read along with me. 'Jesus Christ the same yesterday, and today, and forever.'" Amens could be heard throughout the sanctuary.

Cass presented the word with boldness that the Lord had laid on his heart the preceding week. Convicting words spilled from his mouth, piercing his own heart. He'd spent far too much time lamenting situations in his life, which were beyond his control. Instead of concentrating on the changing scenes around him, he'd choose to keep his focus on the one constant in his life—an unchanging God. When he finished, he concluded it was one of the best sermons he'd ever delivered. Perhaps it was because it was the message he needed most to hear.

CHAPTER 19

When Cass arrived home, Goat was waiting for him and ran out to meet the car. His voice cracked with emotion. "Father, I am so ashamed. I don't know what came over me. Those words were coming from my mouth before I could think what I was doing. Did you get fired?"

Cass hugged his son tightly. "Fired? If you meant fired-up, I'd have to answer yes. You should've stayed for the sermon. I delivered what might possibly be the best message I've ever delivered."

Goat reared back, locking his gaze with his father's. "Then . . . then, you aren't angry with me?"

Cass chewed the inside of his cheek. "I'm furious with you."

"But you said—"

"I said I preached an outstanding sermon. I don't see how that has anything to do with your shameful outburst in church."

"I see." He swallowed hard. "Are they gonna fire you?"

"For preaching? I don't think so."

"I was afraid you'd lose your job because of what I said."

Cass laid his hands on Goat's shoulders. "Son, I don't have a job."

Goat put his face in his hands and moaned. "I'm so sorry, Father. I know how much you enjoy preaching."

"You're right. I love to preach, but it isn't a job. It's a calling. But to ease your concerns, unless I hear otherwise, I still have a place to preach at Friendship Community Church. But if that door closes, God will open another. What are we waiting for? I'm hungry. Let's go inside to eat."

Everyone was seated at the table—everyone but Grandpa. Cass asked the blessing on the food, then complimented Rebekah on the delicious-looking meal. He dipped a hearty helping of pot roast and passed it down to Goat. "How's Gazelle and Grandpa feeling?"

"I just checked on Gazelle and she's still asleep. I wish we could find something to relieve those headaches. They've been happening more frequently."

"Poor kid. And what about Grandpa?"

She lowered her head. "He isn't here."

Cass laid down his cornbread and took a swig of tea. "What do you mean, he's not here? Not here at the table? I can see that."

Emphasizing each word as if it stood alone, she repeated her words. "He's. Not. Here." Seeing the confusion on Cass's face, she said, "Apparently, Papa and Liberty have been communicating by phone, because shortly after you left, Papa came out dressed in his best suit and before I had an opportunity to find out what was going on, Liberty showed up."

"Liberty? What did he want?"

"He came to get Papa to go to church with him."

Cass's brow furrowed. "I see."

Rebekah bit her lip. "Do you? Because I don't. I am miffed with him for choosing to go to Liberty's church, when I know how much you enjoyed discussing the sermons with him. I can't imagine what possessed him to do such a thing."

"Hon, that's not a bad thing. Sure, I'll miss his input, but it's good that he's reaching out beyond the family. We all have outlets. He shouldn't be expected to be glued to us everywhere we go. Grandpa is trying his wings."

Badger pulled at his father's sleeve and flapped his arms. Cass signed to let him know he didn't understand.

Goat laughed. "I think he read your lips. You said Grandpa was trying his wings, and Badger is asking you if Grandpa can fly."

Cass looked Badger in the eye and shook his head. Then smiling, he said, "I suppose we'd better be very careful what we say from now on. He's nobody's dummy."

The front door opened and the chatter around the table ceased at the sound of wheels rolling against the wood floor.

Goat looked at Badger and without signing with his hands, he mouthed the words, "Grandpa is home."

Badger quickly slid from his chair and ran in the hall to meet him.

Goat grinned. "I told you he could read lips."

Grandpa rolled into the dining room, with Badger in his arms. "I hope ya'll didn't eat it all. I'm starving. That preacher didn't know when twelve o'clock came."

Cass chuckled. "Well, I'm sure if you continue to go, he'll learn fast."

"I didn't mind. He's a good preacher." Reaching for the cornbread, he added, "Not as good as my son-in-law, mind you, but he's young. He'll learn. I was joking about the time. As long as a preacher is presenting the Word of God, the way that young fellow did this morning, it's a joy to listen."

Rebekah passed the peas to her father. Attempting to find out what prompted him to go to church with Liberty, she said, "How's Liberty and Elsie doing?"

"About the same as when you saw them two nights ago, sugar. This is a mighty fine pot roast. You outdid yourself."

She lowered her head, feeling that he knew exactly what she was attempting to do. So why didn't he go ahead and explain?

Cass laid his napkin on the table. "The meal was delicious, sweetheart. Excuse me, please. I'd like to go up and check on my sweet girl."

Rebekah said, "Wait and I'll fix her a plate in case she doesn't feel like coming downstairs."

After filling the plate, Rebekah laid a checkered napkin over the food, then handed it to her husband. "If her head still hurts, try to encourage her to take an aspirin powder. I couldn't get her to take one this morning and I could tell she was in pain. Her eyes were swollen from crying."

Grandpa pushed back from the table. "That was delicious. All this good eatin' is putting some meat on my bones. Liberty said this morning that I looked like a different man. I reckon I feel like a different man."

Rebekah smiled. "I'm glad you enjoyed your meal, Papa. Cass and I were just saying last night that you must've gained fifteen or twenty pounds since arriving. I think you were malnourished."

He rolled his eyes. "Weren't nothin' wrong with me, 'cept I let the devil get a stronghold in my life. I was an ornery old goat, wasn't I?" He chuckled when Rebekah didn't respond. "You don't have to say it. I knew nobody liked me and I didn't blame 'em. Shucks, for years I didn't even like myself."

Cass came down the stairs, holding the plate with the napkin still in place. "Gazelle won't eat. I tried to force her, but she said it would make her throw up. She pitched a fit when I told her I was gonna call doc to come take a look at her, but she can't go on like this. We've got to get her help. Don't we?"

Rebekah shook her head slowly, indicating she had no advice to share. "Do what you think best, dear. I'm at my wit's end. I don't know what to tell you. I don't know how to help her if she continues to refuse to take anything for the headaches."

He walked over and picked up the telephone. "Shirley, get me

Doc Brunson, please."

Before the operator had time to connect, he heard Gazelle's voice. "Wait, Father. Don't call. I'm feeling much better."

Cass hung up and met her on the stairs. "Oh, honey, you don't know how good that makes me feel. How about some dinner, now?"

"I'm really not very hungry. I'll eat a little later."

Rebekah said, "But you didn't eat breakfast. Are you sure you don't want to eat just a bite?"

"No thank you." Looking around, she said, "Have you seen Goat?"

Cass said, "I left him sitting outside in the swing trying to untangle some fishing string."

"Thanks, Father. It's a beautiful day. I think I'll join him."

"I'm sure he'll appreciate the company. He's had a bad day, but I wouldn't bring it up if I were you."

Rebekah's eyes widened. "Really? I wasn't aware he'd been anywhere—except church. What happened?"

"It doesn't matter. It's over now. Where'd Badger go?"

"Taking a nap with Grandpa."

"And MyEwe?"

"Taking a nap in her crib."

Wrapping his arm around her waist, he led her into the bedroom. "How many times do we get the rare opportunity to take a nap in the middle of the day? Let's see how long it can last."

"But I haven't finished the dishes."

"Forget the dishes. They'll wait."

****

Goat threw his fishing line down when Gazelle walked out on the porch. "Hey, it's good to see you rambling around. Feeling better?"

"I guess." Her chin trembled. "Goat could we take a walk?"

"Sure, Sissy. I imagine you're tired of being shut up in your room. A walk will do you good. I need to go down to the river anyway, to check on my trot lines."

"But it's Sunday."

"I know but you won't tell Father—will you?"

"Of course not."

When they got to the river, Gazelle sat down on a rock at the edge of the water and waited for Goat to check his lines.

He walked back up. "I'm finished. You ready to go?"

"No."

He sat down beside his sister and wrapped his arm around her. "Sissy, I'm so sorry. Father and Rebekah are very naïve not to know what's wrong with you. Why don't you tell them? They'll understand."

She burst into full-blown sobs. "Tell them? Are you serious? How can I tell them? Do you know what this will do to Father's ministry?"

"The fact that you fell in love with a wonderful fellow who loved you dearly? There's no shame in that."

"Goat don't you get it? I'm pregnant."

He slung back his shoulders. "You're what?"

"You heard me. I'm going to have Ryker's baby."

"Yikes." He buried his face in his hands. "Give me a minute to absorb this news. I don't know what to say."

"Well, you'll be the only one who doesn't know what to say. There'll be plenty of talk when the word gets out."

"How . . . how far along are you?"

She counted back. "February, March, April, May. I'm not sure, but no more than four months. We married the twenty-second of January."

"Whoa! Run that by me again. You . . . and Ryker? You two got married?"

"Yes, and Father will be furious when he finds out."

"Hey, not nearly as furious as he would've been if you weren't married. Don't you see? He can't be angry with you when he finds out you put the horse before the carriage. Come on, let's head back to the house and we'll tell him together."

"I can't, Goat. I simply can't."

"Yes, you can, Sissy. Putting it off will only prolong the misery." He took her hand to lift her off the rock. "Let's get it over with. I'll be there to support you."

CHAPTER 20

When Goat and Gazelle reached the house, Grandpa was waiting on the porch in his wheelchair. He yelled out, "Goat, where've you been, boy? I'm ready. Let's do it."

Goat's eyes widened. "Now?"

Gazelle looked at her brother. "What's he talking about? Ready for what?"

"It's a surprise for the family that he's been working on for months. I tried to talk him into sharing it a couple of weeks ago, but he said he wasn't ready. Sissy, this is very important to him. Do you mind if we wait to break your news?"

"Mind? I wish we could put it off forever."

"You and I both know that's not possible."

Tears welled in her eyes.

"Aww, Sissy, please don't cry. It'll all work out, I promise."

"It'll never work out, Goat. The love of my life is gone, and I didn't even have the chance to say goodbye." The words Ryker spoke on their wedding day came back to haunt her. *One day, there'll be no more good-byes.*

As soon as they walked inside, Rebekah marveled at how good it was to see Gazelle feeling better. "I'm sure the walk was good for you. I don't know what Papa is up to, but he's been antsy waiting for Goat to get back."

Gazelle shrugged. "Goat said he has a surprise for the family."

Grandpa wheeled into his room and Goat followed. Ten minutes later, Goat came out and asked everyone to gather in the Parlor.

Cass grabbed Badger when he tried to follow Goat into Grandpa's room. Rebekah signed for him to wait. "Grandpa will be out shortly."

When he signed back, "Grandpa walk?" She smiled and corrected by showing him how to sign wheelchair. He formed a pout and Cass laughed. "He's a Marlowe. He doesn't like to be told he's wrong."

The door to the Parlor opened and Lonnie stood in the doorway. Then as he carefully put one foot in front of the other, Rebekah screeched. "Papa! You're walking."

Badger punched her and signed, "No wheelchair. Grandpa walk."

She grabbed him up. "Right, Badger. No wheelchair. You knew and you tried to tell me, didn't you?"

Cass said, "Lonnie, I can hardly believe it. When did this

happen?" Then he laughed and said, "You're a lot taller than you look in that chair."

Goat said, "We've been working at it for months."

Gazelle gave him a hug. "Well, we're all real proud of you, Grandpa. You look . . . different."

He smiled. "Good different, I hope."

She nodded. "Yessir. Good different."

"I'm glad because my date should be here soon."

Everyone laughed. Cass said, "I see a sense of humor came with those new legs."

Goat shook his head. "He's serious, Father. He has a date, and he plans to walk her to her car, so don't embarrass him by offering to help."

The old man blushed. "I know what ya'll are thinking. Who'd go out with an old geezer like me?"

Rebekah's gaze locked with her husband's. Then turning her head slightly, she said, "Papa, that's not what we're thinking at all. We're happy you can walk and if you ever meet a lady friend that you feel you'd enjoy being around, there's nothing that would thrill me more."

He saw car lights pulling into the yard. "Well, that's good to know, daughter, because I think she just drove up."

"She? Who?"

Goat opened the door. "Come in Miss JoElle. I think Grandpa went to get his hat. Won't you have a seat?"

"Thank you. What a nice young man, you are. Such manners."

Cass marveled at the kid who never ceased to amaze him.

Grandpa walked out, smiling. "Evening, Jo. I believe you've met all my family. I'm ready if you are."

Rebekah glanced at her husband and smiled. He winked and mouthed, "*Jo?*"

Lonnie crooked his arm and JoElle blushed like a new bride as they strolled toward the door.

Rebekah said, "Papa, wait! If you insist on walking, at least let me give you the crutches Goat used when he broke his leg."

"I don't need no crutches. There'll likely be more crutches than needed at the church."

"Are you serious?"

Lonnie glanced at Cass who winked, indicating he understood the symbolism.

Church Crutches

Rebekah held her breath as she peeked out the window and watched her papa approach the edge of the porch steps. Then, with her hand over her breast, she slowly exhaled when he sauntered down the doorsteps with his head held high and his shoulders thrown back, like a thirty-year-old man.

The family was buzzing with questions for Goat. "Slow down. I don't have all the answers, but I'll tell you what I can. Grandpa began to get the feeling back in his legs about three months after the accident. I went to see Dr. Brunson and told him about the tingling in his legs and asked him if it were possible that Grandpa might walk again. He couldn't say for sure, but he admitted it had happened before. He gave me a book that tells all about the nerves in the body and exercises for Grandpa to try. It was rough at first. He fell a lot. I'm sure ya'll heard the racket in his room."

Rebekah nodded. "Yes! I wondered what was going on in there."

Goat laughed. "I wanted to quit. I was afraid he'd break a bone and be in even worse shape, but Grandpa's a tough ol' bird. He wouldn't give in."

Cass said, "But I don't understand why he didn't let us know. We might've been able to help with the exercises."

"I suggested it, but he said he wanted to surprise you. I only found out by accident that he was trying to get his legs back. Badger came and got me by the hand one afternoon and pulled me into the room. And there was Grandpa, sprawled out on the floor." He chuckled. "He begged me not to tell. I agreed to keep his secret,

195

with the condition that he'd allow me to help. I told him a couple of weeks ago that he was ready for his debut, but he wanted more time." Goat grinned. "Then, I saw how he was making eyes at Miss JoElle when she came to the party. After everyone left, I went to his room and reminded him of all the eligible widowers in this town. I said, 'Grandpa, if you plan to make your move, you'd better get your game going, fast.'"

Cass smiled. "So that's why he decided to go to church in Citronelle."

Goat nodded. "Yessir. When I realized how crazy he was about her, I encouraged him to give her a call."

Rebekah groaned. "For crying out loud, Goat, he's your grandpa, not your teenage buddy."

"Well, he might be my grandpa, but after all we've been through together, he's become my buddy. He was nervous that Miss JoElle might feel sorry for him. I was afraid he was gonna give up without a fight. So, I told him I felt sorry that he was too much of a coward to make the call."

Cass laughed, though Rebekah didn't seem to find humor in the situation.

Goat said, "Well, that got his goat. I thought he was gonna whoop me right then and there. Grandpa looked me straight in the eye and said, 'Coward, am I?' He wheeled the chair around, rolled down the hallway, then grabbed the phone and made the call. To be honest, I think she scared him speechless when she invited him to go with them to church. So, that's how it all came about. Liberty came to get him Sunday morning so he could put the wheelchair on the truck and Elsie and Miss JoElle met them at the church. When Grandpa got home, he told me the next time he went courting, he'd be doing it on his own two feet."

Rebekah's brow furrowed. "I am still stunned that he can walk. But wooing a woman at his age? What do you think about all this, Cass?"

"I don't think it's any of my business, hon."

Rebekah grimaced. "Papa, courting? That's crazy."

Cass shook his head, "Nothing crazy about it. There hasn't been a woman in almost twenty years capable of turning his head. I think it's wonderful." Glancing about the room he asked, "What happened to Gazelle?"

Rebekah said, "She slipped out, shortly after Goat began to explain. She's probably embarrassed to learn her grandpa is acting like a love-sick teenager at his age."

Goat's face turned red. "You're wrong, Rebekah. If anyone would understand what it feels like to be in love, Sissy would. She's heartbroken because she's just lost the love of her life, and everyone around her is going on as if nothing happened."

Rebekah's brow shot up. "What in the world are you talking about? If you're referring to poor Ryker, don't you think you're being overly dramatic to refer to him as the love of her life?"

Cass bit his lip. "Hmmm . . . Don't be so quick to dismiss Goat's theory, Rebekah. He may be on to something."

"For heaven's sake, Cass, I know she was fond of the man, but surely you don't think she was in love with Ryker. I would've known if she had been. She tells me everything."

"Not Ryker, sweetheart. But I haven't heard her mention Jeremiah in quite some time. Is that it, Goat? Is that why she's been so moody, lately?"

Goat threw up his hands. "Jeremiah? Where have you people been? She hasn't been interested in Jeremiah in months. Your daughter was head-over-heels in love with Ryker Adams and he loved her passionately."

"Passionately?" Cass smiled. "That's a mighty strong word for a fourteen-year-old boy. But I hope one day you learn what it means to passionately love a woman."

Rebekah didn't comment, but shot a harsh glare at her husband, which he interpreted as "You have crossed the line. Drop the subject."

She said, "Goat, you have it all wrong. Naturally, she admired Ryker and perhaps even had a crush on him when he first came to town. But she realized he had eyes for someone else."

Cass said, "I know where this crazy notion is coming from. Goat, I'm afraid you've been buying into the gossip, but Horace was wrong."

Rebekah said, "Horace Redding? What has he got to do with Gazelle?"

Goat's jaw tightened. "Ya'll aren't listening. You never listen. That's why you have no clue what Sissy is going through." He stormed out of the room and hurried upstairs.

Rebekah's eyes widened. "What in the world has gotten into him? Into them both? And if I dare ask, what did *you* mean by that remark about Horace?"

Cass related Horace's ridiculous allegation, claiming that the reason Gazelle fainted at the party was because she'd been seeing Ryker on the sly and caught Diphtheria from him.

"How do these ludicrous stories get started? A girl gets a headache and suddenly the town fabricates a story that doesn't even resemble the truth. That makes me so angry."

Cass rubbed her shoulders. "Don't get yourself riled up, sweetheart. We know the truth. What difference does it make what others think?"

She looked up, gazing into his big brown eyes. "You're right. Let's go tuck the twins in bed. I bought them both a new book last Friday, so I'm sure they're still awake, reading."

Cass followed Rebekah upstairs. He wanted to be as confident as she was about Gazelle's situation, but something in his gut told him there was more to the story than they'd been led to believe.

After tucking the twins in bed, Rebekah took Cass by the hand. "Should we wait up in the parlor for Papa?"

"No, sweetheart. I'm sure he'd be offended at being treated like a teenager on his first date."

She cringed. "He shouldn't be offended, since he's certainly acting the part. It's embarrassing."

"Rebekah, why don't you go on to bed without me. I'll be in there shortly. I want to check on Gazelle."

"That's a good idea. Perhaps you should warn her about the rumor circulating, so she can be prepared when the idle gossip finally reaches her, for I'm sure it will. I think it would be better for her to hear it from you first."

CHAPTER 21

Cass knocked on Gazelle's door. "Sweetheart, may I come in?"

Goat cracked the door. "Uh . . . Father, she doesn't feel like talking."

"Then perhaps you should come out and let her rest."

Detecting the irritation in his father's voice, he stepped out and nodded. "Yessir." He walked down the hall with Cass, then suddenly stopped. "This is not going away. I don't know what I was thinking."

Cass frowned. "You're talking in riddles."

"It's Sissy. She has something to tell you, and the sooner you find out, the sooner we can come up with a way to help her through this."

"Son, I know you mean well, but she said she doesn't want to talk and we should respect that. I'm sure she's upset over the rumors, but the best way we can help her, is to let the talk die down, instead of fanning the flames. When folks discover that she doesn't have diphtheria, they'll also find out the rumors about her and Ryker were also false."

"You have it all wrong, Father. Please? Let's go and let her get it over with."

"Get it over with? Good grief, son, the way you're carrying on one would think she was dealing with a life-or-death situation."

"As a matter of fact, it's both a life *and* a death situation. I shouldn't say anything more. It's her place to tell you."

"Fine." He turned and walked with Goat back down the hall to Gazelle's bedroom. "I don't suppose anyone knows her better than you and if you're convinced that she needs to get something off her chest, I'll give her that opportunity. But I don't think we should press her and cause her more headaches."

Whether Goat heard him or simply chose not to respond, Cass couldn't be sure.

Knocking on the door, he said, "Sissy, may I come in?"

"Sure." Her eyes muddled with tears when she looked up and saw her Father standing there. She glared at her brother with trembling lip. "You told him?"

"No. It's not my place to tell, but I think you should."

Gazelle quickly turned over in the bed, burying her face in her pillow. "I can't Goat."

Cass's throat tightened. He sat on the edge of the bed, and stroked her long, dark locks. "Baby, I don't know what kind of burden you're carrying, but I love you, sweetheart and I want to carry it for you. That's what Fathers are for."

She quickly rolled over and glared into his eyes. "Trust me, you don't want to know about this burden, and no one can carry it for me."

"Honey, you know that's not true. I love you. Please tell me."

Her body shook with sobs as he wrapped her in his arms. "Father . . . I'm . . . I'm carrying Ryker's baby."

His arms fell to his side and she screamed. "I told you that you didn't want to know."

Cass closed his eyes and sucked a heavy breath of air into his lungs. "Give me a minute." He rubbed his hand over his mouth. "Honey, I'm sorry. I do want to know about anything and everything that concerns you. I just needed a minute to collect my thoughts. Do you mind if I ask a few questions?"

"I suppose you'll have to."

"Why didn't you tell me Ryker had taken advantage of you. When did it happen?"

"Took advantage? What are you saying?"

Goat chimed in. "He wants to know if you were raped."

His father shot him an evil look. "Thank you, son, but I was trying to be more sensitive."

Gazelle wiped the tears with the edge of the bedsheet. She mumbled, "I wasn't raped."

Cass felt the blood rush to his face. "Are you saying you were in love with him?"

She screamed. "Of course, I was in love with him. Do you

think I'd be in this predicament if I hadn't been in love with him?"

Rebekah opened the door. "What's going on? I could hear the commotion from our room, downstairs."

Cass sat with his head in his hands and blurted out, "Gazelle is pregnant."

Gazelle, said, "I told you, Goat. I told you he wouldn't understand. Well, I won't embarrass you, Father, by staying in town. I'll go away and have the baby where no one knows you. When Elsie was at the party, she told me about staying at a boarding house in North Alabama that's run by Miz JoElle's cousin. I'll go there. After I have the baby, I'll take in ironing to pay for my board. Folks will think I've gone off to Boarding School."

Rebekah glared at her husband. "Are you going to sit there and let her bear this alone or do you plan to help her through it?"

Raking his fingers through his hair, he shook his head. "I'm sorry. This has been such a shock. I can't seem to think straight."

Rebekah walked around to the opposite side of the bed and sat down. She pulled a lace handkerchief from her bodice and gently blotted Gazelle's tears. "You don't have to go away, dear, and there's no need for you to think you'd have to take in ironing. You'll stay in this house and have that baby here. And you certainly don't have to worry about how you'll provide. We have all the provisions you and this baby will ever need. You've made a mistake, but let him who has no sin, cast the first stone."

Cass said, "Rebekah, I don't think any of us need to be

making plans for the future until we have time to process the news. You call it a mistake as if it's something that will disappear with an apology. I think we should all—"

He stopped talking when Rebekah jumped up. "I heard a car drive up. I think it's Papa. Cass, please go downstairs and help him up the steps."

Goat said, "He can do it. I know he can. You'll embarrass him if you rush out to help him."

Cass chewed the inside of his bottom lip. "I think Goat's right. But we've all said enough for one night. Let's go to bed and sleep on it. Things may look totally different in the morning."

Gazelle murmured. "I hope not. I'm glad I'm pregnant. A part of Ryker is still alive inside me."

Cass jerked around and pointed a finger in her direction. "Young lady, if you had any idea what life will be like—" He felt Rebekah's hand on his back, guiding him toward the door. His hand fell to his side and he walked out without another word.

"Hey, where is everybody?" Grandpa yelled.

Rebekah said, "We're upstairs, Papa, but we're on our way down. I expected you back an hour ago. I was beginning to worry."

He cackled out loud. "Were you worried for me or for Jo?"

In no mood for jokes, she ignored the comment. "There's left over chicken in the ice box if you're hungry. Cass and I are on our way to bed."

They met downstairs in the hall and Lonnie said, "Sorry if I worried you. Liberty and Elsie invited several friends over to their house after the evening service and they had food left on the table from dinner. We pulled back the cloth and oh m'goodness, I've never seen such a spread. Jo's a great cook. There were left-over pork chops, turnip greens, candied potatoes, butter beans—"

Rebekah wasn't up for chit-chat. "So, you've eaten, already. Fine. Goodnight."

His brow furrowed. "Is something wrong?"

Cass said, "Sorry, Lonnie. We've encountered a problem, but it's nothing to concern you. Rebekah's upset—we all are—but we'll figure it out. I'm glad you enjoyed your evening. Goodnight."

Goat said, "Sissy, why didn't you tell Father and Rebekah that you and Ryker were married?"

"What difference would it have made?"

"Are you kidding? It would've made a lot of difference."

"Why? Father was furious months ago when he caught Ryker sitting beside me in the swing. If he'd allowed us to see one another, there would've been no cause to slip off to get married. Don't you get it? Father is furious with me for slipping around behind his back to see Ryker against his wishes. To hear that I secretly married him would be one more thing for him to hold against me."

"No, Sissy. You aren't thinking straight. When word gets out that the Preacher's daughter is pregnant, the talk will be ugly. I can just imagine ol' man Horace Redding having a hay-day with the news. But if Father can tell them you and Ryker were married, it'll make things much easier for him."

"I'm sorry, Goat, but I don't feel it's my place to make things easier for him. When you told him I was pregnant, what did he do to make things easier for me? He covered his face as if he couldn't look at me and screamed out, 'Gazelle is pregnant.'"

"It was a shock to him."

She shrugged. "I'll tell him, soon. But I need him to have time to decide whether he wants to disown me and my baby or if he can love us unconditionally. Right now, I really don't care what he does with us."

"Of course, he loves you unconditionally, Sissy. I'm going to bed but try to get some sleep. It's all gonna work out. You'll see."

Cass tossed and turned in the bed, unable to get his daughter off his mind.

Rebekah rolled over and cuddled close. "Can't sleep?"

"No. I don't suppose you can, either. Where did I go wrong, Rebekah?"

"What makes you feel it's your fault, Cass?"

"I was on the road more than I was home. I should've been here for her."

"Stop torturing yourself. You've been a great father and a wonderful example. Gazelle is old enough to know right from wrong and to make her own decisions. Unfortunately, she made a wrong decision, but it's not the end of the world."

"Then why do I feel that it is? You know how she'll be treated as soon as word gets out that she's pregnant. And what about the baby? Poor little thing won't stand a chance. You know the names that will be attached to them both." His voice cracked. "Rebekah, anytime Gazelle has ever had a problem, she's always come to me and I've been able to fix it. But this, I can't fix. I don't know what to tell her. Should she stay here and suffer the ridicule and embarrassment? Should she sneak out of town and let everyone assume she's away at school? I don't know. I don't know anything, anymore. My thoughts are like confetti. They've been shredded and are flying around, with no hope of piecing them together. I'm her father. I should have answers, but I don't."

"Then, why worry over something for which you have no control? Perhaps it's time to turn loose and allow her heavenly Father to take the reins. After all, he loves her even more than we do."

His throat tightened. How many times had he preached that sermon to other people? "Don't you think I want to, Rebekah? I try, but then I find myself pulling back. It's not as if we have a lot of time before coming up with a plan. I looked at her last night and she's showing already. When I pressed her, she said she thinks she's around eighteen weeks. I knew she was putting on a little weight and her face was fuller, but I never in a thousand years would have imagined this could happen to my daughter. However, after news circulated that she was slipping around with Ryker, I can imagine there were some who were scrutinizing her more closely than I. What do I tell people?"

"Your daughter needs you now more than she's ever needed you in her life. And you're more concerned about what people might say or think? Why do you think you have to tell them anything, Cass?"

"Maybe, because she's my daughter and I'm their pastor. Things like this aren't supposed to happen in a preacher's family."

"Well, lying here worrying over the situation isn't helping her nor you."

Rebekah had just dozed off when she heard Cass whispering her name.

"Sweetheart, are you awake?"

"I am now. What do you want, Cass?"

"I've been thinking about the age-old debate about nature vs. nurture. What do you think?"

"I have no idea what you're talking about, but if it's all the same to you, I'd rather discuss it in the morning."

"Sorry."

She could hear him breathing heavily next to her and could tell the short breaths were accelerating. "Cass, honey, what's done is done. You need to let it go and get some sleep."

"Nature vs. nurture is a debate that questions whether a child is influenced greater by the environment or genes. Maybe you're right, Rebekah. Maybe I have been a good father. The Lord knows, I've tried to bring her up to know right from wrong. But if I did do a good job, then maybe it's a sign that nature is more powerful than the nurturing I gave her. And that scares me to death. I never worried about Goat. And the other kids are too young for me to discern which way they'll go."

Rebekah moaned. "Which way they'll go? You aren't making sense. Cass, please go to sleep."

"I never told you this, sweetheart, but I've been concerned for a long time that Gazelle might've inherited more than her mother's looks. Amelia was never happy if she didn't have every man in the room sparring for her attention. She never knew that I found out she was sneaking around with the Fuller Brush salesman."

Rebekah turned over, facing him. "Why were you afraid to tell her?"

"Afraid? I suppose I was. But we had two babies who needed a mother. I knew she didn't love me, but I was frantic that she might leave the kids and I didn't know what I'd do if that happened." He sucked in a heavy breath. "However, in a few years and three kids later, I found out what I'd do. I'd do the best I could, without her."

"Gazelle is not Amelia."

"Then, are you saying you think environment is a stronger influence than genes?"

Rebekah attempted to suppress a yawn, "Cass, we aren't going to have an answer to your philosophical question tonight, so could we please go to sleep?"

CHAPTER 22

Monday morning, the family gathered around the breakfast table, but the somberness was quite chilling.

Grandpa looked around at the solemn faces, and quipped, "Did somebody die?"

Goose's little lip turned down. "Yessir. Ryker died." She slid out of her chair and ran off, sobbing.

Grandpa cringed. "Well, I reckon I put my big foot in my mouth again. I didn't mean it, literally. I was just pondering the downcast looks. Anybody care to tell me what's going on?"

No one spoke up. Then Gazelle threw her napkin on the table and said, "Well, if no one else wants to tell you, Grandpa, I will. I'm a huge disappointment to my family because I'm gonna have a baby. That's why everyone looks like the world is coming to an end." She immediately clasped her hand over her mouth as she glanced over at Gander. She blew out a puff of air when she discovered he was too busy feeding the dog under the table to pay attention to the conversation.

Grandpa said, "So, we're gonna have two more little feet running around here. How about that? Goat, would you please pass the biscuits down this way."

Cass glanced at Rebekah, who acknowledged her bewilderment with a shrug.

After breakfast, Cass kissed his wife before leaving for the church office. "Don't hold supper for me. Andy Stringfellow is in the hospital over in Mobile, and I promised the family that I'd pay him a visit this afternoon."

"What's his trouble?"

"Not sure, but they aren't expecting him to live much longer. Rebekah, God seems to have given you the gift of discernment. I'd be mighty obliged if you'd overlook all my recent rantings and pray for me that I'll know how to help my daughter. I'm not asking you to tell me what would be easier for me. She's my concern and I can't afford to mess this up."

"God will give you all the answers you're seeking, Cass, but I will be praying for you both."

Rebekah was finishing up in the kitchen when Goose rushed in crying. "I think Gazelle is gonna die."

She dried her hands and bent down to hug the child. "Oh, sweetie, why would you think your sister is going to die. Didn't you see how beautiful she looked at breakfast?"

"But she's frowing up. Maybe she's got Ryker's sickness."

"You go outside and play with Gander and I'll go see about Gazelle. But stop worrying. She's not dying. Remember when you threw up when you had the measles?"

She nodded.

"Did you die?"

Smiling through the tears she shook her head. "No'm. I'm still here." She held out her hands as proof. "See? "

"I do see. And you'll see that your sister isn't going to die just because she's a little sick on her stomach."

Goose threw her arms around Rebekah and gave her a quick kiss before running out the kitchen door.

****

Goat went fishing and Rebekah asked Gazelle to watch the young'uns while she went over to the Griffins' field to pick a mess of beans and squash. "I may stop by to look in on the Widow Harris before coming home. Will you be okay?"

Gazelle rolled her eyes. "Please stop treating me as if I'm an invalid. Of course, I'll be okay."

"Sorry. I didn't mean to sound like I was coddling you. I left a hamper of little lady peas on the porch. I'd appreciate it if you'd shell enough for tonight's dinner."

Rebekah had only been gone thirty minutes or less when Grandpa walked out on the porch with Badger following on his heels. Grandpa pulled a few marbles from his pocket and handed to Badger, who sat on the floor, rolling them back and forth. One rolled off the porch and Grandpa signed for him to put them in his pocket and play with them in the yard. Then the old man went back in the house and came out with a dishpan.

He reached into the hamper and filled his pan. "I'll help you."

She forced a smile. "Thanks, Grandpa, but you don't have to."

"I know I don't, but I want to."

Her eyes filled with tears. "Why?"

"Why? I saw you sitting out here alone, and I thought you might need someone to talk to."

She should've known. He wanted to pump her and get all the details. "Sure, we'll talk. I suppose you want to ask how a nice girl like me wound up in my predicament."

"No, sugar. I'm an old man and I know exactly how a nice girl like you wound up in your predicament. I have no questions for you. I'm content to sit here in silence, helping you shell these peas."

She tried to hold back the tears, but they were pushing their way out. "I'm sorry, Grandpa. I can't seem to think straight. I didn't mean to offend you."

"No offense taken, sugar. I reckon if anyone can come close to understanding how you feel, I'd come pretty close to being the one. We both lost the one who made our heart beat, and when the heart ceases to beat, the life goes out of you."

Her eyes glistened with the tears. "That's it. That's exactly how I feel. You do understand."

"More than you realize. Just don't make the same mistake that I did."

"What mistake is that?"

"I grieved so for my Lois that I began to blame the baby for her death. Of course, what I was really trying to do was to take the guilt from my shoulders and put the blame on someone else. The guilt ate away at me like a cancer."

"Grandpa, how long does it take for the pain to go away?"

"Shug, I'd be lying to you if I didn't tell you it takes a lifetime to forget, but that doesn't mean you can't get on with your life. I didn't move on and I regret it. I look back at the wasted years and the pain I caused my sweet Rebekah, because I refused to let Lois go. She would've wanted me to carry on and to be a good daddy to our little girl." He stopped and began to sign.

Gazelle said, "I'm still learning to sign. What did you just say?"

He smiled. I was mocking what my sweet Lois would be saying to me if she could. She'd say, "Shame on you, Lonnie Brewster, for wallowing in self-pity. If you want to honor my memory, you'll be the man I married. I want you to love and be loved. Enjoy our Rebekah and all those little children who now call you Grandpa." His eyes twinkled. "Yes ma'am, that's exactly what she'd be saying if she could." He stared out into space. "So, what do you suppose Ryker would be saying to you, sugar, if he could speak to you from the grave?"

"I don't know. I don't want to think about it, Grandpa."

"That's okay. Just be careful that you don't follow in my footsteps. Don't wait until you turn into a despised, bitter old woman before you decide to think about it. I wouldn't want that for you." He reached for her hand and gave it a gentle squeeze. "I have a feeling Ryker wouldn't want that for you, either."

****

Cass came home for lunch and after the family left the table, he sat staring at his plate.

Seeing he only ate half his sandwich, Rebekah apologized. "I'm sorry I didn't have time to cook." She jumped up and rushed over to the refrigerator. "I could warm you up a little stew left from last night."

Cass shook his head. "Don't bother."

"Are you sure I can't fix you something else? I left Gazelle and Papa here this morning to watch the kids while I gathered vegetables and time got away from me. By the time I got back home, it was too late to prepare a meal."

"The sandwich was fine, hon. I reckon I'm just not hungry."

She sat down and gazed into her husband's drawn face. "What's wrong, Cass?"

"Maybe you should ask what's not wrong."

She knew her husband well enough to know not to push him.

He stood and walked over to the kitchen window. "Well, it took less than twenty-four hours for the gossip train to leave the depot."

Rebekah was anxious to hear more, but she waited, giving him time to gather his thoughts.

"Rebekah, why? Why did she allow it to happen? She's not

that kind of girl. Is she?"

"What do you mean—that kind of girl, Cass Marlowe?"

"You know what I mean. Like her mother."

"Cass, I'm ashamed that you would even think such. Every tub must sit on its own bottom, as they say."

"And what's that supposed to mean?"

She snickered. "Now, that you ask, I'm not really sure. But it seemed to fit. What I'm trying to say is that you can't compare Amelia to her mother. We can't help what color eyes, hair or skin we have. Those are inherited traits. But each one of us is responsible for our own sins. Don't saddle Gazelle with Amelia's sins."

"Is that what you think I was doing?"

"Weren't you?"

"I don't know. Maybe subconsciously. But I had lunch at Maude's today with Liberty. You should've seen the stares. I could hear the whispers. I think I liked it better when they were accusing Gazelle of getting Diphtheria from Ryker. Now, they've heard what she really got from that child molester."

Rebekah's jaw dropped. "Shame on you, Castle Marlowe that you would stoop so low to speak evil of the dead. Gazelle has told you she wasn't raped. The act was consensual. She was in love with Ryker, made an error in judgment and got caught. She's not the first girl, nor will she be the last, but to blame it all on Ryker is to deny the truth. Gazelle told you she was in love with him and he with her."

"And you believe that, Rebekah? You really think a twenty-two-year-old man was in love with a fifteen-year-old girl? I don't buy it." He wrung his hands together. "After I got back to the office after lunch, I received a phone call from Horace, saying the deacons wanted to meet with me this afternoon at two o'clock. I suppose you know what that means. I'll be given my walking papers."

"So, what if they fire you, Cass? It's not as if we need the meager salary they pay you."

"Don't you understand? I don't preach for the money. I preach because God has called me to preach, and now they're about to snatch away that opportunity."

"What God has begun, he will finish. Don't you still believe that?"

He nodded, though unconvincingly.

"God has called you to preach, Cass, and he'll provide. If not here, somewhere. I've learned to appreciate the scripture that says, 'Wait! Wait I say, on the Lord.' It's a good reminder that we need to slow down, take a deep breath and allow God to work out the details, without getting ahead of him."

He pulled out his watch. "Well, I might as well get back to the office and face the music. I'll probably be back shortly after two. I don't think it will take long for them to say what they have to tell me."

He put on his coat, kissed his wife and said, "Thank you for the pep talk. I needed the reminders." He was getting into his car when Gazelle came running out. "Father, wait."

"Hon, I'm in a bit of a hurry. I have a meeting in a few minutes."

"I know. I was standing at the top of the stairs and heard you and Rebekah talking."

He clinched his eyes shut. "Oh, sweetheart, I am so sorry. I didn't mean half those things I was saying."

"I know. But there's something you don't know. Ryker was a good and honorable man. He never took advantage of me, nor am I the harlot folks would have you to believe. He loved me and I loved him. We were married, Father. We had plans to announce it at my sixteenth birthday, but when he died before the party, I was so hurt by the ugly allegations, I decided to let folks think what they chose to think about me. I didn't care. I didn't care about anything, anymore."

"Whoa! Hold on." His gaze locked with his daughter's. "Say that again, slowly."

She smiled. "All of it?"

He shook his head. "Just the part about being married."

"It's true. I skipped school one morning and we drove to a preacher's house and got married. This baby was conceived in love, so all the evil talk about me being a fallen woman is a bunch of hooey. Don't believe a word of it."

Cass's brow fixed in a frown. "What was this preacher's name?"

Her mouth gaped open. "You don't believe me?"

"Of course, I believe you. I probably know him if he lives within fifty miles of here."

"I don't remember. I think Ryker called the wife Aunt Annelle? That sounds about right."

"Where do they live?"

She shrugged. "I don't really know. I was so excited on the way there and back, I didn't pay attention. I think it took about an hour to get there."

Cass pulled out his watch again. "Thanks, sweetheart. I've gotta run. There are a few men I need to set straight." He kissed her on the forehead. "I'm sorry I ever doubted you."

CHAPTER 23

Cass parked in front of the church and counted six cars. The deacons were all there, waiting in the office when he strode in.

"Sorry, I'm late, fellows." He walked over and plopped down in the chair behind his desk.

Horace said, "Preacher, I don't suppose we have to tell you why we're here."

Cass smirked. "Maybe you don't have to, but out of courtesy, I'd think you would."

Horace's lips pursed. "Fine. If that's how you want it, I'll lay it out on the line. It's your daughter."

"What about my daughter, Horace?"

"Really, Preacher. Are you gonna make me say it?"

"You're the one who called this meeting. I think the least you can do is to lay out the allegations."

"As you will. It has come to the attention of the deacons that your teenage daughter has gone and got herself pregnant. The

Bible clearly states that a minister must be able to control his children and it's obvious that somewhere along the line, you lost control. You must know what kind of signal this sends to our youth. Therefore, the deacons are bringing a recommendation to the church next Sunday, asking for a vote to dismiss you as Pastor of Friendship Community Church. Naturally, we feel we have the authority to do it without a vote, but we have no doubt how the vote will go, and it will keep our people from feeling as if the decision was made without their consent."

Cass reared back in his chair. "Are you finished, Horace?"

He nodded. "That's about it. Do you have any questions?"

"No questions, but I have plenty to say. I appreciate your giving me an opportunity to present my side of the story to the church, Sunday."

"Your side? Cass, I'm sorry if you feel we're on separate sides. You're a good preacher and a good man. The only thing we fault you for is your failure as a parent—not that we don't understand. We do. Your first wife was a Jezebel in every sense of the word. Shoot, it's a known fact that if every man in Vinegar Bend whose head was turned when she'd bat those big eyes at them was run out of town, there wouldn't be enough men left to run the town." He hid his smile with his hand and looked around the room, though no one dared look at him. He cleared his throat. "And although we all love Rebekah, she can't be held responsible, since that daughter of yours was half-grown when Rebekah entered the picture." He looked around. "Do you fellows have anything to add?"

Five heads shook. Then Cass said, "I do."

"I'm sorry. Go ahead. You have the floor."

"How many of you are married?"

Looking puzzled, they eased up their hands, one by one.

"I see. Now, how many of you have children?"

Again, all six lifted their hand.

"Were your children conceived before or after the wedding?"

They all looked at one another and chuckled, as if it were a trick question. Horace, said, "Cass, this isn't about us. What are you getting at?"

"You said I had the floor, Horace. Please allow me to finish."

He shrugged. "Fine, but I promised the fellows we wouldn't keep them long."

"And we won't. One more question. Were your children conceived in sin?"

Horace grimaced. "For crying out loud, Cass, make your point."

"My point is, you want to remove me as Pastor of the church because of Gazelle's actions. Is that right?"

"I think you know the answer to that. You've forced me to lay it out. I wish it hadn't come to this. But we are all aware that your daughter got herself pregnant by a man several years older than her."

"I see. So, is that the charge? It's a sin for a female to marry an older male?"

"Don't be facetious. Age has nothing to do with it. It's the fact that she permitted him to have his way with her, which has resulted in bringing an illegitimate child into the world." He pulled at his vest. "That's about as kind as I can say it."

"Thank you, Horace, for your kindness. That's exactly what happened. Gazelle permitted her husband to have his way with her, and now she's carrying their child. Their legitimate child."

Dennis Thurmon said, "Hold on. Did you say . . . her husband?"

"I did."

Horace's face glowed red. "It's a lie. I don't believe it."

"I haven't asked you to, Horace. You have a habit of believing what you wish to believe."

Dennis said, "Well, I recommend that we hold off on making the recommendation, since we have apparently been misled."

Reuben Grisham nodded. "I agree. We may have jumped the gun. We need to look into it and make sure we have our facts straight before proceeding."

"Poppycock!" Horace pounded his fist on the table. "As chairman of this committee, I insist we stick to our plan. If the girl did indeed marry Ryker Adams, let her prove it. But if she fails to do so, then we shall bring the recommendation before the church, Sunday, to relieve Cass of his duties."

Cass stood and thrust out his hand. "Good day, gentlemen. If this meeting is adjourned, I'll see you in church, Sunday."

Cass could hardly wait to get back home that evening. He kissed Rebekah, then said, "Where's Gazelle?"

"Cass, she's not feeling well. Please, whatever you have to say to her, can wait."

"Did she tell you?"

"Tell me what?"

"She and Ryker were married."

She dropped the dishrag. "What are you talking about?"

"So, you haven't talked to her."

"No. She's been in her room since you left."

"Well, just as I was leaving after lunch, she ran out and told me that she and Ryker ran off and got married."

"And you believed her?"

"I have no reason not to. She may be high strung and stubborn as a mule, but she's not a liar. She said she skipped school one morning and she and Ryker drove over to a preacher's house and got married . . . so, yes, I believe her. Don't you see, Rebekah? When we let people know that she was married when she got pregnant, that will squelch all the vicious rumors circulating."

"Cass, I've recalled a conversation on the porch the day you became so upset when Ryker was sitting beside Gazelle in the swing. Do you remember what he said after you overreacted?"

With his tongue stuck in his cheek, he grinned. "Overreacted? Okay, so I did. But no, I didn't really care what he had to say at the time. I was more interested in getting him gone."

"I remember well. He said 'Sir, I love your daughter.'" Then, he stood up to you and said he'd continue to see her, with or without your blessings. She shrugged. "Well, that may not have been his exact words, but it was close."

"I do seem to recall something like that. But after I had time to cool down, I knew he was just blowing off steam and saying it to get back at me."

"I thought so to, at the time. But now, after all that's happened, I believe he meant it with all his heart. Cass, he was deeply in love with Gazelle."

"Maybe he was, maybe he wasn't. But I'd much rather think he was in love with her, than to believe he took advantage of her. Well, say a quick prayer that I'll have the right words."

"Do you prefer to speak to her alone, or do you mind if I go up with you?"

"I want you to hear it from her."

Rebekah knocked on her door. "Gazelle, may we come in?"

"We?"

"Your father and I."

"Sure."

Rebekah said, "Your father tells me you and Ryker were married."

"That's right."

"Oh, sweetheart, why didn't you tell us? That makes everything different."

Her face twisted in a scowl. "Does it? What is different, Rebekah? Tell me. Does it bring Ryker back? Does it make my baby less real? More real? Does it vilify me as a mother? Or has my slate been cleaned now that I've dispensed this tidbit of information."

Cass spoke up. "Gazelle, I know you've been through a lot, and I realize you're hurt and you're angry. But I won't have you speaking to my wife in such a manner. Rebekah has been your only ally at times. She's never condemned you or allowed anyone else to speak ill of you."

Gazelle's chin quivered. "I know. You're right. I'm sorry, Rebekah. I wasn't angry at you. I heard Father tell you at lunch that the deacons were considering firing him because I'm pregnant. I've been up here, fuming at the thought that a few self-righteous men would hold someone responsible for another person's sin. The baby I'm carrying was probably conceived the afternoon after we were married that morning. Certainly not before. But suppose the rumors had been true, and we weren't married. Would it be right to hold Father responsible?"

Cass said, "Don't be so hard on the deacons, sugar. I don't condone the way Horace handled the situation, but the men were attempting to abide by a scripture in Timothy that admonishes preachers to be able to control their children, and there's a reason for that being in there. You remember the story of Eli in the Bible, and what happened when he lost control of his two wayward sons. Not that I'm comparing you with Phineas and Hophni, but I'm just saying the deacons are within their right to question me about the conduct of my children."

"But they were judging me, Father, without knowing the truth."

"I can't argue with that. But instead of judging them, I think we should present them with the proof and let it become a lesson to all of us."

"What proof?"

"The marriage certificate. Where is it?"

Her brow furrowed. "Ryker took it. I was afraid to bring it home. Afraid you or Rebekah would find it and we didn't want you to know until I turned sixteen." She sighed. "At least I didn't want you to know. Ryker thought we should tell you immediately."

Cass sucked in a heavy breath, then blew out. "I see."

Rebekah said, "Don't worry about the certificate. We'll go and ask the preacher who married you to verify the date you and Ryker were married. That should satisfy the deacons."

Cass raised a brow. "That might be difficult. She can't remember his name nor where he lives."

Rebekah said, "The ring. He did give you a ring, didn't he? I'm not sure that would prove anything, but maybe Mr. Snodgrass at the jewelry store could tell when he bought it."

Gazelle shook her head. "No ring. We borrowed the preacher's wife's, and I gave it back after the ceremony." She glanced first at her father's expression, then to Rebekah's. "Ya'll don't believe me, do you? I wouldn't believe me, either if I were you. It does sound suspicious, but I promise you we were married."

Cass said, "Hon, it's not a matter of us believing you. And it's not for my reputation that I want them to know the truth. It's for your sake and the baby's that I want the truth known and for the whispers to cease." He lowered his head. "But you don't need to worry. The truth will come out and the truth shall set you free."

CHAPTER 24

Sunday morning, Cass dressed for church and kissed Rebekah goodbye.

"Cass, I still don't understand why you don't want us to go with you. I feel you should have your family sitting on the front row, supporting you."

"No, sweetheart. Anything is likely to happen, and I haven't forgotten Goat's reaction to Horace's accusations, and this could turn out to be much worse. Horace will be there with an agenda and he has a lot of sway. I won't have my family subjected to a bunch of wild accusations."

The church auditorium was filled, thanks to Thelma Redding who spent days on the telephone, insisting everyone come to see the circus. Cass had reason to believe that's exactly why twenty-five percent of the people who hadn't been to church since Easter had shown up.

Horace took twenty-five minutes laying out the reasons for the special called meeting. He ended by exclaiming in his most sanctimonious voice, "Jesus said, 'Let him who is without sin cast the first stone. Folks, I'm not here to cast stones. Lord knows, we've all made mistakes, but what we're dealing with here is not something as minor as letting a naughty word slip or failing to pay a debt on time. The claim the preacher wants us to believe is that his fifteen-year-old child married the doctor's assistant." He chuckled. "Sounds a little suspicious to me, since the man is dead and unable to corroborate her story. However, if I'm wrong, I'll be more than willing to admit it." Horace held out his hand. "Show us the marriage certificate, Preacher, and that should clear it up. Then, you can keep your job and we can put the rumors to rest."

Cass was glad he insisted the family stay home. Things appeared to be taking shape just as he had imagined.

Prancing back and forth across the platform, Horace looked out at the crowd and facetiously said, "What? No Marriage Certificate? What happened? Did the dog eat it?" Giggles could be heard around the auditorium.

"No, Horace. Ryker kept it."

"Ahh! We have no proof because Ryker kept it and of course, he's dead. Another convenient coincidence. It's bad enough that your inability to control your children has come to light but lying for them is also a grave offense. Preacher, at this time, the deacons and I would like for you to step outside while the members vote on whether we feel it's in the best interest of the church for you to continue serving as our Pastor."

Cass walked down the steps of the podium and down the aisle of the church. Several members on the end of the pews reached out to shake his hand as he passed by them on his way out the door.

He debated whether to get in his car and drive home, rather than to wait. He knew how it would go. There were some who would believe him and vote in his favor, but the rest? Could he blame them? Though he trusted his daughter and knew she was telling the truth, he had to admit it sounded fishy. He went behind his car and fell on his knees. "Lord, You've given me a promise from your word—Faithful is he who calleth, who also will do it. I know without a doubt you called me to this church. You began a good work here, and I don't think you've finished what you started."

The time seemed to drag as Rebekah paced the floor, waiting for her husband to return. She ran outside as soon as she heard a car pull up. She attempted to hide her disappointment when she realized it was Lonnie, Elsie and JoElle, bringing Papa home. "You folks get out and come on in. Cass isn't home yet."

Liberty said, "We had the Lord's Supper and church was dismissed afterward, so we got out a little early."

"Well, stay for dinner, if you will. I've cooked enough for an army." She offered out of courtesy, yet hoped they'd refuse, since she was eager for the opportunity to talk to Cass in private as soon as he returned.

Elsie said, "That's mighty hospitable of you, Rebekah. I think we shall. It's been way too long since you and I have had a chance to chat. I've really missed you."

Rebekah was surprised. Elsie sounded perfectly fine. Like her old self. She watched out of the corner of her eye at her papa and JoElle sitting in the back seat. He got out and opened the door for his lady friend.

Liberty stopped in the yard to push Goose on the tire swing. Rebekah and Elsie went into the kitchen to set three more plates, and Lonnie and JoElle sat in the swing on the porch.

Rebekah kept glancing at the clock, eager for Cass to get home. "Well, Elsie, you're looking good. How do you feel?"

"I feel great. Oh, Rebekah, Liberty is wonderful. I couldn't ask for a better husband, and JoElle takes such good care of us both. I'm so thankful she's with us." She leaned over and whispered, "And she's crazy about your Father, and when he looks at her it's so cute the way he lights up. But I want to know about Gazelle."

"I suppose you're talking about the rumors."

She thrust her hand over her heart. "Oh thank goodness. I was hoping it was rumors and not the truth. I couldn't imagine that sweet baby being pregnant. Aren't people cruel to spread such lies?"

"I think you misunderstood me, Elsie. Gazelle *is* pregnant."

"Oh, no! Bless her heart."

"What you probably haven't heard is that she and Ryker

Adams were secretly married."

"You don't say. Well, bless her heart. I'm not surprised, though. I remember the night I lay on her bed and she talked for hours, telling me how much they loved one another. Sweet little thing was terrified that her father would find out they were seeing one another, so I had to promise not to tell. Did she hold you to the same promise, or did you convince her to tell Cass?"

Rebekah swallowed hard. Gazelle confided in Elsie? It hurt— hurt bad, knowing that she didn't come to her. Not wanting to admit it, she simply smiled and said, "She told her father."

"That's good. I told her it needed to come from her, and I encouraged her to tell him. I wish I'd been around when Ryker asked her to marry him. I'll bet she was floating on clouds. I remembered what it was like to be young and in love, and it thrilled me that she'd confide in me. It was so cute the way her eyes would light up when she talked about him."

Rebekah blinked, hoping to hold in the tears.

****

Cass stopped praying. He stood and brushed the dust from the knees of his trousers when he heard loud applause and people shouting. Reuben Grisham stuck his head out the church door and yelled. "Come on in, Preacher. The vote was seventy-nine to two."

Cass met Horace and Thelma coming out the door as he walked in. He walked up to the pulpit and said, "Thank you, folks. I appreciate your confidence in me. My heart is too full to preach a sermon and besides, it's already past twelve o'clock and I don't

234

want to be responsible for these ladies going home to burnt roasts."

Several laughed out loud, and women nodded.

"So why don't we all stand and sing 'Bless Be the Tie that Binds,' and go home. I'll see you back here tonight at seven o'clock."

****

The front door opened, and Rebekah heard men's voices coming down the hall. She ran to meet her husband and when he bent down to kiss her, she whispered, "Are you . . . did they?"

Understanding perfectly, he winked. "Yes, I am and no they didn't."

She threw her arms around him. "That's wonderful, darling. You fellows tell the kids to wash up and everyone get to the table before the food gets cold."

The twins were the first to the table and as always, Rebekah sent them back to wash their hands. Badger walked in with Grandpa and JoElle, and Goat brought MyEwe to the table.

Gazelle walked over to take a seat next to Elsie.

Rebekah's heart sank. She'd tried so hard to win her stepdaughter's trust and until today, she thought she'd succeeded. How could she have been so wrong? Why would Gazelle have shared her deepest secrets with Elsie and not with her?

After everyone had finished the meal, Rebekah went to the kitchen and brought back a large pan of banana pudding topped with a golden, mile-high meringue. Oohs and ahhs were heard as she dipped the delicious-looking pudding into dessert dishes.

Elsie walked over to Goat and said, "Could I hold little MyEwe?"

Liberty's face turned white. "Uh, honey, she doesn't really know us. Perhaps we should let her stay with Goat."

Cass understood Liberty's concern. She seemed to be doing so well. What if holding a baby would bring back all the painful memories and cause her mind to snap again? What a travesty it would be if she should have a relapse.

Liberty said, "Honey, I think we should be getting back home. Rebekah, it was a wonderful lunch. Thank you for inviting us."

Elsie shook her head. "We aren't in a hurry, sweetheart." Smiling, she said, "And I'm sure JoElle agrees with me. Right, JoElle?"

JoElle blushed when heads turned her way.

Elsie reached for MyEwe. "I want to hold the baby. Rebekah, is it alright if I feed her a little pudding?"

Rebekah flinched. "I think Goat fed her a good lunch. I don't think she's hungry."

Goat handed the baby to her. "But she loves sweets. I'm sure she'll love having you feed her pudding."

MyEwe proved Goat right and finished off the last bite. Everyone bragged on what a great dinner Rebekah had prepared, and she invited them into the parlor.

Liberty said, "Elsie is accustomed to taking a rest after lunch. I really think we should go, but it was so good being with all of you, today." He said, "Hon, give the baby back to Goat and get your pocketbook."

She frowned. "Do I have to give her back?"

Rebekah gasped and reached for her child.

Elsie giggled. "Don't look so frightened, Rebekah. I was teasing. Although I wouldn't mind keeping her. She's a sweetheart. Funny, how I never wanted children until I married Liberty. Now, I'd give the world to be able to have a child to call my own."

Cass, Rebekah and the kids followed them outside. Lonnie held JoElle's hand as he walked her to the car. After Liberty drove away, Goose said, "Grandpa is Miss JoElle your girlfriend?"

Gander feigned a gag. "Eeeyew!"

Goat punched him. "What's wrong with Miss JoElle, Gander? I think she's swell."

Gander turned up his nose. "Grandpa? With a girlfriend? He's too old."

Rebekah expected her papa to be embarrassed, but from his expression, she wondered if he wasn't amused at the idea.

Patting Gander's head, he said, "Sonny boy, I once thought as you do, but one day, you'll learn that love has no age limits."

As they walked back into the house, Rebekah said, "What happened to Gazelle? I thought she came out with us."

Goat said, "I saw her run out the back door when we started outside. I checked on her and she was leaning over the porch rail regurgitating. I wanted to stay with her, but she insisted I leave her alone."

CHAPTER 25

The week drug on and instead of morning sickness, Gazelle seemed to have the twenty-four-hour sickness. Rebekah tried every remedy she knew, but nothing helped. Wednesday morning, she sat beside Gazelle, wiping her head with a wet rag. "Sweetheart, I'm going into town. I need to pick up groceries and I plan to run by the doctor's office to see if there's something he can prescribe for the nausea."

"No! I told you Rebekah, I don't want to take medicine. It could be bad for the baby."

"Dear, the doctor wouldn't give you something that could be harmful. I can't stand to see you so sick." She wrung the cloth out and hung it on the rack above the washstand. "The twins walked across the field to visit the Calloway children. Badger is with Papa, of course, and I'm taking MyEwe with me, so you have nothing to do but lay here until you feel better. Goat promised to look in on you and get you anything you need while I'm gone."

"The only thing I need is to be left alone."

Rebekah drove away, and Gazelle heard Goat running up the stairs. "How 'ya feel, Sissy? Can I get you something?"

"I'm feeling better."

He sat down in a chair near the bed. "If you need something, let me know." He sat there popping his knuckles and fidgeting.

She grinned. "I don't need a babysitter. Why don't you go fishing?"

"Nah. I'm fine. I want to be here for you if you need me."

"I'm telling you, I don't need you."

He jumped up. "If I'm not needed, then maybe I will go fishing. But are you sure you'll be okay?"

"Positive. Now, go."

Goat barely had time to leave the yard when there was a knock on the door. When it got louder, she crawled out of bed and went to the edge of the stairwell. She called out, "Grandpa, could you please answer the door?"

The knocking persisted and she grabbed her robe and made her way down the stairs, feeling a bit woozy. She opened the door and glared, then fell to the floor.

Minutes later, she came to with a familiar face staring down at her. "Ma'am, are you okay? Can I do something for you?"

"Who . . .are . . . you?"

"My name is Quint. I'm your husband's brother."

"I thought when I first saw you, you were Ryker. You look so much like him."

"Yes ma'am. We were twins."

"Twins? He told me he had a brother, but he never mentioned you were twins."

"If I could be so bold as to invite myself inside, I'd like to talk to you."

"Yes, I would like that. Give me a minute. I'm still dizzy."

"Allow me to help."

Before she could respond, he swept her up in his arms and carried her inside and laid her on the sofa in the parlor. She said, "Forgive me, but I can't stop looking at you. It's eerie how much you favor him." Her brow creased. "Wait! You called him my husband?"

"He was, wasn't he?"

"Yes, but how did you . . . oh, he told you?"

"No. He never mentioned it. And forgive me for being so bold, but after seeing you, I can't imagine how he could've kept it a secret. You're as beautiful as he told me you were, the night he met you at a party. A taffy-pull if I remember correctly."

"He didn't tell we were married because I asked him not to tell anyone until I could break the news to my Father, which I had planned to do on my sixteenth birthday. However, Ryker died before we could announce it. But if he didn't tell you, how did you find out?"

He reached in his pocket. "That's why I'm here. I came to Vinegar Bend with Mama and Dad on the train to bury him, which we did—but Mama asked me to stay to take care of his affairs."

Her throat tightened. "Affairs? He had no affairs."

"You know—pack up his things, sell his cottage, order a tombstone for his grave, and that sort of thing. Then I had planned to drive his car home."

"Oh!"

"It was while I was packing that I found the marriage certificate in his drawer. I thought you'd want it, but I also wanted to meet the girl I'd heard so much about."

Gazelle raised up. "I'm sorry, I need to go."

"Go? If I said something to offend you—"

"It's nothing you said. "Excuse me, please." She jumped up and rocked back and forth on her feet, trying to get her balance.

Quint grabbed her shoulders to brace her, and suddenly she threw up all over his coat. Hysterical, she sobbed, "I've never been so embarrassed. I'm so sorry. I won't ever be able to look you in the face again."

"Hey, no problem. I didn't want to wear a suit over here, anyway. It's almost a hundred degrees outside. Point me to the kitchen and I'll get you a glass of water."

He came back and held her hand steady as she took the glass and drank from it.

The front door opened, and Goat walked in. "Ryker? Oh m'goodness. Is it really you?"

Gazelle said, "Goat, this is Quint. Ryker's twin. Please take his coat."

"I didn't know he had a twin." He glared at the soiled coat and held his nose. "Ooh, I see she didn't make it to the bathroom. It's on your shirt, too. Well, looks as if you've just passed the Marlowe initiation. Take it off and I'll bring you a clean shirt. You look to be about Father's size."

Quint pulled off his shirt and handed it to Goat. "Much obliged."

Taking the glass from her hands, he said, "I'm afraid I don't have my brother's medical knowledge, but a little wine is good for the stomach. Where does your father keep it?"

She heard Goat laughing as he walked up the stairs.

"Father doesn't drink wine."

"Oh. No problem. I brought a few bottles with me. I can go over to the cottage and get you a bottle."

"Thank you, you're kind to want to help. But I'm afraid it might not be good for the baby." Seeing his jaw drop, she followed with, "I'm sorry. I forgot you wouldn't know because I never had a chance to tell Ryker."

"So, I'm gonna be an uncle?"

She nodded.

His eyes glistened with tears. "That's wonderful. I can't wait to tell Mama. I appreciate the loan of the shirt. I suppose I should go now. It was nice meeting you and Goat."

"Will you come back?"

"Uh . . . yes. Tomorrow. Tell your Father that I'll have the shirt laundered and back to him by morning."

"I will. Thank you for bringing the certificate."

After he left, Gazelle went into the kitchen and pulled a dressed hen out of the refrigerator, put it on to boil and rolled out a pan of dumplings on a newspaper.

Rebekah walked in with a load of groceries and sniffed. "Chicken and dumplin's? You did all this?"

Gazelle smiled. "I'm feeling much better."

"Undoubtedly. Thank you, dear. I forgot to put the hen on before I left, and I was already fretting over what I'd feed your father for lunch, since I knew I wouldn't have enough time for it to boil. I'm so glad to see you up. I suppose Goat was itching for me to get back so he could go fishing. I had asked him to stick around to take care of you. It looks as if he did a great job."

Grandpa and Badger came into the kitchen and Badger held up a handful of wildflowers for Gazelle, and flashing a big smile, he signed.

"What did he say, Grandpa?"

"He said he hopes you get well. It's a lovely day out. We took a nice long walk in the woods and he wanted to bring you the flowers."

She laughed. "He said all that?" She signed back. "Thank you, Badger. I love you."

He grinned and told her he loved her, too.

The phone rang and Mrs. Calloway asked Rebekah if it would be alright for the twins to stay and have lunch. "The children are having such a grand time. I've been canning tomatoes all morning and they're playing so well together. It's been nice having Robbie and Kate occupied and out of the kitchen. God love 'em, but I get so much more done when they aren't underfoot."

Rebekah acknowledged that she understood but asked to speak to Goose and Gander. After giving them strict instructions to be sure to thank Mrs. Calloway for lunch, she insisted they be home before dark.

Cass came home for lunch and gave a loud shout as soon as he walked through the door. "Is that chicken and dumplings I smell?"

He walked into the kitchen and stuck a fork in the pot. Rebekah swatted at his hand, but not before he was able to stick a dumpling. Blowing it slightly, he put it in his mouth and let out a delightful groan. "Delicious."

"Your daughter rolled them out and cooked them while I was out shopping."

"Gazelle? You did this?"

She smiled. "Are they too salty?"

"Too salty? Are you kidding? They're perfect. You sure know a way to a man's heart." The minute the words escaped, he flinched. Her feelings stayed on edge so much of the time that he never knew what might bring on the tears.

Halfway through the meal, Goat said, "I suppose Sissy told you about Ryker's brother?"

Rebekah refilled her husband's tea glass. "He has a brother?"

Gazelle lowered her head and nodded. "I was going to tell you after lunch."

Cass took a swig of tea. "Yes, I heard he came with his parents to bury—"

Rebekah said, "Now that you mention it, I do remember hearing about a brother. It would've been nice if we could've met Ryker's folks, but of course the emotions were so intense at the time I'm sure it was best that they came and went back as quickly as they did."

Goat said, "But Quint didn't go back."

"Quint?"

Gazelle blotted her lips with a napkin. Why it was so hard for her to look her father in the eye, she didn't know. "That's his name, Father—Ryker's brother."

Goat snickered. "He's a good egg. Sissy through up all over him and he didn't even seem to mind."

Cass held up his hand. "Hold on just a cotton-picking minute. What am I missing here?"

Goat said, "I came home and he was—"

Gazelle's lip trembled. "I'll tell it, Goat. Father, he came by this morning to bring me the Marriage Certificate. He didn't go back with his folks but stayed in Vinegar Bend to pack up Ryker's belongings. That's how he found it. He said he knew I'd want to have it."

Cass left his seat, bent over and wrapped his arms around Gazelle's neck. "That's wonderful, dear. That should slow the wagging tongues in this town."

Gazelle pushed back and threw her napkin on the table. "May I be excused?" She left the table in a huff.

Cass lifted his arms in surrender. "What did I do? I can't talk to her anymore. Anything I say, lately, seems to be wrong."

"Sweetheart, I know it hurts you for folks to accuse her of being . . . uh . . . intimate, outside of marriage, but I don't think your daughter really cares what people are saying and I have a feeling she wishes we didn't put so much emphasis on it. Her heart is broken. Not only has she lost her husband, but her baby will never know its father. Can't you understand that's the only thing concerning her? Not the idle gossip."

"Is it so wrong for me to want to protect her reputation? I merely meant the marriage certificate would prove she wasn't promiscuous."

Gander said, "What does promise cutest mean?"

If looks were daggers, Rebekah's sharp glance directed at her husband would've pierced the skin, at the very least. "It's grown-up talk, sweetheart. If you're through eating, you and Goose can go wash your hands and go outside to play."

After the children left the table, she leaned in. "You still don't get it, do you, Cass?"

"I guess not. I have no idea why she became so upset."

Goat said, "Maybe I can help. Father, I think she feels you weren't so much worried about her reputation as you were your own."

Rebekah said, "That's not true, Goat. Your father may have

trouble with his words not coming out right sometimes, but I know his heart and he never puts his feelings ahead of you kids."

The corner of Cass's lip turned up in a wry smile. "Thank you, hon, but I'm having trouble trying to decide if you're my prosecutor or my defender."

Goat rolled his eyes. "I wonder if I'll be this hard to figure out when I get to be an old man."

Rebekah giggled. "I can answer that. You're your father's son. The older you get, the more you begin to act like him. But that's a good thing. I wouldn't change a thing about either of you."

Cass glanced at his watch and said, "Good grief, where did the time go? I'm expecting a phone call at the office from the church treasurer in ten minutes." He kissed his wife and hurried out the door.

That evening at supper, there was no talk of gossip, or Ryker, or his brother, Quint. Gazelle spent as much time as possible alone in her room. She posted the Marriage Certificate on the wall beside her bed. "Oh, Ryker, I miss you so much. I wish the gossip about diphtheria had been true and that we could've died together." Her heart palpitated, and as if her words could somehow become a self-fulfilling prophecy, she cried, "Lord, I didn't mean it. I don't want to die. I have to live. I need to live for my baby's sake. *Our* baby."

CHAPTER 26

Thursday morning Gazelle was in the bathroom, throwing up when she heard a knock at the door. Quickly wiping her mouth, she heard Rebekah walking down the hall. Listening, she heard Quint's soothing voice.

"Morning, ma'am, my name is—"

"Oh m'goodness, you don't have to tell me who you are. You are the spitting image of your brother."

"So they tell me."

"I'm Rebekah. I'm Gazelle's step-mother, although I cringe at the word. Not that I'm not proud to be her stepmother, I was referring to the connotation that goes along with the title."

"Yes ma'am. I understand. Is Gazelle home."

"She is, but poor dear is very sick and I'm afraid now would not be a good time to visit."

Gazelle called down. "I'm coming, Quint. Please have a seat in the parlor and I'll be down, shortly."

Goose ran through the front door, yelling. "Where's Ryker? Where did he go?"

Gander stalked out of the Butler's pantry with a jar for catching tadpoles. "Ryker? Ryker's dead."

"No, he's not. I was up in a tree and I saw him, and he came in the house." She ran to the parlor and sailed into Quint's arms. "I knew you weren't dead. I knew it."

Gazelle walked in and said, "Goosy girl, that's not Ryker. His name is Quint. He's Ryker's brother."

She clung to his neck. "No, he's not. He's Ryker."

Quint kneeled down, holding her on his knee. "Your sister's right, I'm not Ryker, but I can see you loved my brother very much and that makes me love you."

Her lip pushed out in a pout. "You're really not Ryker?"

"No. I'm his twin. That's why we look so much alike."

"Me and Gander are twins, but we don't look alike."

"That's because Ryker and I were identical twins and you and your brother are fraternal twins. That means you don't look alike."

"Oh. I was gonna marry Ryker when I got big, but Gazelle married him first."

Rebekah stepped inside the door and insisted Goose run back outside. Then, closing the door, she left Gazelle and Ryker to talk in private.

He said, "I meant to bring the shirt back this morning, but I forgot to wash it last night. I'll be sure to get it back either tonight or in the morning. Please make my apologies to your daddy."

"He won't mind. I doubt he knows it's missing. Won't you have a seat?"

"Thank you."

For the next few minutes, they sat in silence with Gazelle wringing her hands, and Quint popping his knuckles. "Gazelle, I came because I wanted to let you know that I won't be selling the cottage, since it now belongs to you."

"To me? No, it doesn't."

"Yes, it does. When Mama and Daddy left me here to sell it, we didn't know Ryker was married. As his wife, it now it's now yours."

She wanted to refuse. Perhaps she should. After all, she and Ryker were married such a short length of time. But the thought of bringing up her baby in Ryker's house, where their love was consummated, made her heart quiver. If she continued to live at home, Father would continue to see her as his little girl. She needed to grow up and grow up in a hurry. The only way that would be possible would be to take her baby and leave home.

Quint said, "You also now own a car."

"Oh, no. You'll need it to drive back to Florida."

"I can go by train. That's how we came."

"I simply won't allow it. I'll take the cottage, but you take the car."

"You're very sweet, Gazelle, but Ryker would want you to have both. I know he would."

"How long will you be staying in Vinegar Bend?"

"I plan to leave tomorrow." He popped his knuckles, then smiled and apologized. "Nervous habit."

She grinned. "Do I make you nervous?"

"A little."

"Why?"

"I don't know. I wish Mama and Daddy could've met you. They would've loved you and I think you would love them."

"After meeting you and knowing Ryker, I'm sure I'd love the folks who raised you."

"You could you know."

"I could what?"

"Meet them."

Her eyes widened. "When will they be here?"

"Oh, they aren't coming. Daddy has lung cancer and the trip was hard on him."

"Lung cancer? I'm so sorry. Ryker never mentioned it."

"They didn't want him to know. They knew how much he loved his job and the girl that he couldn't quit talking about."

"But I thought you said I could meet them."

"I meant you could drive me to Florida, let the folks meet the woman carrying their first grandchild, then you could drive the car back to Vinegar Bend."

She laughed as if he'd cracked a joke.

His face turned red. "I shouldn't have suggested it. It was a dumb idea."

Chewing on the inside of her cheek her gaze locked with his. Then a slight smile inched across her lips. "Not dumb at all. I'd love to meet my baby's other grandparents. What time shall we leave in the morning?"

"Are you serious?"

She giggled. "I think I am. But I must warn you, I'm still having morning sickness, but I'll try to stay at a reasonable distance. I'm still embarrassed that I upchucked on you, yesterday."

"Hey, forget it. I wasn't worried about my clothes. I was worried about you. You were green."

She rubbed her hand across her chin. "Maybe I should just let you take the car and go alone. I'm afraid you'd have to stop too many times on the way there. It could take a very long time to make the trip."

"I'm not in a hurry. Please. I'd love . . . the family would love for you to go."

She lifted a shoulder. "If you're game, I am."

"Fine. Is seven o'clock in the morning too early for you?"

"Seven is fine. I'll have your coat ready by then."

He stood and looking quite awkward, stuck out his hand. Gazelle ignored it and gave him a hug. "Thank you, Quint. I look forward to meeting your parents."

Gazelle was upstairs when her father came home from lunch. He kissed Rebekah, then said, "How's Gazelle?"

She shrugged. "I heard her throwing up this morning, but I haven't seen much of her."

He grimaced. "That's not good. It probably means she's been too sick to come down."

"Oh, no. She spent a good deal of time downstairs . . . just not with me."

"Really? What's she up to?"

"Perhaps you should ask her. Ryker's brother came by the house and stayed an hour—maybe longer. After he left, she went upstairs, and I haven't seen her since."

"That was nice of him to visit her."

"You should see him, Cass. He's the spitting image of Ryker. It's eerie."

"I hate to be in a rush, sweetheart, but I need to sit down and eat. I received a call from Deacon Hall that Mrs. Hightower is not expected to live much longer. I plan to run by and pray for her before going back to the church office."

"Poor ol' soul. I reckon if anyone is ready to meet their maker, it would be Mrs. Hightower. The food is ready and on the stove. I'll feed the kids after you leave."

"Thank you. Don't bother putting it on the table. I'll fill my plate to save time." He ate and left with a corn pone in his hand.

Gazelle had little to say at lunch.

Rebekah said, "That was very kind of Ryker's brother to visit you."

She nodded. "Yes, he's very nice."

"Did he indicate how long he intends to stay in Vinegar Bend?"

"Pass the okra, please, Gander." She raked a helping on her plate and handed the platter to Goat. "Oh, I'm sorry. I believe you asked how long? He's leaving in the morning."

"Oh. You two talked a good while."

"Yes. He's easy to talk to."

Goat said, "He and Ryker look so much alike, I wonder if they ever tried to fool their schoolteachers by pretending to be the other twin."

Gazelle laughed. "I'll have to ask him."

Rebekah said, "I thought you said he was leaving in the morning?"

"That's right."

"So are you expecting him to come by before he leaves?"

"Yes, didn't I tell you?" Then lifting a shoulder, she smiled. "I don't suppose I did. I'll be going with him."

Rebekah's jaw dropped. "You'll be doing what?"

"Going with him. He wants me to meet Ryker's parents and let them get to know the mother of their grandchild. I think it was sweet of him to suggest it."

"Oh, honey, you can't do that."

Her teeth ground together. "Who said?"

"I didn't mean to indicate I was forbidding it. I simply meant it's quite a drive to Tallahassee, Florida and you know you're likely to throw up on the train."

"We aren't going by train. We're taking Ryker's car."

Goose said, "Can I go? I'm gonna marry Quint."

Gazelle giggled. "You're very fickle."

"What's that mean?"

Rebekah said, "Enough talk, Goose. Finish your lunch."

Gazelle picked up her plate and took it to the sink to wash. "Thank you for dinner, Rebekah. It was all good."

"You hardly ate a thing."

"I had plenty. I need to go pack."

"I think you should wait and speak with your Father before proceeding with your plans to leave."

"Why? I've already told Quint I'd go." She didn't wait for an answer but hurried up the stairs to her room.

Thirty minutes later, she came downstairs with a load of clothes and headed out to the wash house.

Rebekah picked up the phone to call the church to let Cass know of his daughter's plans. After trying numerous times, she gave up, assuming he stayed longer at the hospital than he'd intended.

CHAPTER 27

Cass was late getting home for supper. He walked in the house and tossed his hat at the hat rack in the hall. Blowing out a heavy breath, he sighed, "What a day." Then seeing Goose and Gander playing on the hall floor with jacks, he said, "Goose, sugar, would you mind going to my room to get my slippers and bringing them to the parlor?"

Gander jumped up. "I will. I know where they are."

Goose screamed, "He asked me to get them. Father, tell him you asked—"

"Forget it. Stop that bickering before I tan you both. I'll get them myself."

Rebekah walked out of the kitchen, drying her hands on her apron. "My, you're in a foul mood."

"You'd be too if you'd had the kind of day, I've had. Everything that could go wrong, went wrong." He pulled her down to his lap and kissed her. "Sorry, I was such a booger-bear. I'll apologize to the kids at supper. Right now, I just want to kick off my shoes and relax."

"What happened?"

"I don't want to talk about it. It's nothing for you to worry about, though. Where's your papa? He's usually sitting in the swing with Badger when I get home."

"JoElle came by earlier and they went for a ride. Badger's with them."

"You don't think this is getting serious, do you?"

"I don't know what to think, but I hope Papa knows he'd be making a big mistake if he has any romantic thoughts in mind."

Cass laughed. "I'm sure he's just enjoying having someone close to his own age befriending him. Lonnie, romantic? I can't get that picture in my head."

"Well, he wouldn't be the first old man to forget his age and go running after a woman."

"Hey, sweetheart, we're talking about your papa. I was just kidding when I asked if it was serious. He's got it good here, and I'm sure he knows it. Why would he want to take on a wife when he has no way of supporting her?"

"You're right." She stood up and stretched. "Are you ready to eat, or would you like to rest a while longer?"

"No, I'm feeling better. All I needed was a little snuggle-time with my sweetie."

"It will take me a few minutes to get it on the table. Why don't you go up and see Gazelle?"

"She'll be down for supper in a few minutes. I heard MyEwe waking up. I'll go pick her up and put her in her highchair. If anything can lift my spirits, it's seeing how excited she gets when her 'Fa-da' walks in the room. If only I could have that same effect on everyone . . . Horace Redding, for instance."

Rebekah said, "Now, I understand why you were in the dumps when you got home. A confrontation with your favorite deacon?"

"At least he keeps me on my knees. I'm pretty sure God made two Horace Reddings. One to be the thorn in Paul's flesh and the other to be the thorn in mine."

Minutes later, MyEwe was in her highchair, playing peek-a-boo with her Father. Rebekah smiled at how quickly the cute blue-eyed bundle of joy had wrapped her Fa-da around her little finger.

Rebekah asked Cass to get everyone to the table. He called the twins in, then asked them to find Goat.

Rebekah said, "I forgot to tell you. He finished his chores and asked if he could go catfishing tonight. I told him you'd want him home by nine o'clock. He took a can of Vienna sausages and a sack full of soda crackers with him."

"I see. Well, Gander, run upstairs, please and tell your sister it's time to eat."

He came running back down and said, "Gazelle said for us to go ahead and eat. She's doing something."

"Doing something? What is she doing that's so important that she can't come to the table with the family? I'll go get her."

Rebekah winced. "I don't think that's a good idea, dear. I know what she's doing. Why don't we wait and discuss it after supper?"

He sat down and tucked his napkin in his shirt collar and looked around at the empty seats. "Grandpa, Badger, Goat and now Gazelle think they can decide to come eat when it's convenient for them? I don't like it. We're a family and we eat as a family. I plan to make that clear as soon as we're all together again. It isn't fair to you, sweetheart, to prepare such a nice meal and not have the family to show respect by coming to the table. I'll make sure this doesn't happen again."

"It's fine, Cass. I understand."

"Well, I don't, and I intend to put a stop to it. This is getting out of control."

She whispered, "Not now, while the kids are eating." She nodded toward Gander, who seemed to be taking in every word. "Your rules, remember? I've always been proud that you would never allow bickering at the table."

Gander said, "Father are you gonna whoop Goat?"

Cass tried to hide his smile. "Whoop him? No, son, I don't plan to whoop him. Now, eat your supper. This is good fried chicken Rebekah cooked for us, isn't it?"

He gnawed on a drumstick. "Real good."

After the twins left the table, Cass said, "Now tell me what's going on with Gazelle."

"There's no easy way to say it. She's packing."

"Packing what?"

Rebekah poured out the whole story, from Quint coming to visit, to Gazelle's insistence that she was leaving with him in the morning to drive to Tallahassee, to meet Ryker's parents.

He reared back in the straight-back chair and rubbed the back of his neck. "I see."

"I tried to call you, but you weren't at the office. I wanted to let you know what was going on so you could come home and put a stop to it. But after you got home tonight, I didn't want you to start something at suppertime that might upset the twins. You might want to go up to her room now and explain to her that she does not need to get in the car with a perfect stranger to go stay overnight with folks she doesn't even know."

"I thought you said he was Ryker's brother?"

"That's right."

"And she wants to meet Ryker's parents?"

"Yes."

"That doesn't sound like she's running away to join a badlands gang. I can understand why she might wish to meet them."

"Cass Marlowe, have you lost your mind? Gazelle is very vulnerable at this point. She's going through a grieving process and not only that, but she's pregnant and doesn't need to travel. Her place is at home where we can help her through this tragic loss."

"Seems to me she'd be with folks who'd understand what

she's feeling, since I'm sure they're grieving also. I think it's good that she's going. And it was thoughtful of the boy to invite her."

"Well, this is certainly not the attitude I thought you'd take. I expected you to use a little common sense. Did I mention she plans to drive herself back?"

"Rebekah, first let me remind you she doesn't have a car. We'll allow her to stay a couple of nights getting acquainted with Ryker's folks. I'm sure any reservations we might have about her traveling there will be minimized by the joy those poor grieving parents will receive from knowing our daughter is carrying Ryker's child."

"I know your heart's in the right place, Cass, but you aren't thinking straight. She does have a car. Ryker's brother has insisted that the cottage and the car belong to Gazelle, since she was Ryker's wife."

His brow lifted. "Didn't she tell him she didn't need either? I can take her anywhere she needs to go, and she has a home. Why would she need a cottage?"

"I suppose she could sell it."

He chuckled. "As if she needs the money? That's ridiculous. I'm sure she'll tell them so."

Gazelle came downstairs. "Ya'll still eating?"

Rebekah waited for Cass to respond.

"No, sweetheart, we're talking about your trip tomorrow."

"Are you angry with me for going?"

He stood and wrapped his arms around her. "Now, why would I be angry?"

"I don't know. I suppose I thought you'd try to stop me."

Cass laughed. "Sugar, if I wanted to stop you I wouldn't try. I'd do it."

Gazelle clinched her lips tight as if the words in her head would spill from her mouth if she didn't fight hard to hold them in. Her father was being much more agreeable than she had anticipated and now was no time to cross him.

He said, "But let's get one thing straight. You won't be driving back home by yourself."

"And who will be coming back with me, Father?"

"My point is that you won't be driving. You can stay a couple of nights, which will be ample time to get acquainted. After church Sunday, I'll go get you and bring you home."

There were all kinds of objections going through her head, but why upset him?"

Rebekah volunteered to help her pack, but Gazelle assured her she had everything packed already. She picked up a biscuit from off the table and her father insisted she sit down to eat it. He passed her a pork chop, though she declined.

"Honey, you need something nourishing. You're eating for two, now."

Things were going so much smoother than she'd anticipated. She forked a chop and cut it up in small pieces, hoping to keep it down. If she mentioned the real reason she didn't want to eat, her father would insist she was in no condition to take the trip. He might even insist on taking her himself, which not only would make her seem immature in the eyes of Ryker's parents, but it would be terribly humiliating

As soon as she finished the last bite, she quickly excused herself from the table to hurry upstairs, hoping she could hold it in until she reached the bathroom.

CHAPTER 28

Liberty ambled into the house and slumped down on the sofa. Elsie walked over and bent down to pull off his boots.

"You look exhausted, dear. I'm sure must've worked hard today. Why don't you stretch out and relax a bit before supper?"

He pulled her down and kissed her. "You worry too much about me. I didn't do much at the farm so I'm not physically tired. But I had some business with Judge Sawyer, and while I was there, I heard some sad news, which has left me emotionally exhausted."

"What happened?"

He explained that while he was at the Court House in Chatom, a woman from Child Welfare brought in little Lucy Granger.

"And who is . . . oh, Liberty." She gasped. "That's Dorie's child, isn't it?"

He nodded. "They're saying Harlan is in prison."

"I'm not surprised, but where's Dorie?"

"She was found dead, although the cause has not yet been determined."

"Oh, m'goodness. That poor child. That is so sad."

"I was told by the Social Worker that there was a full docket and her case probably wouldn't be heard for hours. The Court House was packed, and the poor kid looked like a little scared rabbit. I've never seen so many folks waiting for their turn in court. It was so full, many were sitting on the floor, and it was hot as blue blazes in there."

"What will become of the poor dear?"

"Unless she has a relative to claim her, I suppose she'll be carried off to the orphanage."

Elsie's eyes watered. "Well, why are you still lying there. Come on."

He sat up, scratching his head. "Where are we going?"

"To rescue that poor baby, that's where. We can't let her be shipped off to an orphanage. We'll bring her home with us until a relative steps up."

He grabbed her in his arms and wrapped her tightly. His throat tightened. Why did he have to blurt it out? Shouldn't he have known this would be her reaction? Elsie had mentioned more than once the compassion she felt for the child from the day she saw her with Dorie in front of the store. If he refused to take her to Chatom, could it cause her to have a relapse? What if they arrived too late for the hearing? But suppose they were granted permission to bring the little girl home, and then her deadbeat kinfolk showed up at their door to claim her? What would it do to Elsie if she had to let her go?

How could he make her understand that her health meant more to him than anything in the world? Sure, his heart broke for the child, but wasn't his first responsibility to take care of his wife? If only JoElle were home. She'd know how to advise him. But JoElle wasn't home, and Elsie was pulling on his arm, urging him to hurry.

Liberty and Elsie arrived at the Court House and when he didn't see the child, he feared the case had already been heard and she'd sadly been taken away. Then, he eased open the big double doors leading to the courtroom and saw little Lucy asleep on a bench beside the woman from the Welfare Department. He suggested Elsie wait in the corridor and allow him an opportunity to speak with the woman, but Elsie insisted she go with him.

After presenting their proposition to the woman, she appeared elated. Cass concluded she was more concerned about disposing of a case, rather than finding a home for a child. When Lucy's name was finally called at almost six o'clock, the three adults walked to the front and appeared before the judge. Lucy continued to sleep.

Liberty had expected to be drilled with questions, but it became apparent the judge was ready to go home. The woman handed the judge two papers, which he quickly signed, then shoved them into Liberty's hands and yelled, "Granted!" It was the only thing he said before rapping his gavel on the podium and yelling,

"Next!"

Liberty turned and looked at Elsie. His knees turned to jelly when he heard her sobbing. What had he done? It was too late to second-guess the decision. She said, "Pick her up, Liberty."

He slid his arms underneath the child, gently lifted her and took her to the car. Elsie sat down and said, "Now, give her to me."

The little girl squirmed and rubbed her eyes. She stared into Elsie's face, then looked over at Liberty. "I know you. You came to my house and gave me my baby doll."

Liberty explained the doll had been Elsie's. "But she wanted you to have it."

Elsie glanced at Liberty and his shoulders relaxed, seeing her smile. She said, "That's right, sweetheart. That baby doll was very precious to me, but I knew you'd be very good to her and love her as I did."

"Miss June said the judge would send me to the orphanage. Is that where you're taking me?"

"No. We're taking you to our house. Is that okay?"

Her eyes lit up. "Forever? To be your little girl?"

Liberty spoke quickly before Elsie could answer. "You'll be with us until you are placed in a permanent home."

"Like the orphanage?"

"No, I meant until you have a relative who will come and take you home with them."

Lucy burst into tears.

Elsie's heart broke, seeing her so sad. "Honey, please don't cry. I know you miss your mama but we'll take good care of you, I promise. Do you know of a relative who might come get you? Maybe a grandmother . . . or an aunt?"

"I have a step-sister, but she's mean. I don't want to go live with her."

"Then you don't have to, so let's don't even think about it."

Liberty rubbed the back of his neck and questioned his own sanity. What was he thinking when he told Elsie about the child's situation? She was already convincing the little girl that she didn't have to go live with her sister, when the courts would surely rule otherwise.

JoElle had the porch light on for them when they arrived. Her eyes brightened when they walked in with little Lucy.

"Well, my goodness, looks like we have a visitor." She looked at Liberty for an explanation, but when it became apparent one would not be forthcoming, she said, "I'm Mother Jo, sugar, and what name do you go by."

"Lucy. My whole name is Lucy Ann Granger."

"Well, what a pretty name. I suppose you're all hungry. I left the food warming on the stove."

Liberty said, "Thanks Mother Jo. I could sure eat something."

Elsie's eyes had never looked brighter. "I'm not hungry, but I'm sure Lucy would like to eat."

JoElle took the child by the hand and said, "Why don't you come with me, sweet pea, and let's find something you might like to eat."

Elsie thanked her and said, "I want to go fix up her room. Liberty, when you finish eating, would you please go look in the big cedar chest in the attic and bring down the pink chenille bedspread, and the matching curtains? There's a Mary Had a Little Lamb lamp up there, also." She started down the hall, then quickly went back to the kitchen. "Oh, Liberty, I forgot. Look in the chifforobe and you'll find a Sunbonnet Sue quilt. My grandmother made it for me when I was about the age of Lucy."

"Honey, it's summer. Do you really think she'll need a quilt?"

"I'll just lay it at the foot of her bed. It's fun to look at all the pretty little girls with their Sunbonnets. She'll love it. I know I did."

JoElle was dying for an explanation but didn't want to probe in the presence of the child. But for whatever reason the little girl was there, it had to be an act of God. How many times had she prayed for the Lord to send Liberty and Elsie a child? This wasn't how she imagined it would happen, but it was perfect. Already, she could see the love in Elsie's eyes.

After making Lucy a cup of hot cocoa, she went into the bedroom where Elsie was busy cleaning out drawers. "Mother Jo, I'd like for you to go with me in the morning to buy her some new clothes. And we'll go by the Five and Dime and pick up a few toys."

"Sure, hon, we can do that. While she's still in the kitchen, brief me on what's going on. How did you and Liberty happen to get custody of her?"

"We went to a hearing at the Court House."

"Really? When did this all come about?"

"Today. Liberty happened to hear about it, and he came and got me. We told the judge we wanted her, and well—here she is—ours."

Liberty came down from the attic in time to hear the conversation. He threw his hands to his face. Walking into the room, he stood between the two women, glancing at one and then the other. "Mother Jo, Elsie means she'd be happy if it were to turn out that we could raise little Lucy, but the truth is, she has a step-sister who will be notified of her whereabouts. As Lucy's nearest kin, she'll be awarded custody, unless for some reason she isn't capable of raising a child."

Giant tears welled in Elsie's eyes. "Liberty McAlister, I don't think you even want her."

"Don't be silly. I'd love for her to stay here forever. I'd like to be the one to walk her to her first day of school, teach her to dance, and walk her down the aisle on her wedding day. But the truth is, we caught the judge at the end of the day when he was exhausted. I have a feeling the reason he granted us temporary custody was because he was ready to go home."

JoElle bit the edge of her lip. "Temporary custody? So she'll be leaving?"

Elsie's heart raced when she looked up and saw Lucy standing in the doorway. The child ran across the room and sailed into

Elsie's arms, sobbing. "Don't let them take me away. I want to stay with you."

"Shh, shh! My sweet little one, don't you cry. Mama's not gonna let them take you anywhere."

Liberty groaned and stalked out of the room, with JoElle following.

He said, "What have I done? I know Elsie has had a mental breakdown, but she's been doing great. I think she's intentionally leading the child to believe that no one can remove her from this house. And did you hear her refer to herself as Mama? Oh, Mother Jo, why is she doing this?"

"She wants to believe it so badly, she's convincing herself it's true."

"You mean the way she convinced herself that the doll was real? If this keeps up, she'll be as loony as she was at the asylum. I can't go through this again. I can't!"

"Son, do you know what I think? Elsie's greatest fear is losing Lucy, so she's attempting to combat that fear by convincing herself that no one can ever take her away. You, on the other hand, have the same fear. I see it written on your face, every time you look at Lucy. You're terrified of losing custody, but instead of convincing yourself that no one can take her away, you've convinced yourself that they will. Therefore, you're as frightened as Elsie."

He paced back and forth across the floor. "Okay, I'll admit it. I'm scared to death. What can we do, Mother Jo?"

"Enjoy her while you have her and pray that all things will

work out for little Lucy's good. Trust the Lord and lean not to your own understanding."

"Thank you." Her smile was so angelic—so confident looking, that he felt an overwhelming sense of peace that whatever happened, they'd all survive it."

She said, "I think Elsie must've laid Lucy down. I heard her walking across the hall to your bedroom."

"Good. I'm beat. Maybe things will be clearer in the morning. Goodnight, Mother Jo."

He tiptoed into the dark room and undressed for bed. When he pulled back the covers, he saw a tiny little body cuddled up next to Elsie. He rolled over with his face buried in his pillow. "Lord, I do pray for you to work this out for Lucy's good, but could you please make it coincide with our good, too?"

****

Quint showed up at the Marlowe home at exactly seven o'clock Friday morning.

Cass went up to her room to get Gazelle's bag and instead of a small overnight case, she had two suitcases packed. "You aren't planning on taking both of these are you?"

She giggled. "I couldn't decide what I might want to wear while I'm there."

There was no need to argue. He grabbed one in each hand and carried them downstairs.

Quint said, "Let me get those, sir. I'll put them in her car."

Cass cringed at hearing him call it "her car." It wasn't her car.

She didn't need a car and though Goat had taught her to drive, Cass didn't approve. He saw no reason a female would ever need to drive a car, unless she happened to be an old maid or fatherless, and his daughter was neither. But this was no time to stir up trouble. Quint helped her into the automobile, and she sat there smiling. It was the first time Cass had seen a smile on her face since Ryker died. He glanced at Rebekah and winked, indicating he was convinced he'd made the right decision by allowing her to go. He waved and said, "I'll go get you Sunday afternoon, shug. I should be there by three or three-thirty. Have your things ready when I get there, because we'll be turning around and driving straight back to Vinegar Bend."

Quint whispered, "Didn't you explain to him it won't be necessary to come for you?"

"I did, but he either wasn't listening or misunderstood. Just wave, smile and let's go."

He saw all the hands waving in the air, and following Gazelle's instructions, waved and drove away. "But what if your Father shows up, Sunday? Didn't you want to make sure he understands?"

"I promised to call him collect after we get to your folks' house to let him know I'm okay. He's been overly protective since I've been sick. I'll remind him when I call that I plan to ride the train home."

"Train? But you have a car." He smacked himself on the side of the head. "Oh, you can't drive, can you? I can teach you."

"My brother taught me to drive, but I wouldn't feel right taking the car. I want you to have it."

"Me? No, I have a car. You don't. Or at least you didn't, until now."

He winked and smiled and for a brief second, he looked so much like Ryker she longed to have him reach his arm over the seat and pull her close—the way Ryker would do. She could feel a blush painting her face. Could he read her thoughts? Feeling overwhelmed by guilt, she suddenly questioned her motive for wanting to take this trip. Was it really to meet her baby's grandparents—or was it to spend time with Quint, pretending he was Ryker?

She grabbed the door handle and yelled for him to stop. He pulled off the side of the road and she opened the door and threw up until she was heaving. Tears streamed down her cheeks. "I'm so sorry. So sorry."

He pulled a handkerchief from his pocket and wiped her face. She felt his arms folding around her, and a broad hand gently pulled her head to his chest. His voice was calming. "It's okay. I'm sorry you're sick, but just keep in mind this is but for a season and the harvest will be great. You're gonna have a baby. Isn't that wonderful?"

Her heart pounded hearing his soft voice consoling her. It was exactly the type thing Ryker would've said. He would've pulled her close with her head resting on his chest and repeated those exact words. She tried to look at him without being obvious. He wasn't Ryker. He was Quint. And regardless of how much they were alike, he could never take Ryker's place. Shoving back to her side of the seat, she said, "You're very kind. I'm fine now. We can go."

CHAPTER 29

Liberty yanked at his boot, getting ready to go to work. After tossing and turning half the night, he felt more exhausted than when he went to bed.

Elsie and JoElle were getting dressed to go shopping when the phone rang.

Liberty hobbled down the hall with one boot on and the other in his hand. "I'll get it."

It was a lady from the Court House saying the judge wanted them to bring the child to his chambers at ten o'clock. He dreaded telling Elsie, but she took it much better than he'd expected.

Her response surprised him. "Oh, dear. I wish the judge had waited until tomorrow, so I'd have something decent to dress her in. Mother Jo and I are planning to shop for her clothes today."

Liberty found her attitude baffling. Did she not realize that the only reason the judge was sending for them meant someone had shown up to claim little Lucy?

He had to be strong. He'd prayed with all his might and now he had to trust.

Elsie brushed Lucy's hair and then tied it with a pretty yellow bow ribbon she took from one of her favorite dresses. "You look adorable, sweetheart."

Lucy wrapped her arms around Elsie and said, "I'm glad you're gonna be my mama. When we go out today can we go by my old house and let me get my baby doll? Becka Lou misses me."

Elsie's smile stretched from ear to ear. "So you call your baby doll Rebekah Lou?"

"When Daddy gave her to me, he said that was her name."

"That's exactly right. And I think it's time for Rebekah Lou to come home. I miss her, too."

Liberty's breath caught in his throat. *Did she call me Daddy?* He'd always wondered what it would feel like to hear a child call him Daddy. Now, he knew. It was gut-wrenching. He turned his back to keep them from seeing the moisture in his eyes.

When they reached the Court House, they were directed to a backroom that had the judge's name on the door. They walked in with Lucy between them, holding their hands.

Liberty swallowed hard, seeing a young woman sitting there, barefooted and puffing on a cigarette. She eyed Lucy, then remarked, "You've growed since I seen you."

The judge made small talk with Lucy, then in a more serious tone, he said, "Lucy, this is your sister, Elma."

Lucy hid behind Elsie's skirt. "I know who she is. I don't like her."

Elma threw her cigarette on the floor and stomped it out with her barefoot.

Liberty's eyes widened in amazement.

The girl raised her pencil-drawn eyebrows and said, "Well, I don't like you, either, Squirt and there ain't no way I'm gonna be saddled down raising somebody else's kid. How do I even know my old man was her daddy? Can't nobody prove it. Shucks, I can't start taking in every little waif who claims to be the offspring of Harlan Granger."

If the judge heard her rant, he didn't let on. He seemed preoccupied with the papers in front of him. Flipping from one page to the next, he picked up his pen and wrote something. Then looking up from his desk, he handed the papers to Liberty. "Take good care of this baby."

Elsie said, "Then she's—?"

The judge looked up from above the top of his spectacles. "Yours. That is what you wanted wasn't it?"

"Yessir. Yessir, it's what we all wanted. Thank you, sir."

When they got into the car, Liberty looked at Elsie. "Well, that was a surprise."

"A surprise? No. I knew she was ours. 'For this child I prayed, and the Lord hath given me my petition which I asked of him.'"

Liberty scratched his head. "I've heard that exact phrase somewhere. The Bible?"

She nodded. "It's recorded in First Samuel. It didn't mean much to me when I read it weeks ago, but the moment I saw Lucy napping on the Court House bench, the words came back, verbatim. It was as clear as if they were being audibly spoken by God and I knew she was ours."

Liberty's chin quivered. "I thought it odd that Lucy called you mama and me daddy without any prompting. The fact that she became attached so quickly frightened me, because I didn't know how she'd cope—how any of us would cope—if the judge removed her from our home."

Elsie placed a hand on either side of his broad, square jaw and smiled. "What a blessed child our little Lucy is, to have you for a father."

He threw his arms around his wife. "We have a child, Elsie. Our very own little girl. I hope if I'm dreaming that I'll sleep for a long, long time."

****

Saturday morning the phone rang while the Marlowe family was eating breakfast. Cass said, "That must be Gazelle." He shoved his chair back and hurried to answer. "Gazelle? Gazelle, hon, is that you?"

He heard the familiar giggle and relaxed. "Yessir, Father. It's me."

"I've been quite concerned. Are you okay?"

Rebekah was pulling on his shirt sleeve. "I'd like to talk with her. Don't hang up until I have a chance to—"

He cupped his hand over his mouth and whispered. "Shh, I can't hear while you're talking." With his mouth pressed to the telephone he shouted, "What's that, dear? I didn't understand. I thought you said you were planning to . . . never mind. Repeat it."

"I said I intend to stay with the Adams until after the baby comes."

He licked his dry lips. "Honey, you can't . . . no, that's not a good idea. Have your things together and I'll come get you today. I'll leave in a few minutes."

Rebekah said, "For crying out loud, Cass, what's going on? Please tell me."

"Hold on, Rebekah."

Gazelle said, "Father, I can hardly wait for you and Rebekah to meet Ryker's parents. They are so sweet and so good to me. I know the Lord sent me to them. They're excited over the baby. Mama Jean has pulled out all Ryker and Quint's old pictures, and I Suwannee, I can't tell one from the other, but she can. It's eerie how much they were alike. And you and Papa Joe would hit it off immediately. He's a rancher. I told him our best friend, Liberty, is also a rancher."

"Honey, slow down. That all sounds fine. I'm glad they're good folks and have responded kindly to you, but you can't stay there."

"Father, I'm sorry you don't approve, and it breaks my heart to have to go against your wishes, but this is something I must do."

"Sweetheart, is it because of the negative talk that spread

around town in the beginning? It's been squelched. I posted the Marriage Certificate in the paper to make sure everyone understood. You have nothing to be ashamed of, now."

"Father, I had nothing to be ashamed of before they knew the truth."

"Of course. You're right. I just thought maybe the gossip played a part in the decision you're trying to make."

"The decision is made. I'm sorry you don't approve, but I have two families now and I want my child to know how blessed it is to have four such wonderful grandparents, and lots of fantastic aunts and uncles. I should go now. Mama Jean has breakfast on the table, and I think they're waiting on me. Give my love to Rebekah and the children and tell them I'll write soon. Bye now."

His hand dropped, still holding the phone.

Rebekah grabbed it. "Gazelle? Gazelle?" She glared at Cass as she laid it on the receiver. "I wanted to speak to her. What did she say?"

"She's not coming home."

"But why?"

"I don't know. I can't imagine. All she would say was that they're good folks and she intends to stay until after the baby is born."

Rebekah took his hand. "We have to let go, Cass."

"Why? She's still a child. Sixteen."

"Do you remember when I was sixteen?"

He shrugged. "That was different."

"Let's go finish our breakfast. The children have already eaten and left the table."

"I'm not hungry. I guess I'll go on to work since she insisted that I not go get her. Where did I fail, Rebekah?"

"Cass, you have never failed any of us. You're a wonderful husband and a great father. But there comes a time in a woman's life when she must make her own decisions and not rely on her father. Remember when Ruth married Boaz? What was it she said?"

He mumbled, "'Whither thou goest, I will go.' I suppose that's what you're referring to?"

"Yes, but you didn't finish. 'Ruth said, 'Thou people shall be my people.' I believe Gazelle loved Ryker so much, that she's made that same commitment to love his people. She understands it's what he would've wanted. We can't fault her for that."

"You're right." His lip curled in a soft smile. "She sounded extremely happy and that's what we want. Right?"

"That's exactly right. We'll write her often and it isn't so far that we can't pay her a visit now and then."

"Have I told you lately how much I love you, Rebekah? I need you. I'm in awe at how God uses you to reveal his truth to this bull-headed preacher." He headed toward the table. "I sure hope the kids didn't eat all the fried ham and red-eye gravy. I'm starving."

CHAPTER 30

October, 1920 . . .

Grandpa was pushing Badger on the tire swing in the front yard, when a fellow on a fancy new automobile drove up. "Mornin' sir, I reckon you're looking for my son-in-law, the Reverend Castle Marlowe, but he ain't here. You can find him at the Friendship Community Church—that is, if he ain't out visiting the sick."

"I didn't come to see Mr. Marlowe. I'm looking for a Mr. Lonnie Brewster."

Lonnie squinted. "That would be me." He pulled Badger from the swing, then signed for him to go inside the house. "How can I help you?"

"Maybe I can help you. You say you're Mr. Brewster?"

"That's what I said, but you ain't told me who you are."

The man extended his hand and said, "I'm Gastin Meriweather, and I'm here to discuss your late sister's Last Will and Testament with you."

"What are you saying? My late sister? I only got one sister and last time I heard she wadn't late."

"Was Nellie Brewster your sister?"

"She is."

"You apparently haven't heard. Your sister was found dead a few days ago. From all appearances, she either had a heart attack or a stroke while milking. They found her in the barn beside the turned over stool. A bucket of milk was spilled on the ground. I'm sorry to have to break the news."

"Well, I'll be dogged. I'm mighty sorry to hear that. I reckon I need to talk to somebody about planning for a funeral, but that ain't your worry. I'm sure my daughter can help me figger all that out."

The man ran his hand over the top of his bald head. Lonnie had a feeling it was a habit he probably had, back when he had hair. He'd often seen Cass doing the same thing, except there was something up there to rake through.

"Funeral? I guess I forgot to mention it, sir. Nellie's last request was that when the life went out of her that she be turned over to the gravediggers and promptly laid in the ground. No preacher, no funeral—nothing. She even made it plain she didn't want to be embalmed. I don't mean any disrespect, sir, but your sister was a rather peculiar lady."

"Yessir, she was right peculiar." He chuckled. "I reckon it runs in the family. It was mighty nice of you to go to the trouble of finding me to let me know."

"That isn't the purpose of my visit. I assumed you'd already been notified of her death."

"I don't reckon none of her friends woulda known how to find me to let me know."

"I understand. I'm the attorney representing her Last Will and Testament. As her only living heir, she has named you to be the beneficiary of her estate."

"Aw, shucks. I don't know what kinda trick you trying to pull, but Nellie Brewster didn't own no state."

"I said the estate. Her belongings."

"Well, you still barking up the wrong tree. I ain't seen her in years, but I'm pretty sure she didn't have nothing worth worrying over. She's lived her entire life on that run-down dirt farm that belonged to Pappy. It was between the railroad track and the mill, so nobody in their right mind would want it. But we were po' folks and it was all Pappy could get his hands on."

"Sir, that run-down dirt-farm as you call it is now prime property and worth quite a bit of money. For years the mill has tried to purchase it from Miss Nellie, but she refused to sell. They've asked me to deliver their offer to you."

Lonnie rubbed his eyes twice and kept glaring at the paper. "Does this say what I think it says? Are all those zero's in the right place?"

"They are, sir."

"Shoot fire, where do I sign?"

He chuckled. "Not so fast. If you could be at the Court House in Chatom tomorrow afternoon at two o'clock, I'll have Mr. Donnell from the mill and the Bank President meet us there to finalize the transaction."

Rebekah could hardly believe it when her papa shared the news. "I'll call Cass and see if he can take you to Chatom tomorrow. I'm sorry we didn't get the word about Aunt Nellie in time to attend services."

"Much obliged, sugar. If this goes down like the fellow said, I reckon I'm gonna be a rich man."

She smiled. "And what would you do with so much money, Papa? Don't you have everything you need, right here?"

"You and Cass have been mighty generous, but I'd like to think I didn't have to be dependent on you. The first thing I wanna do is learn to drive. Then, I'll buy me a car. It don't have to be no fancy automobile. Just sump'n to get me from one place to the next. I ain't never drove nothing but a horse and buggy, but I figger if Goat can do it, I oughta be able to drive one of them contraptions. Just one thing bothers me."

"What's that, Papa?"

"I been praying for a week or two for the Lord to show me a way to stand on my own two feet."

"I think he answered that prayer a few months ago."

"No, I don't mean like this. I was praying that I wouldn't be dependent on Cass for my provisions."

"Oh, Papa, you know he doesn't mind. He's glad to have you

staying with us. We all are."

"He's a good man, Rebekah, and he's treated me right, ain't no doubt about it. But a man don't feel worth his salt as long as he's lettin' another man carry his load. When I first got here, I couldn't do nothin', but it's different now that I got my legs back. It ain't right to let him keep supporting me. It's time I quit being a burden."

"Don't be ridiculous. No one in this household considers you a burden."

When Cass came home from work, Lonnie went out to meet him. "Cass, how long you reckon it would take you to learn me how to drive this vehicle?"

"How long? I have a feeling you'll catch on right away. It's really not that difficult, once you learn to shift. Why don't you hop in and we'll drive down to the field and let you get a feel for it?"

Rebekah stood at the window smiling as she watched them ride off together.

CHAPTER 31

Friday afternoon, Rebekah stood back and admired the two-tiered birthday cake she made for the twins. The bottom tier was chocolate icing—Gander's favorite—and the top tier was strawberry, Goose's favorite. Grandpa had Badger sitting atop the ice cream freezer as he turned the crank. He yelled, "I hope they'll be here soon. The cream is ready."

Goat yelled, "Here comes Liberty and Elsie."

The twins ran to meet them, and Gander jumped on the running board as Liberty pulled into the yard. Goose waited for Liberty to lift four-year-old Lucy from the back seat, then she took her by the hand.

"That's a pretty dress, Lucy."

"Thank you. My mama bought it for me."

"I like your doll, too. What's her name?"

"Becka Lou."

"That's a fine name. We have a seesaw in the backyard.

Would you like to seesaw?"

She nodded and they ran off together.

Elsie and Liberty looked at one another and smiled. Liberty said, "That was sweet of Goose to make Lucy feel welcomed, since she's a bit older. I hope we can do as good a job raising our little girl as Cass and Rebekah have done with their kids."

Everyone gathered in the backyard and Rebekah and Elsie exchanged hugs. Rebekah said, "Where's JoElle?"

Liberty chuckled. "Didn't Cass tell you?"

His brow furrowed. "Tell me what?"

Cass had a sheepish grin. "I let Grandpa take the car to go pick up his date."

Rebekah's mouth gaped open. "You did what? He can't drive."

Cass and Liberty exchanged glances and laughed as if they were privy to a joke that no one else had heard. "He can drive, sweetheart. What you meant is 'He can't drive well.'"

Heads turned when Cass's automobile came rolling into the yard with gears grinding as it came to a sudden halt, barely missing the Pecan tree.

Rebekah whispered. "Have you lost your mind, Cass? He could've killed them both."

"But he didn't. He's back with his girl and his self-esteem intact. Be happy for him, hon. I've never seen him so happy."

After enjoying the cake and ice cream, Rebekah invited everyone inside to watch the twins open their gifts.

Goose proclaimed it to be the best birthday any girl had ever had. She turned to her brother for confirmation. "Wasn't it, Gander?"

He shrugged. "How do I know? I'm not a girl," which brought forth laughter.

Cass said, "I'm afraid he's learning to be a real comedienne like his big brother, Goat."

Grandpa said, "I agree, Goose. This has been a fine birthday, party. There's nothing like getting together with good friends. And that's why I've chosen tonight to share something that I've been praying about for some time now. When I came here, I was a lonely, bitter soul. I wanted to die. I didn't think I'd ever walk again, and I was pretty sure no one would care if I did keel over. But through love and patience, Cass, Rebekah and the kids helped to lift me from the depths of despair. I stopped hating everyone and discovered they didn't hate me. They hated my ways. So with God's help, I changed my ways. I began to gain back my self-respect and no longer wanted to die. Then I met the most wonderful, loving soul when Miss JoElle Jernigan came to town." All eyes turned toward JoElle. She fanned the blush rising to her cheeks.

Grandpa called her to stand beside him. "I wanted to surprise her tonight by getting on my knees in front of all our kin and friends and ask her to marry me. I changed my mind for two reasons. One, I was afraid she might say no and that would be embarrassing, but the second reason was that I knew it would be even more embarrassing if I got on my knees and she'd have to help me up."

He held up his hands to quell the laughter. "So, I did the next best thing. I asked her before I brought her here and I'm happy to report she's agreed to become my wife."

The women squealed and ran up to hug them both.

Lonnie said, "Wait! There's more. As you all know, I came into some money a couple of weeks ago when I sold the family homestead. I've offered to build my bride her dream house anywhere in the world she chooses to live."

JoElle said, "I told him I didn't want a fancy house. I wanted something small, but comfortable, near town so I could walk to see my little granddaughter, Lucy, anytime I chose. And Lonnie has found the perfect place."

Cass said, "Really? Where?"

Lonnie said, "We've bought Ryker's cottage from Gazelle. It's perfect. It's close to the church, the clinic, town and most important, close enough for little Lucy to walk down the street by herself when she wants to spend the night with Gram and Grandpa."

Lucy ran up and grabbed him around the waist. "I love you, Grandpa."

The phone rang and Cass excused himself to answer it. He yelled from the hall. "It's Quint. Gazelle is in labor."

They all rushed to the hallway and listened.

Cass said, "You tell her we'll leave first thing in the morning.

No, no. That's not necessary. We wouldn't want to impose. But if you could make reservations for us to stay in a nearby Hotel, I'd appreciate it."

Goat said, "We'll need more than one room. No way can two adults and six kids fit into one room."

Cass said, "You're right. Quint are you still there? We'll need two rooms."

Grandpa yelled, "Tell him to make it three." He glanced at JoElle, who nodded as if she read his thoughts. He laughed. "Correction. Make it four."

Liberty looked at Elsie, then shouted. "Add another to that."

Quint said, "I've gotta go. I promised her I wouldn't be gone long, although the doctor says he expects it to be a lengthy labor. How about if I reserve the entire top floor?"

"That sounds good. You take care of my little girl, you hear?"

"Yessir. I intend to."

The entourage arrived at the hospital before noon, Saturday morning. Grandpa volunteered to stay at the hotel with all the children under twelve, since they weren't allowed in the hospital.

The nurse announced that only two family members could go into the patient's room. When they walked in, Quint was by her side. Cass didn't know why it bothered him. Shouldn't he feel grateful that she hadn't been left alone? Still, it didn't seem right, somehow, and he wasn't sure why. "Quint, I'm sure Gazelle was frightened when she went into labor and it was very thoughtful of you to stay with her until we arrived. I'm sure you have things to do, so I'll take over from here."

Quint gazed down at Gazelle and she reached for his hand, which Cass assumed was her way of thanking him and letting him know he was free to leave.

He didn't let go. Instead, he said, "Much appreciated, sir, but I have no where I need to be. The doctor made rounds about thirty minutes ago and he said she's still got a way to go before she's dilated enough for the baby to make its entrance."

Cass wanted to admonish him for speaking so boldly about such a private matter, but Rebekah appeared to read his mind and shot a cold, hard stare his way. He understood it to mean, 'keep your thoughts to yourself.'

Gazelle looked at Quint and squeezed his hand. Cass stiffened. He was sure he didn't imagine it. It was definitely a squeeze and then the boy reached up and brushed a lock of hair from her face. He smiled. She smiled back. Cass jerked at his collar. Was something going on or was he being paranoid? He glanced at Rebekah who failed to see what had just taken place. For if she had, he was certain the looks exchanged between Quint and Gazelle would've troubled her as much as it troubled him. He tried to think of something to say to his daughter, but his mind was reeling with questions.

"Uh . . .sweetheart, I suppose you and the baby will be coming home as soon as the doctor approves? I know you've enjoyed your nice long visit with the Adams. I'm eager to meet them."

Quint said, "Mama and Daddy are in the waiting room. They said they wanted to give Gazelle's family an opportunity to spend as much time as possible with her."

Cass nodded. "That was kind of them."

Gazelle clenched her eyes tight and moaned.

Quint leaned over and stroked the back of his hand across her cheek. "Pain?"

She nodded. "It's gone."

He said, "Preacher, I've tried to decide when would be the proper time for me to say this, but I reckon this is as good as any. I'm in love with your daughter and . . ."

Cass shook his head vehemently. He shot an open palm in the air. "No. Stop! I'll not have you putting ideas in her head at a time when she's most vulnerable. Perhaps you should leave, young man."

Gazelle said, "Father, you didn't let him complete his sentence. Finish, Quint."

He nodded. "And she loves me. We got married last night after I brought her to the hospital."

Cass felt his knees grow week. He grabbed hold of the metal bed post. "You what?"

"We got married."

"No. Please tell me you're making this up."

Gazelle's lips trembled. "We hoped you'd be happy for us."

"Happy? Honey, I know you miss Ryker, but just because his twin looks like him is no reason to marry him. You don't love him.

This is ridiculous."

Rebekah said, "Cass, I think it's wonderful. Why would you think it's so ridiculous?"

"She's only been here a few months. She's still grieving over Ryker. Don't you see? She hasn't had time to fall in love with him."

Rebekah raised a brow. "Really? How long did it take you to fall in love?"

"That's different. Stay out of it, Rebekah."

Gazelle said, "You're wrong, Father. I do love him with all my heart and soul. I miss Ryker, but I've learned to love Quint and he loves me, too."

Rebekah said, "Congratulations to you both. I'm happy for you and your father will too, when he has time to let the news soak in."

Cass lowered his head. "Gazelle . . . honey, are you sure you love him?"

"Yessir. Very much."

He turned to Quint. "And you love my daughter?"

"More than I ever thought it possible to love anyone."

"And you'll be good to her? And the baby?"

"It's my heart's desire, sir."

Cass chewed on his lip. Then sucking in a lungful of air, he held out his hand. "Welcome to the family."

Refusing to take the hand, Quint wrapped his arms around Cass's neck. "Thank you, sir. I can hardly wait to meet all of this wonderful family I've heard so much about."

Gazelle screamed out in pain and a nurse rushed in. "I'll have to ask everyone but the father to leave."

Rebekah hurried out, then looked around, ran back and grabbed Cass's hand. Didn't you hear the nurse? She said we should leave."

"She said everyone but me."

"No. She meant the father of the baby."

He whispered, "But he's dead."

"No, he's not. Quint is now the baby's father, just as I'm the mother of five children, none of which I brought into the world."

CHAPTER 32

October 21,1920

Cass walked the floor in the waiting room for two hours until Quint finally came to the door and announced, "It's a girl and they're both doing fine."

Rebekah said, "That's wonderful news. Have you and Gazelle named her?"

"We named her Rykelle. If she'd been a boy, we would've called him Ryker, but Rykelle was as close as we could come to naming her after Daddy One. As soon as she's old enough to understand we'll tell her all about Daddy One and how Daddy Two came to fall in love with her and her beautiful Mommy."

As soon as the doctor allowed them to see Gazelle and the baby, Cass, Rebekah, Goat, Liberty, Elsie and JoElle all agreed little Rykelle was the most beautiful baby they'd ever seen.

Later in the evening, lying in bed at the hotel, Cass said, "Isn't it amazing?"

Rebekah laid her book down on the bedside table. "What, dear?"

"The way God works. I was just thinking about how it all began. It was the day I met you standing at the train depot, barefooted as a yard dog." He laughed. "And so young, you were. I was shocked to learn you hadn't yet seen your sixteenth birthday."

"I'm still amazed that you didn't put me back on that train and send me back to Sipsey Ridge."

"If it crossed my mind, it didn't dwell there long. Looking back, I realize we had absolutely nothing in common, yet I was furious with Roy for not wanting to marry us. But he did and now, here we are."

"God really worked that out for our good, didn't he?"

"Yes, but after I got you home, it seemed our future together would end before it began. Gazelle was such a little brat, she ran you off before we spent one night together."

Rebekah reached up and turned off the lamp. "She was a pill, for sure, but now, I couldn't love her more."

"I often wonder if Goose hadn't come down with the measles, if we would've ever gotten back together."

"Strange, the things God can use to work out his purpose. Even measles."

"We've come through a lot together and made it to the other side, but when Amelia showed up from the grave, I really thought everything I held dear was slipping away from me. Goat ran away, thinking I'd lied to him and I wasn't sure I'd ever see him again. I've never prayed as much as I prayed then. I was terrified that Amelia would come between us, turn the children against you and destroy our marriage."

"But it never happened."

"No, thank the Lord, it didn't. Then when Badger had to have the transfusion, and Amelia refused to give blood to her own child, I thought sure we'd lose him."

"And we didn't."

"No, thanks to you."

"But I really thought I'd messed up when I brought your Papa to live with us. I wasn't sure you'd ever forgive me."

She laughed out loud. "Nor did I. But what a blessing that turned out to be."

"You didn't think so the night he blurted out that you were pregnant."

"You're right. I was so angry with you for not noticing and of course I was looking for a reason to justify my anger toward Papa. He certainly provided the justification."

"And remember all the trauma we went through with Badger before discovering he was deaf?"

"How could I forget? Those were rough days, for sure. But look at him now. It's amazing how quickly he's learned to sign. If he doesn't know the correct sign for a word, he makes one up and it's typically easy to understand."

Cass let out a painful-sounding groan.

"What's on your mind, now?"

"That ghastly time when Elsie went through the false pregnancy."

"Aww, yes. That was heartbreaking. It still makes me shudder to think about what she went through. If Liberty had any knowledge of her obsession with you, he never let it show."

"Her weird fixation put me in an awful position, and I didn't know how to handle the situation."

"But you didn't have to handle it. God did. He did it his way, and that's always the best way."

"All those things were bad, Rebekah, but I'm not sure anything hit me as hard as finding out my little girl was pregnant—and on top of that, learning she was a widow. All the agony I'd previously endured, paled in comparison to the pain I felt for Gazelle. I can deal with my own anguish, but I can't take it when I see you or one of the kids suffering. I'd always felt it was my duty to protect Gazelle and suddenly things had spun out of my control. I felt helpless."

"That's not a bad place to be. That's when we learn to rely on God."

"Absolutely." He wrapped his arm around his wife. "I have a confession to make. Remember how upset I was when Gazelle phoned, saying she wasn't coming home, and planned to stay with Ryker's folks?"

"I do."

"I'll admit, that cut to the bone."

"Really? Why?"

"I considered it a slam against her own family. I know now that it was my pride that was hurt. I concluded she was choosing them over us."

"Now, what do you think, Cass?"

"I think I need to stop drawing conclusions. Several years ago, I arrived at a schoolhouse early, and to save time, I sketched my illustration on the blackboard before the lecture was to begin. When I finished, I looked at it and judged it to be perfect. But when I stepped out to get a drink of water, some kid went in the room and scribbled all over my illustration with chalk, turning it into something unsightly. I was mortified."

"Did you fix it?"

"No. There was no way to fix it. I decided the only option would be to grab the eraser, clean the board and do a new thing. As it turned out, it was a much better idea than the original sketch. And tonight, as I reflected on all the things that's happened in our family, I suddenly saw an amazing parallel."

"What do you mean?"

"God is the Master artist who created us in his image. He says we are wonderfully and fearfully made. But we grab the chalk and scribble, marring his beautiful work. Then we fret and fume and worry over how we're gonna fix the mess we've made. So we keep scribbling. But the more we scribble the worse it becomes. Finally, we lay down the chalk and look toward the Creator to fix the creation. He wipes our slate clean, making ready for him to do a brand-new beautiful thing in our lives. Isn't that exciting, sweetheart?"

He rolled over and wrapped his arm around Rebekah. "My heart is overflowing with gratitude. And now, we have a precious little granddaughter with an incredible mother. When Gazelle was growing up, I lamented over her strong will. I called it being stubborn."

"And now, what do you call it?"

"A blessing, for sure. She has solid convictions that can't be swayed by cunning tongues or strange doctrines."

"Or of family members who mean well?"

With tongue in cheek, he said, "Yeah, that too. And if you won't tell anyone I said so, I'm growing right fond of our son-in-law."

Giggling, she said, "I won't tell a soul . . . but stay away from the chalk."

"Goodnight, Rebekah."

"Goodnight my love."

I've won numerous literary awards throughout the years, but the awesome friends I've met on this journey have been my true reward. Below is a listing of my novels:

VINEGAR BEND SERIES

    *Chalkboard Preacher from Vinegar Bend – Book 1

    *Chalkboard Preacher Drawing Conclusions -Book 2

    *Chalkboard Preacher A Clean Slate – Book 3

SWITCHED SERIES:

    *Lunacy – Book 1

    *Unwed – Book 2

    *Mercy – Book 3

GRAVE ENCOUNTER SERIES

    *When the Tide Ebbs – Book 1

    *When the Tide Rushes In – Book 2

    *When the Tide Turns – Book 3

THE KEEPER SERIES

    *The Keeper – Book 1

    *The Prey – Book 2

    *The Destined – Book 3

HOMECOMING SERIES:

    *Sweet Lavender ---Book 1

    *Unforgettable – Novella - 2

    *Gonna Sit Right Down – Novella- 3

    *Hello Walls – Novella - 4

*PLOW HAND – Book -Stand-alone

*A GIRL CALLED ALABAMA – Book - Stand-alone

Thank you for choosing my books. An Amazon review would be greatly appreciated.

Made in the USA
Columbia, SC
23 March 2021

34517328R00186